The Game Ended in Sudden Death. But Who Was Calling the Plays?

Phyllis Randolph—the merry widow of sports czar Charley Randolph was now sole owner of the L.A. Marlins, ready to tackle marriage #5. She had the means and the motive to kill the man who'd made her rich. But did she have the guts?

Lane Randolph—the sexiest, most arrogant woman Lujack had ever seen. She was a cool gambler who could win or lose $50 G on a roll of the dice. Did she really want Lujack to find her brother's killer . . . or was she cruising for something else?

Hiram Hotel—a black bookie with his finger on the Mafia pulse. He claimed to know a lot about the Randolph killings. But how much would he tell his old friend Lujack—before setting him up?

Frank Nimmo—a Chicago mobster moving in for the kill. He's ready to take on the Marlins and L.A. with blackmail and blood, but first he needs a legitimate front . . .

(more . . .)

Raves for . . .
THE GOOD BOOK

"Raymond Chandler lives! A cracking good, gritty Southern California mystery in the best hardboiled Chandler tradition. You can almost smell the dusty palm trees and hear the traffic on the interchange. Thoreau has the family gift for clarity of expression and a cop's eye for the seamy underside of LA-LA land."

—Jim Murray,
Los Angeles Herald-Examiner

"David Thoreau tells a story with wit and a street understanding. Establishing what he sets out to do, he brings off his material in a way genuinely entertaining."

—Mel Durslag,
Los Angeles Herald-Examiner

CITY AT BAY

"A wonderfully written, swift-paced novel by a writer with intimate knowledge of his material."
—*West Coast Review of Books*

"A fine ride on the wild side of town."
—*San Francisco Chronicle*

"This portrait of a city on the verge of exploding is beautifully drawn."
—*Los Angeles Times Book Review*

THE SANTANIC CONDITION

"A first-rate thriller."

—Sacramento Bee

"Thoreau hammers his adventure to a driving finish."

—Detroit News

"A top-notch adventure-mystery."

—South Bend Tribune

"A big book . . . Professionally put together."

—The New York Times Book Review

DYNASTY OF POWER

"Fascinating . . . A fast-paced drama heavy in action-packed suspense."

—Santa Ana Register

"Fast-paced . . . The author obviously knows his way around the upper reaches of California society."

—Publishers Weekly

THE
GOOD BOOK

DAVID THOREAU

POCKET BOOKS
New York   London   Toronto   Sydney   Tokyo

This book is a work of fiction. Names, characters, places and
incidents are either the product of the author's imagination or
are used fictitiously. Any resemblance to actual events or locales
or persons, living or dead, is entirely coincidental.

Another *Original* publication of POCKET BOOKS

POCKET BOOKS, a division of Simon & Schuster, Inc.
1230 Avenue of the Americas, New York, N.Y. 10020

ISBN: 0-671-64525-0

First Pocket Books printing May 1988

10 9 8 7 6 5 4 3 2 1

POCKET and colophon are trademarks of
Simon & Schuster, Inc.

Printed in the U.S.A.

To Alison and Scott

Chapter 1

WHAT A FACE. THE kind of face a wide-angle lens could love. Long jug-handle ears and droopy eyelids seemed to pull at a perpetually furrowed brow. Everything about the face was outsized; the nose, the jowls, the ears, all made him tragic in a baggy, warm-hearted fashion. The sad clown, Jimmy Lujack thought. Maybe that's why moviegoers liked Burt. They could identify with the face without having to live in it.

Lujack caught Burt Masters's green eyes examining him and remembered why he was at the actor's palatial Holmby Hills home—to pay the man fifty-six thousand dollars. The very successful, very rich, sad clown.

"You don't dress as conservatively when you collect, Jimmy," the familiar voice chuckled, appraising Lujack's subdued sport coat and slacks.

"If a bookie looks like a banker when he pays off, the player feels comfortable. If he looks like a bum who just hocked his wife's jewelry, maybe the player starts shopping around."

"But when the player's a loser?"

"Shut up and deal."

"You got that part right." Masters smiled.

The actor was one of Lujack's biggest clients. Over the three years they'd been doing business, he'd beaten Masters out of close to a quarter of a million dollars on college football and the baskets, only to lose most of it back on professional football. Masters knew the pro game. Their arrangement was simple enough. When the tab got to be above fifty thousand dollars one way or the other—pay up. They usually met at the Director's Room at Hollywood Park or Lujack's office above the Chin Up restaurant. This was the first time he had ever been to Masters's home.

The actor glanced down at the leather briefcase.

"Fifty-six," Lujack volunteered, knowing Masters disliked accounting.

"Tough week, huh?" Masters commiserated.

"Goddamn Dodgers," Lujack grumbled, handing Masters the briefcase. "They had to be playing the Yankees. L.A. gamblers love to bet against the Yankees."

"Sort of like screwing the boss's wife, huh?"

"Yeah, sort of," Lujack agreed without enthusiasm.

"Come on out on the patio," Masters said, spreading an arm in the direction of a large pool area on one side of the Tudor-style mansion. "My wife's always wanted to meet the infamous Jimmy Lujack."

"Thanks, Burt, but I should be getting back. Mondays are pretty busy for us. We got the Monday night game, and I like to tinker with the early lines for the weekend."

"No rest for the wicked."

"Something like that."

"What's the opening spread on the 49ers?"

"Minus six," Lujack said, quoting the morning betting line from Nevada One, his handicapping service. He liked Nevada One because it was tied into Frank Nimmo's Super Bowl Sports Book in Las Vegas. The marketplace made the best betting line, not the handicapping, and Nevada One reflected the betting market like Dow Jones reflected the stock market.

Each pro football team was like a blue chip stock. An investor bet his team was going to win by the point spread the odds makers set. As the kickoff approached, the odds changed according to the amount bet. The more money bet on one team, the worse the odds.

"Give me a coupla dimes on the Niners. They're hot."

Lujack nodded. Masters was betting two thousand dollars that the 49ers would beat the Bears in next Sunday's game by more than six points. If they won by more than six, Masters won; if they won by less than six or lost, Lujack was the winner. If the 49ers won by exactly six, the game was a "push," and nobody won. As with all football bets, Masters put up eleven dollars to make ten, the difference being the "vigorish," the bookie's ten percent commission.

"What about tonight's fiasco? Marlins still minus four?"

Lujack nodded again. The L.A. Marlins were four-point favorites to beat the New Orleans Saints in the Monday night game.

"How about the over under?"

"Forty-five."

"Give me two more dimes on the Marlins and another dime on the over," the actor said. Lujack wrote the five thousand dollars' worth of bets next to

Masters's number—17. Lujack and his partner, Tommy Chin, had about forty regular customers who each had a number.

"My wife's having some people over tonight, so I'll probably end up watching the game. Can't stand watching a game without betting on it, even if it is the Marlins," Masters explained, watching Lujack for a reaction.

Lujack knew better than to play that game. The meteoric demise of the Marlins since the death of their owner, Charles Randolf, had been the big story on the local sports scene. From Super Bowl runner-up to NFL doormat in two short years. A bookie's dream come true. Lujack and Tommy had made close to three hundred thousand dollars off Marlin bettors over the past two seasons.

"If any team can make the Marlins look good, it's the Saints," Masters continued. "Rumor has it Mick Mayflower actually threw a spiral in practice this week."

"I didn't say anything." Lujack smiled, knowing there was nothing he could say, even if he wanted to, that would dissuade Masters from betting on the Marlins or anything else. The man was a player. He'd wager against yesterday if he could get odds. As with many of Lujack's customers, there was a coin constantly flipping inside Burt Masters's head. At a million dollars plus per picture, Masters could afford to keep that coin in the air for quite a while.

"You heard about Phyllis's latest miracle cure? She's imported a preacher from Arizona to give the game plan his blessing before the game."

"The Church of the Christian Pyramid."

"Right," Masters said, shaking his head. "Last week in Chicago, one of the local sportswriters dubbed the Marlins defense the 'Holy Rollovers' . . .

I don't know how Charlie Randolf could have done it . . . left the team to that birdseed-brain wife of his."

"I always heard Charlie had a strange sense of humor."

"Not that strange," Masters muttered, then flashed his famous smile.

"Who am I calling stupid? I'm the one bettin' on 'em."

It wasn't like Masters to be self-deprecating. Lujack wondered who he'd been talking to.

"You and Tommy must be cleaning up on the Marlins," Masters continued. "When the home team loses, the bookies get rich."

"Things haven't been too bad . . . until the goddamn Dodgers."

Masters put a friendly arm around Lujack and began walking him to the car. With his free hand, the actor picked up the briefcase containing the fifty-six thousand dollars. No sense leaving it untended.

"Ever wish you were back with the cops?" the actor asked as they approached the Shelby-Mustang GT.

Lujack could not recall telling Masters he'd even been with the cops. A vice detective, to be exact, on his way to robbery-homicide . . .

"Only when I get a parking ticket," Lujack said, getting into the Mustang and starting the engine.

The guttural roar put a prompt end to their conversation. That roar was one of the many things he liked about the car. Masters waved and turned to go back into the house to count his money. Lujack took the Mustang down the actor's driveway twice as fast as he should have. A startled gardener sidestepped into a hedge.

Lujack ran the Mustang near five thousand rpm all the way down Sunset, even though he was in no rush to get back to the office. He'd lied to Masters; he'd already set the early lines. But then, he assumed Masters had lied about his wife wanting to meet him. Bookies and wives were natural enemies. When he was working vice, many of the gambling collars they had made were on tips from wives. Bookies or collectors threatening their husbands, calling up at all hours. That the husbands had bet money they didn't have was one thing; that the wives had to lose sleep or a new pair of shoes, or found out that the son of a bitch's life insurance policy had been cashed out . . . that was something else.

He took the 405 south past the V.A. Hospital. He had the Mustang cruising in third gear at seventy. Anna had thought he was crazy when he bought the blue and white monster during the height of the gas shortage, but the price was irresistible. Now that gas was back to under a buck, he'd had offers for three times what he'd paid for the car. He wasn't sure why he hadn't taken any of them. After two tickets, his insurance rates damn near wiped out the savings on gas.

The Sawtelle exit flew by. His second or third year on the force, Lujack had worked out of the Purdue Street station not far from the freeway. He'd answered dozens of calls from irate West L.A. citizens complaining about the crazies from the V.A. Hospital. There was one Vietnam vet who used to dress up as an orange and walk around the Sawtelle area. At first the residents didn't mind "Agent Orange" wandering around the neighborhood in his costume, and the children loved playing with him. It was only when he began to peel, showing ugly splotches of infected skin, that the locals got upset and Orange's pass was revoked. Twice after that, Agent Orange somehow managed to get out, and twice Lujack brought him back. His third and last escape took place on the

Sawtelle baseball diamond, near second base, with a can of gasoline. Anna had hated it when he told her that story. Of course, he'd known she would.

The Chin Up was on Pico near Robertson, in a Jewish neighborhood slowly being gobbled up by the ever-expanding Mexican, black, Asian ghetto that was Los Angeles. When Tommy Chin's father opened the Chin Up in the thirties, the Chins were the only Orientals north of Gardena and west of Vermont, Cathay Circle and Grauman's Chinese theaters included. The Chin Up was a favorite watering hole of the MGM stars of the period. And in the 1930s, that was just about every star who counted. But after the war, both MGM and Chinese-Americans lost a little of their luster, and Benny Chin was forced to cater bar mitzvahs for the local merchants and office parties for the car salesmen on Olympic and Wilshire boulevards. When Tommy came back to the business in the sixties, after a stint in the Marines, the neighborhood had begun to integrate. As the second-generation Jews moved to the San Fernando Valley, Tommy began buying up their property. Tommy told Jimmy he had made more money off the Watts riots than Smith and Wesson.

The outside of the restaurant looked like a movie-set version of what a Chinese restaurant should look like. There was a fake Marco Polo roof, with fake bamboo siding covering the corrugated tin walls. The style of cooking was now advertised as Mandarin or "Peking style." Tommy had changed it from Cantonese during the Nixon, low-fat, me-generation seventies, when detente was in and greasy food was out.

Lujack's senses made the automatic adjustment from the warm October sun and smog to the cool darkness, the sound of running water, and the smell of fried food that always permeated the Chin Up. The customers, typically few on Monday, were composed of "Chinese junkies," as Tommy referred to his regulars. A smattering of Century City–Beverly Hills deal makers who liked the tradition of the Chin Up as well as the relatively low prices. And the locals—Dr. Davey Rosenbloom, owner of Optic City; Sid Green, manager of Beverly Hills Vacuum, which in fact was two doors down, not in Beverly Hills at all; Pete Colima, senior partner of Pete's Barber Shop across the street on Pico. The Colima family had been in the neighborhood even longer than the Chins. Fifty years cutting hair in the same shop, and pretty much in the same shape. Pete didn't like Chinese food, but he didn't mind the well scotch.

"How about those Dodgers, Jimmy?" Pete cackled as Lujack walked by. "I told you, buddy."

"You and everyone else in town, Pete," Lujack said, forcing a smile and peeling off a ten-dollar bill from his pocket roll. Goddamn Dodgers.

"Did you hear the one about the Polack who found his wife in bed with another man?" the old barber asked.

"Think I missed that one."

"He pulled out a revolver and put it to his temple. 'What do you think you're doing?' his wife asked. 'Shut up, woman, you're next!'"

"You're a fuckin' riot, Pete," Lujack said and kept walking. He wondered if Pete knew that his wife, Anna, had left Lujack for his partner, Marty Kildare. And that Marty had shot himself in the temple three months after Marty and Anna were married. And that Anna was now in a mental hospital looking out at . . . looking out at what?

"What do you have for the Marlins tonight, Jimmy?" the barber yelled after him.

"Minus four," Lujack told him. Pete was too old to remember even if he had known.

"Minus four?" the old man said indignantly. "The *Herald Examiner* has 'em at minus six."

"Then bet the *Examiner,*" Lujack snapped back.

At the end of the bar, his black-rimmed glasses scrunched up to the top of his head, the phone screwed into his ear, and a scowl on his face, was Tommy Chin. Tommy would be forty in December, but his looks denied it. The East-West syndrome, Lujack observed. As the head of the Chin family since the death of his father in 1969, Tommy had been forced to shoulder the responsibilities of his mother, two brothers, and two sisters from the time he turned twenty-two. When he married and began to raise a family, those responsibilities increased. In the Chinese community, he was a distinguished and respected son, husband, and father.

Then there was the other side of Tommy Chin. The bookmaking, gambling, womanizing side which Lujack knew. The owner of a Chinese restaurant who hated Chinese food. The husband who had hookers sent up to his second-floor office in a dumbwaiter. The successful bookie who had never been to a professional football game. To Lujack, Tommy would always be the hustler he'd met in a Gardena poker parlor ten years ago. The bookie he'd busted and then arranged bail for. His good and dear friend.

"Two moves. Five hundred on Dallas minus five. Two hundred on San Francisco at plus six," Lujack overheard him repeating as he walked by. Tommy always repeated the bets—his slight accent had once caused an expensive mistake. No matter how long it took, Tommy always double-checked every bet with the client.

When he saw Lujack, Tommy's expression changed.

The cranky man-in-the-moon frown parabolized. His eyes drifted upward. There was a visitor.

"Who is it?"

Tommy shrugged. "Never seen him."

"Lo fan?" Lujack asked.

Tommy nodded. *Lo fan* was Cantonese for "white man."

"Rich boy," he added, giving Lujack the diabolical smile he reserved for a privileged three or four friends.

"How's the take?"

"Heavy on the Cowboys."

Tommy didn't need to check the list to know how much money had been placed on each team. He was a walking computer . . . who hated computers.

"How heavy?"

"Thirty-four hundred."

"Better move the line down half a point. I'll tell Susie when she comes in."

"We better do better than that, partner," Tommy said, taking a bite of the hamburger he had stashed behind the bar.

Lujack knew it was coming. Since he and Tommy had started the Good Book, they had never laid off any of their action to the larger books in town. "Laying off" was the gambling parlance for insurance. If a bookie took too much action on one team, he simply passed it on to a larger bookie, thereby covering himself against a big loss if the heavily bet team was a winner. Most bookies didn't like to bet. They were content to even their bets and take their five percent profit. By not laying off, the Good Book had more exposure on a given game for winning or losing, but, just as importantly, they were their own bosses. They didn't have to deal with the mob-run books in L.A. or Vegas. Until this year, they had been lucky.

But now they were in trouble. Football started slow, and the Dodgers winning the Series had killed them. Already Tommy had gone into the reserve fund for a hundred fifty thousand dollars, and football season wasn't half over. Not to mention the bowl games, the heaviest betting period of the year.

"If things don't change by the end of the week, I'll call Hiram," Lujack said.

"Things won't change."

"You and I have been winning big for three years. What makes you think things won't change?"

"Year of Ox. Ox good luck for gamblers, bad luck for bookies."

"I wish you'd told me sooner."

"I didn't know sooner. My uncle only told me last week."

"Last week? It's October. We've lost nearly two hundred grand in the last three months."

"Uncle's been very sick."

"What's the matter with him?"

"He lost all his money gambling, tried to kill himself."

"I thought you said the year of the Ox was good for gambling."

"Uncle's been in a coma since last year. Year of Rat. Year of Rat is bad for gamblers, but very good for bookies."

Tommy popped the remainder of the hamburger into his mouth. The phone rang before Lujack dared to ask what kind of luck next year's Chinese critter would bring.

Lujack pushed back the beaded curtains at the end of the bar and walked up the stairs that led to the second-floor offices. The first office was Tommy's. He was the bankroll man. It was his money that financed the operation—although he and Lujack split the profits equally. The second office—marked "East-West Enterprises"—was the phone room, the official home of the Good Book. Every afternoon about this time, Susie Katz, the phone man (actually a sixty-five-year-old woman), would come in. Office hours were usually three to six-thirty P.M. during the week, and Saturdays and Sundays from nine A.M. until one P.M.—the kickoff time for the second of the NFL games. There were two phones in Susie's office: one outside line for customers and one inside line for either Tommy or Lujack to notify Susie of any line changes, circle games (limited betting), or games off the boards (no bets accepted). The office at the end of the hall was Lujack's own. In the organizational triad of the Good Book, Lujack was the backup man—the man who moved the lines, kept a separate record of the day's play in case of an act of God or the vice division, and did the payouts and collections. In the four years he and Tommy had been in business, Lujack's collection rate had been damn good. He'd never used the strong-arm, leg-breaking tactics that were prevalent on the East Coast, but the fact that he'd been a five-time police light-heavyweight boxing champ didn't hurt his percentage.

It was an efficient, old-fashioned setup. He and Tommy didn't believe high technology was necessary to run a profitable book. The lower the profile, the lower the risk. Lujack had seen too many computerized bookies convicted by their own electronics. As Tommy said, the Chinese had been gambling for three thousand years before anyone ever heard of the exclusionary rule.

Chapter 2

THERE WAS SOMETHING VAGUELY familiar about the conservatively dressed young man sitting in the solitary chair outside Lujack's office. Lujack guessed a financial type—maybe socialite.

"Mr. Lujack?" the man asked anxiously, rising to his feet.

"You got me."

A well-manicured hand was extended. Lujack guessed him to be in his late twenties. He had a weak chin.

"I'm Kurt Randolf. Morris Breen sent me over."

Lujack unlocked his office, and Kurt Randolf followed him inside. The office was furnished more stylishly than downstairs but in the same tropical-exotic motif. Wicker chairs, bold-colored print upholstery, brass lamps, a Gauguin reproduction—"Chinese Restaurant CPA," his decorator friend called it. The only non sequitur was the police academy picture he had on the wall. Elysian Park summer class of 1973.

Kurt Randolf sat in the chair opposite Lujack's desk. Lujack, of course, recognized the name and now remembered the face. Kurt Randolf was the son of the late Charles Randolf, maverick owner of the Los Angeles Marlins pro football team. The son had none of the father's rugged, dynamic presence. The face was tanned but soft and unformed. Lujack remembered seeing young Randolf on the sidelines at a Marlins game years earlier. He was one of the Marlins water boys, and during one time-out he wasn't quite fast enough for his father, who physically shoved the boy out on the field. Charles Randolf had always been an active owner, whether it was fighting with the commissioner, firing coaches, trading players, or pushing around the water boys. A real bastard was old Charlie.

"Morris said you occasionally worked as a . . . go-between for people who need help. Believe me, Mr. Lujack, I need help. Of course, I'll pay whatever you think . . ."

"Most people who need help go to the police," Lujack said firmly.

"I've been to the police," Randolf said with exasperation. "I've been to the San Diego district attorney three times in the last two years. He says the matter is closed. My father died of a heart attack. The attending physician at Rancho Verde Resort signed the death certificate, the coroner concurred, and that's the end of the matter."

"What is it Mr. Breen said I could help you with?" Lujack asked, not sure he was tracking the young man's story.

"Morris said you used to be a policeman. A vice cop. He said you also had certain connections on the

14

shady side of the street. He said you were a man with a unique taste in friends."

"What, exactly, is the nature of this trouble, Mr. Randolf?" Lujack asked again, in no mood to wait for this oblique young man to come to whatever point he was going to make.

"I think someone is trying to kill me," the other man said softly.

"Oh? And what gives you that impression?"

"Three nights ago, I was driving home from work. My office is in Century City, and we live on Beverly Glen up by Briarwood Park. I left the garage after eight and drove down Santa Monica. I took a left onto Beverly Glen and noticed that a car that had followed me out of the garage was still behind me. There were two men in the car, a late-model Cadillac or Buick. When I crossed Sunset and the car was still there, I began to get apprehensive. Probably because of the inquiries I've made recently concerning my father's death."

When Lujack didn't comment, Randolf continued. "After Sunset, there's a little park and then the turnoff for Westlake School, then a straight stretch with no access roads, so I floored it. My Mercedes has a lot of guts, and I was probably going seventy in a matter of seconds, but this car stayed right with me. That was when we came to the roadblock."

"The roadblock?"

"Luckily, at least for me, there'd been a small fire in the Glen, and the cleanup was still going on. When I slowed down to pass through the fire marshal's barrier, the car behind me pulled into a driveway and turned around. I had a brief conversation with the fireman and drove home."

"You couldn't see who was in the car?"

"It was dark. I could only see the outline of two figures when I first noticed the car on Santa Monica."

"This happened three days ago. Have you been followed since?"

Randolf shook his head.

"You said you found out something about your father's death that may have put your life in danger?"

"It's the only thing I can think of. Of course, my real estate business is very successful, but my competitors aren't the kind that would put out a contract on me."

"It sounds like someone's trying to scare you, not kill you," Lujack said matter-of-factly. "And if someone wanted you dead, it would have been much easier to kill you in the parking garage."

Kurt did not like that remark.

"I'm afraid I didn't anticipate where this might lead," he muttered nervously. "I have a wife and two daughters. I wouldn't want them to be in jeopardy because of what I consider a duty to my father . . . and to myself. Can you help me, Mr. Lujack?"

Randolf's tone was plaintive. The soft face showed fright yet a certain determination. In his own mind, he believed he was in danger. Lujack actually felt some compassion for him, as much compassion as he could muster for a kid who'd inherited twenty million bucks.

"Whatever fee you think . . . Morris Breen said you wouldn't be cheap."

Lujack could imagine Attorney Breen's Dun and Bradstreet mind conjuring up the finder's fee for this one. It was true Lujack had helped a few of Breen's clients out of precarious situations over the past few years and had been handsomely paid. But Lujack didn't want to be an ombudsman for rich people who got their noses dirty. He was a bookie, not a trouble-shooter. On the other hand, there were the goddamn Dodgers.

"Pardon?" Randolf said.

"Nothing," Lujack said, waving his hand, then reconsidered. "My fee will depend on what you want me to do. And so far, Mr. Randolf, I'm not sure what that is."

"Maybe I should start at the beginning."

"It wouldn't hurt."

"For the past two years, I've been conducting an unauthorized investigation of my father's death. But let me set the record straight—although you're probably aware of most of the circumstances. Dad's body was found in the sauna of his suite at Rancho Verde. The attending physician, Dr. Paul Makaris, determined that the cause of death was a heart attack. The San Diego coroner performed an autopsy, and his findings concurred with those of Dr. Makaris. My father's will, dated three months before his death, left the Marlins to his wife, Phyllis, and his real estate holdings were left to my sister and me."

Lujack nodded. He could still hear the "ss" in "Phyllis." Kurt was none too fond of his stepmother.

"In the course of my investigation, I have come across evidence which I think proves, or at least raises the strong possibility, that my father was murdered.

"I know you're thinking that this is sour grapes on my part because of the will," he quickly added, which was exactly what Lujack had been thinking. "But believe me, Mr. Lujack, I know the reason why Dad didn't leave me the Marlins, and I'm reconciled to his decision."

Lujack was, of course, tempted to ask why, but he didn't want to show too much interest. At least until his job and his reasonable unnamed fee were agreed on.

"The first thing that bothered me was the place he died. In a sauna, I mean. Dad hated saunas."

"I don't particularly like saunas either, but I've taken them before, to be social," Lujack said, wondering if the kid was serious.

"Not Dad. He never took them. He hated sweat."

"From the little I know about medicine, it isn't easy to fake a heart attack."

"But there are ways to put stress on a weak heart. And my father's heart, according to the coroner, was ready to go at any moment."

"Did your father know this?"

"I assume so, but Paul Makaris, his personal physician, won't talk to me. He says it's part of the physician-patient relationship. My own hunch is that he wants to protect Phyllis. After Dad died, Phyllis started going down to Rancho Verde. Now Makaris is her doctor."

Lujack thought he knew where Kurt's story was heading, down a familial cul-de-sac with cliffs for gutters.

"You're telling me that your stepmother knew about your father's condition?"

"It's a good possibility. Neither my sister nor I did, that's certain."

"And you think your stepmother had something to do with inducing this heart attack?"

"I think she knows more than she's telling. Let's leave it at that."

Lujack had heard rumors about the timely heart attack of Charles Randolf. There was little question that Phyllis had improved her "lie" financially and socially over the past few years. From Charlie's bimbo wife, she had become peripherally accepted in Los Angeles society. Not a bad trip for a four-time-married roller-derby queen from Gary, Indiana. But, still, a long way from murder.

"About ten months ago, I was put in touch with a maid who used to work at Rancho Verde. She told me she'd seen a very attractive young blonde leaving my father's suite about thirty minutes before his body was discovered. Neither the Rancho Verde private police nor the San Diego sheriff's department ever made any attempt to find this woman, although both were told about her by the maid.

"Also, there was a gash on Dad's forehead that never appeared on the autopsy report. Two witnesses told me about it."

"Did you pay any of those witnesses, Mr. Randolf?"

His face showed some sign of resentment. "Of course not. I did give the maid a little something for her time. But doesn't it strike you as odd that both the Rancho Verde and San Diego police have ignored these facts?"

"What does the D.A. say about your information?"

"He says two doctors examined Dad's body, ruled on the cause of death, and the case is closed."

"Do you think the D.A. and this Dr. Makaris are part of a murder plot?"

"I don't know who is part of it, Mr. Lujack," he replied angrily, defensive. "As I'm sure you know, the NFL owners and the commissioner's office have a lot of influence in this country, and they certainly didn't want my father's death investigated very thoroughly. In fact, I understand they didn't even want the county sheriff brought in. And, of course, my stepmother barely made it to Dad's funeral."

Lujack was beginning to fidget uncomfortably in his bamboo chair. He made a mental note never to date another interior decorator. Randolf's evidence was far from convincing. The fact that Charles Randolf was getting his valves blown out by some local talent during the siesta hour and unfortunately went past the red line didn't constitute murder. Assuming Randolf knew about his weak heart, he should have stayed in the pits. And the fact that the NFL owners hadn't wanted Randolf's final moments on earth framed for instant replay by the press wasn't too surprising either. He was equally sure the twenty-seven living owners weren't exactly anxious to have their wives privy to business practices of an owners' meeting. As much as he hated to admit it, Lujack was going to have trouble taking Kurt Randolf's money.

"Mr. Randolf, I think you can understand why the NFL owners might not want it made public that your father possibly died 'en flagrante,' as it were," Lujack said as tactfully as he knew how.

"I'm no prude, Mr. Lujack. I know that my father was a man of great appetites. Nor am I ignorant of the extracurricular activities that can be provided for men like my father at Rancho Verde. But there is one more thing you ought to know before you make up your mind whether or not to help me."

"I'm still listening."

Kurt Randolf reached into his coat pocket and pulled out a letter. "Two months ago, I received this from a retired FBI agent, Phil Muscagy. Muscagy worked in the Las Vegas office of the FBI for over ten years before retiring last winter. He said he'd heard from a mutual friend, a Las Vegas sportswriter who was also a good friend of Dad's, that I wasn't satisfied about the findings in Dad's death."

Reading from the letter, Randolf quoted: "During the period in question, our office was conducting an authorized wiretap on a phone used by Johnny Stella, a close associate of Frank Nimmo. On three occasions during that period I heard Stella describing Charles Randolf as being a large bettor on NFL football games through a Los Angeles bookmaker, Ernie Barbagelatta."

This time Lujack was impressed. This was one rumor he hadn't heard about Charles Randolf, and the mere fact that he hadn't made it all the more important. NFL owners had been known to bet on games. So had players. But an owner betting big and a bookie like Frank Nimmo, to say nothing of the FBI, sitting on the action—that was interesting. And possibly even dangerous for those who knew about it. Most bookmakers could take a local bust; the fines and sentences were nothing. But an FBI interstate bust, that was six years' hard time and the IRS looking down your throat. Now he understood why the kid had come to him.

"What happened to this investigation?"

"According to Muscagy, the special agent in charge of the Las Vegas bureau, Quentin Rule, came into the office one day and closed down the whole operation. Muscagy thinks that Nimmo found out about the wiretap and called in a few markers. They didn't have my father's voice on tape because he was evidently betting with this Barbagelatta in Los Angeles, and that isn't a federal offense."

"How about Barbagelatta? Was he on the tape from L.A. laying off to Nimmo in Vegas? That's a federal beef."

Randolf looked confused. "I'm not sure. Muscagy has since told me he thought they had some kind of case against Nimmo for interstate bookmaking but the FBI blew it. Muscagy said that was one of the reasons he'd quit. He told me the Vegas office of the FBI has more holes in it than a block of Swiss cheese."

"I've eaten a few of those sandwiches myself," Lujack said wryly. "Do you think your father owed Nimmo or Ernie 'Barbells' any money?"

"I really don't know. That's one of the reasons I came to you. Dad always paid his debts, I know that."

"Have you told anyone about your father's betting?"

"I talked to the commissioner's office. I was hoping this might get Dick Pressley moving. But the son of a bitch just gave me the runaround. 'Of course, we knew Charles made an occasional wager, but never on his own team. Your father was a man of complete integrity, Kurt, you know that.' I also know that he and Dad hated each other's guts."

Lujack enjoyed Randolf's imitation of the NFL commissioner. Pressley was smoother than cream on Jell-O. Unlike player betting, owner betting was tolerated (tacitly) by the commissioner's office. The double standard was attributable to the simple fact that it was the owners who paid the commissioner's salary. In many ways, the NFL reminded Lujack of his days working vice. You could bust all the criminals you wanted, but the only ones who went to jail were the ones who didn't count. Charles Randolf had been the one owner who publicly and privately fought with Pressley. To Lujack, it proved what arrogant assholes both men were.

Lujack tried to lean back in his chair—definitely the most uncomfortable chair he'd ever owned. He suspected that Kurt Randolf was somehow trying to lessen the humiliation of his father's will by his crusade to set the record straight. Maybe the son thought he could reverse the father's action by negating it—hence the murder theory. But it would probably be easier for Kurt to resurrect the USFL than to prove his stepmother, or the NFL owners and commissioner, or the bookmaking syndicates of Frank Nimmo and Ernie Barbagelatta were involved in Charlie Randolf's death. If only those goddamn Dodgers hadn't beaten the Yankees in five games.

"Tell you what I'm going to do, Mr. Randolf. I'll make a few calls. See what I can find out about your father's gambling debts—if he had any. I know a few people in Vegas close to Frank Nimmo. That guy's bad news. I also know Ernie Barbagelatta and some of his people at the Lido Club."

"I can't tell you how much I appreciate this," Randolf said with relief, again reaching into his pocket. He withdrew a checkbook as if paying for something would make it happen.

Lujack waved the checkbook away. "Don't give me any money now. I'll bill you at one hundred dollars an hour and expenses. Promise me that you'll let me do the investigating. You go back to your real estate developments."

"Then you do think I'm in danger."

"When I take on a job, I like to work in a vacuum. I can think better that way," Lujack told him. "But if Nimmo or Barbells is involved, and they think you're trying to crash their party, I wouldn't be leaning out any windows if I were you."

"I'll send you any material I've put together. Is there anything else I can do?"

"Yeah. Tell me why your father left the Marlins to your stepmother."

Kurt Randolf took a deep breath. For the first time since coming into Lujack's office, he seemed reluctant to talk. "It's a long story. There were inheritance tax advantages, but the real reason was that my sister and I never got along very well with Phyllis, and leaving the Marlins to her was Dad's way of punishing us. Me, really. Lane likes polo players, not football players."

Lujack didn't press it. There was a lot more to this particular cul-de-sac than he could see in one afternoon. He only hoped he wouldn't have to get out of the car. A drive-up teller, that's what he needed.

It was two days later, Wednesday, when Lujack picked up the evening paper at the "original out-of-town" newspaper stand on Robertson and saw Kurt Randolf's picture on page one, that he was reminded he hadn't called anyone about young Randolf's problem. It wasn't that he was uninterested or had forgotten, but he and Tommy were suffering through another horrendous week—the Marlins had trounced the Saints, and he'd been in no mood to talk, much less sleuth.

Next to Randolf was a picture of his wife. Her name was Kathleen. She was attractive in a Southern California sorority sort of way. Next to Kurt and Kathleen were pictures of their two daughters, Beth and Marian. Both little girls were very blond and very cute. When they grew up, they might be stunners like their Aunt Lane, except they weren't going to grow up. The caption beneath the picture said that all four members of the Randolf family were dead. They'd burned to death in their million-dollar Beverly Glen home the morning before. The first alarm had been sounded at four A.M. By the time the fire department had reached the scene, it was too late. Lujack scanned the story for mention of arson. "The cause of the fire is under investigation," an LAFD spokesman was quoted as saying.

Chapter 3

T HE FIRST THING LUJACK realized was that he didn't have a hangover. Just a trace of scotch across his forehead. The second was that he wasn't sleeping next to Karen Summers, his sometime squeeze. Thank God for small favors. His third realization wasn't as kind. It was Friday morning, and the Good Book was down eight thousand for the week just on pro baskets. And it was only the first week of the fucking season. If the Lakers had covered against the Blazers at the Forum, they'd be down another fifteen hundred, with college and pro football games still on the weekend menu. Usually, he phoned in for the late-night basket scores, but last night he couldn't. He'd put on a Miles Davis record, sat next to his bottle of Johnnie Walker Black, and slipped into the soothing world of Miles's trumpet, Coltrane's sax, and Wyn Kelley's piano.

He wondered if he were getting sick of bookmaking

and the sixteen- and seventeen-hour-a-day madness that a gambling life entailed. The fact that he and Tommy had lost over two hundred thousand dollars in the past three months could have something to do with his mood. Were the bettors getting smarter? Were the handicappers and bookies getting lazy? He knew other books were having trouble too. With all the different bets possible—over/under on total points, parlays, straight bets—and with the newspapers publishing gambling columns, injury reports, and betting lines as if gambling were legal, sooner or later all this available betting information had to give the sophisticated player an edge. He'd talked with a few books who thought the problem was in the size of the payoff. Bet eleven dollars to make ten. All the bookie's expenses had gone up with inflation—phones, phone men, rent, betting schedules, handicapping services—but the bookies were still only charging five percent of the total take. Lujack thought it would make good sense to change the payout price to maybe six dollars to make five. But that wouldn't change the two hundred grand he and Tommy were down.

Usually, Friday morning was his errand time. He would take his laundry into Brentwood Village, eat breakfast and read the paper, mosey around the village shops looking at the pretty girls in Dolphin shorts and Fila headbands. Even if you didn't jog, you had to dress like you did. Lujack's PAL sweatshirt usually short-circuited any prolonged conversations, which was fine with him.

After errands, he usually went to the Riviera Country Club and played tennis with Morris Breen or one of his other uptown friends. Being a member of the Riviera was one of the differences between being a bookie and a cop. As a bookie, he was an entrepreneur

and was allowed the status of a successful businessman. In fact, two of his clients had sponsored his
membership, which ran him a tidy thousand dollars a
month. As a vice detective, he would have been lucky
to get into the parking lot on a stolen car report, let
alone play in the Club Calcutta. But there would be no
tennis this Friday; Tommy had insisted they do something about the business. Today, not tomorrow—
before the college and pro games went off and they
found themselves down another ten or fifteen thousand dollars.

The phone rang as Lujack was mulling over this
unhappy prospect and trying to unscrew the top of an
instant coffee jar. It was a source of continual frustration to him how such a fastidious coffee maker kept
getting water in his instant coffee jar.

"Yeah?"

"Lunch, twelve-thirty," Tommy said.

"Yeah, yeah. What happened to the Lakers?"

"They won by seven. Cooper hit two free throws
with one second on the clock."

"Shit," Lujack said. The spread had the Lakers
minus six points.

"Right. When it rains, it pours shit," Tommy said,
quoting one of his own favorite Chinese-American
aphorisms.

"That makes it ninety-five hundred dollars down
going into today," Lujack said, scanning the Nevada
One betting schedule of games for Friday, October 22.

"Nothing looks too appetizing tonight. We might
get a little action on the Rice–TCU from the Texans.
Maybe we should knock the spread down a point to
TCU minus nine and a half. Our people don't bet
Rice. Nobody bets Rice."

"Forget the colleges. Sunday is what I'm worried
about," Tommy said, not concealing his impatience.

"We're already twenty thousand heavy on the Steelers, minus four against the Browns, and almost that much on the Jets, plus five against the Dolphins."

"We'll talk about it at lunch. Maybe we can jiggle the lines again," Lujack said, delaying the unpleasantness another two hours.

"We have to do more than jiggle the line, and you know it," Tommy said.

"I talked to Hiram last night," Lujack finally confessed. "We're meeting tomorrow night."

"Good," Tommy said and hung up.

The water was boiling, and he managed to get half a teaspoon of half-soluble coffee out of the jar. The date on the milk carton was October 18, but it didn't smell any worse than he felt. He didn't blame Tommy for wanting to cut down their exposure. By not laying off action, they had, in essence, been gambling more than bookmaking the last four years. The advantages—more flexibility in moving the betting lines and insurance against stiffs—were only advantages if they were winning. Now they were losing. The good business practice would be to balance the book and just play for five percent off the top. Five percent of a two-hundred-thousand-dollar weekly handle was ten thousand dollars. Equal to the amount they were losing now.

But there was a down side to laying off bets that he and Tommy didn't have to mention. The only L.A. bookmaker big enough and reliable enough to take their kind of action was Ernie Barbells, the Southern California syndicate boss and the man who ran the most lucrative bookmaking operation in the country, the Lido Club Book. Lujack had gone into the bookmaking business to make a good living without having to work for anyone but himself. If he and Tommy started laying off with Ernie Barbells, that independence would be gone. He'd be just another grunt working for a crooked boss. If he'd wanted to do that, he could have stayed with central vice and got his twenty-year pension.

The phone rang again. It was Sam Ballard from the LAFD arson squad. The news wasn't surprising. "Traces of C-four on all the exits and enough gasoline around the house to roast the Oscar Meyer Weinermobile. Whoever torched the place didn't want anyone to walk out. We've got a murder-one warrant on the case."

"Any leads, Sam?"

"There are only about twenty guys around capable of pulling off this kind of job. But that's too many to round up. I was hoping you could help."

"Not really. Except that it might not be a local torch."

"Some help," Sam said gruffly and hung up.

The coffee was weak. Lujack's thoughts droned in tandem with the refrigerator motor. He began to feel twinges, jolts of that same helpless, maddening frustration he had felt nearly five years ago when he walked into the second-floor room of the Temple Arms and found three Latino boys stacked in the corner. The bodies had been nude except for a tiny gold cross around one boy's thin neck. Each had been shot once in the ear with a .22-caliber pistol. All had worked for a downtown pimp, Manny Ramos, who specialized in supplying young boys for parties. Lujack interrogated Manny for two hours the day he discovered the bodies. When he was finished, Manny had to be taken to the emergency ward of the county hospital. The next day, Lujack was suspended from central vice, and Lieutenant Kyle Thurgood from homicide was assigned to the case.

A week later, his wife, Anna, moved out. She ended

up with his former partner, Marty Kildare. Anna said Lujack was impossible to live with. He never stopped being a cop. Marty was fun. He looked on the bright side of life. Eight months later, Marty looked on the bright side of a .38 police special and pulled the trigger. Anna blamed herself. Lujack knew better.

The boys' identities were never discovered. It was assumed they were Mexican nationals, but they could have been from any Latin American country. Their ages were determined to be thirteen or fourteen. All had been sexually molested. Three days after their "talk," Manny was released from the hospital. Six hours later, he was found dead in his Lincoln Heights home, shot once through the ear with a .22-caliber pistol. Two months later, Lieutenant Thurgood tucked the Temple Arms file into his unsolved drawer. He had never interviewed Manny Ramos. To Lujack's knowledge, he had not interviewed the two men Manny Ramos said had been at the party. Two very prominent Los Angeles businessmen. But the word of a dead pimp and a crazy vice cop hadn't been enough to rattle those particular gilded cages. Lujack wondered if it was good or bad luck that one of those partygoers happened to be Kurt's father, Charlie Randolf.

Lujack was seriously considering calling Karen Summers and driving to Malibu for a day of gin, tonic, and frolic. Karen was a brass plate of a lady with frosted blond hair, white teeth, and a fresh-smelling crotch. She fit L.A. like Willie Mays fit center field. Maybe that was why she sometimes made him feel like a third-base coach hitting fungoes. On second thought, Karen could wait.

He was trying, and failing, to get all his dirty clothes into one laundry bag when he heard a knock on the door. He didn't get many visitors at ten o'clock on a

Friday morning, and he approached the door expecting to find a Jehovah's Witness or, if his luck was changing, maybe the cute young film editor who lived in the apartment across the way wanting to borrow a cup of sugar . . .

His luck definitely was changing. The woman on his doorstep was the best-looking broad he had ever laid eyes on. Big-time beautiful in a sexy, sultry way, with dark magical eyebrows, tawny skin, and a strong, almost masculine chin. The pictures he'd seen didn't do her justice. She was wearing a white cotton shirt and Levis and still could have been on the cover of *Vogue*.

"Mr. Lujack?"

"You got me," Lujack said, not unmindful that it was the same response he'd given her brother five days earlier.

"My name's Lane Randolf. You knew my brother, Kurt."

"I'm very sorry about Kurt and his family," Lujack said awkwardly, letting the impact of the woman's presence sink in on him.

"May I come in?"

"Of course," he said, acutely aware that he was in his pajama bottoms and the apartment looked like a before ad for Raleigh Hills. "Let me get things straightened up a bit," he said, whisking away the Johnnie Walker from the coffee table. "Can I get you some coffee, Miss Randolf, or some juice? Just let me put some clothes on," he said, hurriedly disappearing into the bedroom for a quick change.

"Coffee would be nice," she called after him.

Glancing in the mirror, he noticed it wasn't one of his good days. A shave wouldn't hurt, nor would a face lift. He put his hand through his hair and tried to restore some order.

Watching her out of the corner of his eye as he scraped for some coffee, he wondered what the hell she was doing here. How had she even found the place? And why?

"You're wondering what I'm doing here?" she asked, fixing him with those dramatic dark eyes. A smudge of redness did nothing to subdue their magnificence.

"It crossed my mind."

"Yesterday, the fire inspector brought me the contents of my brother's safe. There was an envelope addressed to you that you were to get in the event of his death."

She made a brave attempt to sip at her watery coffee. It was his chance to fill in the blanks. He should have known better.

"Miss Randolf, I met your brother only once. That was five days ago," he explained.

"I don't care when you met him, Mr. Lujack," she interrupted. "One of the last things he did on this earth was write you a letter. The least you can do is read it."

If it were possible, she was even more beautiful when indignant. Why she was so indignant, he couldn't understand. Lujack took the envelope; inside was a letter dated October 20, Tuesday. The day after Kurt had come to the Chin Up and the day before the fire.

Dear Mr. Lujack,

If you're reading this letter, it means that my worst fears were confirmed. Enclosed is the information I promised you. It should be self-explanatory. Also enclosed is a check for $50,000 which my lawyer will process through my estate. This check, I trust, will cover any expenses you incur in finding those responsible for my death and the death of my father. Please conduct your investigation tactfully and keep my wife and family out of danger.

Sincerely,
Kurt Randolf

In death, Kurt Randolf was as thoughtful and naive as he was in life. It was unfortunate that his wife and daughters would no longer benefit from that thoughtfulness. He scanned the contents of the envelope. There was the letter from Phil Muscagy and Randolf's notes on subsequent phone conversations. Also the name of the maid at Rancho Verde, Carmen Melendez, and the name of the Rancho Verde doctor, Paul Makaris. Other names, numbers, and notes were included. Lujack didn't immediately realize their significance, although he recognized many NFL movers and shakers. There were even old newspaper clippings about Kurt's stepmother. How a black and white picture of Phyllis Berry skating around the Chicago Arena with an American flag attached to her helmet figured in Kurt's investigation of his father's death, Lujack had no idea. Finally, there was the check for fifty thousand dollars with instructions for payment.

He carefully folded the contents back into the envelope and handed it to Lane Randolf. Her dark eyes widened in anger, and instead he placed the envelope on top of the coffee table.

"Not enough money, Mr. Lujack?" she asked, looking around his disheveled apartment.

"Your brother and I never discussed a fee. I told him I'd make a few calls."

"About his investigation? About Daddy's death?"

"That's right."

"And did you make those calls?"

"No, I didn't," he said weakly, feeling inadequate and angry that this woman should somehow be making him feel responsible for Kurt Randolf's death. "Listen, lady, I'm very sorry about your brother and his wife and his daughters. But I had no idea he was in such danger."

"Neither did I," she said softly, her mind obviously retracing past thoughts and events. Lujack suddenly realized she too felt guilty. "Kurt loved Daddy very much, maybe too much, considering. Why couldn't he have just let the whole thing drop?"

"Your brother was convinced that your father was murdered," Lujack heard himself saying.

"What if he was? A selfish, obstinate, manipulative old man. Is he worth the death of two beautiful little girls?"

Lujack knew the answer to that question by heart but thought it better to keep his own counsel this time.

"I loved my father, Mr. Lujack, please don't misunderstand. But when he died I felt no need to try to resurrect him." She hesitated, glaring at Lujack. "But why am I telling you all this? You're obviously much too busy playing your jazz records and drinking your scotch to be interested in finding Kurt's murderer."

"You said I wasn't interested. I didn't. Who do you talk to when the mirror is broken, Miss Randolf?"

Lane Randolf's gorgeous face seemed to lose its composure. For a second, Lujack thought she might actually be listening to something he said. Or possibly doubting something she said. No such luck.

"Does that mean you're for hire?"

"It means I'm interested in finding out who killed your brother."

"In that case, there's a man I think you should talk

to," she said, recovering her aloof tone. "He works for the arson squad of the L.A. Fire Department. His name is Sam Ballard."

She pulled a card out of her wallet. Sitting upright in his old leather recliner, he couldn't help but notice her breasts pressing against her cotton shirt. She had a figure to match her face. More's the pity. She was an arrogant, self-centered bitch.

"Mr. Ballard believes that the cause of the Briarwood fire was arson. He told me the squad found traces of some kind of explosive compound on the scene."

Lujack carefully put Sam Ballard's card on top of the envelope. She was annoyed but didn't say anything this time.

"I talked with Sam this morning," Lujack explained. "He's far more qualified to follow up any arson leads than I am. The police are now treating the case as homicide. They'll also be assigning personnel."

She looked around his apartment full of records and betting schedules. He wondered if she were comparing him to his counterpart in the LAPD. "If my brother came to you for help, you must be the right person. He was very thorough at that kind of thing. It was one of the few characteristics he had in common with our father. Do you mind if I ask you a question, Mr. Lujack?"

"Be my guest, Miss Randolf."

"What is it you do? Are you some kind of private detective? I know you're not with the police department or the government."

"What I do most of the time is take bets. I'm a bookmaker."

"A bookmaker. Well, well. Did my brother know this?"

"I expect he did. You said he was very thorough about that kind of thing."

"Yes," she agreed, watching him with a little more interest. "Much of what's in this envelope has to do with gambling. My father was a gambler. Was that why Kurt came to you?"

"Probably."

"And these gamblers. Do you think they're the ones who had Kurt killed?"

"It's a possibility. The job was professional. And professional gamblers have been known to do business with professional arsonists."

"Do you think I should tell the police about our arrangement? And about the contents of the envelope?"

"Not if they don't ask you. The fewer people who know about our arrangement, the better. As for the information in the envelope, Kurt kept the authorities informed about his discoveries."

"It didn't seem to do much good, did it?"

"Not much," Lujack admitted. "Who's the executor of Kurt's estate?"

"I am. Along with L. Clark Sterling of Brompton, Hanover, and Sterling."

Lujack smiled.

"You know Clark?"

"Doesn't everyone?" he said of the super-lawyer and, in recent years, super-sports-agent-lawyer.

"Clark was Daddy's lawyer. Kurt always trusted Clark, although I could never understand why. The man is positively unctuous. Even Phyllis can't stand him."

"If possible, I'd like to meet your stepmother."

Lane Randolf raised her eyebrows. "What did Kurt tell you about Phyllis? That she was a crazy, conniving bitch who saw my father as a one-way ticket out of poverty, then cashed that ticket in for an NFL football team?"

"He said that you and he didn't get along with Phyllis very well, and it put a certain strain on your relationship with your father."

"Enough strain for my father to leave Phyllis the Marlins when she didn't know a football from a Frisbee." She laughed bitterly. "After all, the Marlins were the only thing Kurt ever wanted from Daddy."

Suddenly, she caught herself being unguarded. The mirror cracking. Taking a deep breath, she stood up. The quickening of Lujack's heart recorded the event. She was indeed a stunning woman, even at ten-thirty in the morning. She purposely left the envelope on the table.

"I'll see what I can do about arranging for you to meet Phyllis," she said, sneaking a look at her watch, pausing for effect. "I know Kurt wanted you to find Daddy's killer as well as his, but as far as I'm concerned, that fifty thousand dollars is for one job only: to find the people responsible for the deaths of Kurt and his family. I talked with Clark this morning, and he agrees. Why don't you drop around his office next Monday morning about ten, and we'll make it legal?"

The most Lujack could muster was a sad smile. He'd never met such a beautiful, sexy, arrogant woman in his life. He wanted to throw the check in her face, and, as much as he needed the money thanks to the goddamn Dodgers, he wanted, needed, to see her again.

"You'll probably want my phone number," she said, taking a pencil from her purse before he could answer.

"I'm dying for it."

Ignoring his comment, she wrote her address and

phone number on a book of Le Dome matches. She was letting herself out when he called her back.

"Miss Randolf, you must realize that these people your brother suspected of being involved in your father's death may be involved in your brother's death. These are the kinds of people our system of justice doesn't exactly thrive on. They can take care of themselves. They have juice."

"Are you telling me you can't handle the job, Mr. Lujack?"

"I'm just telling you that knowing who set that fire and bringing whoever ordered it to justice are two very different propositions."

"You find the man, or woman, who gave the orders, Mr. Lujack. I'll take care of the justice," she said, and she headed her Calvin Kleined rear end out of his apartment.

Lujack pulled a beer out of the refrigerator. Not surprisingly, it overflowed on the kitchen floor when he yanked off the top. He was in no mood for doing the laundry and kicked the bag from the hall back toward his bedroom, sending the dirty clothes all over the floor. He walked back and forth from the kitchen to the living room, trying to sort out his responsibilities from his emotions, the past from the present. The manila envelope on the coffee table dominated the room and his thoughts like a rectangular evil eye.

His final words to Lane Randolf had been more for his sake than hers. People like Lane Randolf didn't live within the parameters of justice, social or legal. She was too much like her father to believe in such pedestrian concepts. Her reasons for hiring Lujack were to fulfill her familial obligation, nothing else. The girl, for all her outrageous beauty and allure, couldn't become a part of it.

His luck certainly had changed. Except that it

wasn't good or bad luck that had brought first Charlie Randolf and then L. Clark Sterling back into his life. Randolf and Sterling, the two names Manny Ramos had given him. According to Manny, Randolf had been one of the guests; Ramos had recognized him from newspaper pictures. But it had been Clark Sterling who paid the bills. Sterling had been the host. And now, with Ramos and Randolf dead, only Sterling could give Lujack the answers to what had happened to the three boys . . . and, perhaps, what had happened to his own life.

No, it wasn't luck. Luck was chance. It was fate. Fate was destiny. A gambler might confuse chance with destiny, but a vice cop wouldn't. Lujack picked up his wallet from the coffee table. He opened it and took out a tiny gold cross. Carefully, he placed it on top of the legacy of Kurt Randolf.

Chapter 4

IT WAS SATURDAY NIGHT, and every star in hooker heaven was out. Lujack drove east on Sunset past the Strip. "The more things change, the more they remain the same," some Frenchman said sometime. Lujack wondered if the Frenchman had ever spent time on Sunset Boulevard; he would have appreciated it.

Lujack had grown up near Sunset, on Curson, up by the old Wattles mansion. When he was a boy, he and his friends used to go by the Sunset Towers after school and ogle the glamorous girls who always seemed to be about. "Call girls," his father had said with a wink, explaining that things had gotten pretty quiet on the Strip since the days of Mickey Cohen. It wasn't until later that Lujack found out what call girls did and later still when he heard the story of Hollywood's most famous bookmaker.

Working foot patrol during the seventies, Lujack had come across another kind of working girl. The

Sunset Towers was falling down, and tight Lana Turner sweaters and high-heeled shoes were passé. The kind of ass you could buy on Sunset Boulevard in those days wore bikinis, flashed beaver. Some actually jumped into a john's car at the red light. If they could cop the driver's joint before the light changed, they had a sale.

Now, in the bottom-lined eighties, Lujack knew of young runaways being met at the bus terminal downtown by representatives of so-called talent agencies. The representative, a glorified pimp, would supply the girl, or boy, with drugs and promises of a show business career, while in the meantime they turned tricks to pay their mounting drug bills. If a girl was pretty enough and sophisticated enough, she might get a job working out of one of the private clubs along the Strip. Until her tits headed south and her mind turned to mush. A boy might end up with a "producer" for a year or two, until his eyes started to crinkle. Eventually, the girls would find their way down on Sunset working out of plasterboard motels or the backseat of a john's car. The boys would play the hitchhike game on Santa Monica Boulevard, hoping the next trick wasn't the one who gave them AIDS—knowing they'd been exposed years ago. Life on the street had always been a house game. A sucker bet.

Cops and whores. The two were more alike than most coppers wanted to admit. "Want a date? What you want? How much you got? Got a place?" He'd heard those questions hundreds of times in the same high, fake-feminine, come-on voice. At first, when he rousted hookers, there was an underlying sexual tension. It was exciting and stimulating, having girls, many of them under eighteen, in such a vulnerable position. With every arrest, there was an implicit and sometimes explicit offer of sex for freedom. Lujack remembered the one time he had made the trade. He'd been in a down period with Anna (when hadn't he?), and Leanne was irresistible. A streaked blonde from the San Joaquin Valley who said one more bust would put her back on the farm with her lecherous father and stone-faced mother. They'd gone to her apartment, a one-roomed disaster above the boulevard. It smelled like incense and cum. She'd given him a kiss on the cheek when he left. The next day on the street, she'd smiled sweetly, and the day after that she ignored him. His partner, Marty Kildare, told him she was doodling a plainclothes vice cop and was off limits. Cops and whores hadn't been the same to Lujack after Leanne. He didn't hate whores like the other cops did, but he thought he understood how much they hated him.

A billboard advertised a special Halloween car wash. Where Lujack was going, it was Halloween every night. Hiram Hotel had insisted they meet at Salome's Lair, a nude-dancing clip joint on the corner of Sunset and Poinsettia. Lujack couldn't understand why an uptown blood like Hiram would want to meet him at Salome's. The girls who danced there were junkies making one last pass at show business before ending up on the streets. Not at all Hiram's type of girl. He preferred "starlets, not harlots."

The nude neon Salome dancing behind her diaphanous veil would have been more convincing if all of the sign had been working. For those who couldn't fill in the blanks, there was a painting on the front wall of Salome reclining on a couch, studying the head of John the Baptist. Lujack had always thought it the most apropos piece of art in Hollywood. A whore looking at the head of a john on a silver platter.

Lujack parked in the back lot and warily walked around the hot-pink stucco nightclub to the entrance marked by a black curtain. The first thing he noticed was a very thin, very pallid woman's body in a G-string and high heels dancing the night away on an elevated stage. The lighting was out of a nonunion horror film—smudge-pot cinema. What the dancer lacked in tits, she made up for in tattoos. The second thing he noticed was trouble, trouble in the fierce face of Philip Karabian. The last time he'd seen Karabian was in the men's room of an Armenian restaurant on Hollywood Boulevard. Karabian was the maitre d'-bouncer who had a fondness for Quaaludes and busboys.

"Looking for a date, Lujack?" the swarthy man said, putting a thick arm out to block Lujack's passage.

"When did you get promoted, Karabian?" Lujack said, looking past the Armenian, surveying the evening's crowd. There were a few social security perverts at the bar, finishing off a lovely day by drinking up their checks with a floor show. A pimp he recognized was sitting at one of the tables with two of his girls. A little pep talk before they hit the bricks.

"Still the funny one, aren't you?" Karabian said, pushing Lujack a little. "Where's the cute one? Kildare? That's right, he couldn't take it when you lent him your wife. Sucked on a hollow-point lollipop."

Lujack looked down at the heavyset Armenian. He wondered if Karabian was armed. Lujack hated fighting foreigners.

"I don't see anyone in here mean enough to make you disrespectful, faggot. Now why don't you just let me go over to the bar and have a drink while I wait for my friend?"

Karabian gave an odd grin, then took an awkward swing at Lujack with his right hand. Lujack fended off the blow with his elbow and sent Karabian reeling into a table with a stinging left hook. Karabian was still grinning as he remained on the floor. Lujack finally got the joke. He felt two large arms wrap around him. Using a move Tommy had taught him, he raised both feet and violently kicked his heels into the man's shins. The man growled, and the grip released instantly. Ignoring Karabian, Lujack swung around and came face to collar bone with a huge Armenian.

The two men half-circled each other momentarily, the Armenian with his hands at his sides like a gorilla planning to tear Lujack apart, literally. Lujack knew he must move fast. He threw two left jabs. The monster kept coming. Again, two more quick jabs, following with a left-right combination that sent the giant man reeling back into the curtain. Lujack ripped off the rod and smashed it over his head. With one hard kick, he sent the man through the doorway and down the steps.

The girl on the stage was unfazed by the melee, still bumping and grinding as far as her ninety-pound frame could take her. The mustached bartender gave Lujack a silent salute. None of the customers seemed upset. On the floor, Karabian was rubbing his jaw and swearing in Armenian. Lujack toyed with the idea of drop kicking the faggot outside to join his friend but decided it wasn't worth the shoe leather.

The bartender took a step backward as Lujack approached the bar. Lujack, for the moment, was the king of this Casbah.

"Pour me a brandy. A Hennessey, please, not the lacquer thinner in the well."

"Yes, sir," the bartender answered, scampering down the boards.

"Ossifer, ossifer, my license, it's perspired," came a voice from the direction of the curtain.

It was an old in-joke. Hiram Hotel imitating a jive nigger Lujack had once pulled over on Central Avenue.

"Ossifer, I jus' loves you poleece. I done voted you that raise you wanted. Yes, sir! I only wishes it could be radioactive."

Lujack greeted the tall, dapper Hiram Hotel with a hug. As usual, the goateed Hotel was flanked by his Filipino chauffeur-bodyguard, Felix. Hotel was the only six-foot three-inch black man Lujack could imagine who would have a five-foot four-inch Filipino bodyguard, but then Felix was no ordinary bodyguard. He had served ten years as President Marcos's personal bodyguard, and there were few men in the business more lethal.

Karabian was still on the floor. The entrance of Hotel and Felix added another measure of distress to Karabian's already unhappy evening.

"What are you doing here, James?" Hotel said, in his normal rich baritone, after assaying the damage. "Making shish kebab with my management team?"

"I didn't know they were yours."

"We took over Salome's about six months ago. Can't you see the improvement? Look at this talent."

Hotel grabbed the nearest dancer by the back of her neck as he would a cat. The bikini-clad black woman's eyes widened unhappily. Whatever beauty or talent she had once had was long gone. So was her pride; she passively bore Hiram's contempt.

"I thought you were big time, Hiram. What are you doing terrorizing these poor ladies?"

"Goes with the territory, my man. You gotta know that. If we don't put a couple of toll booths down here, every pimp and pusher in Hollywood thinks he can drive through free."

"Crawl through, maybe," Lujack said. It was the first he'd known of Hotel's involvement with Ernie Barbagelatta's Sunset Boulevard prostitution services.

"Scat," Hotel ordered the hooker, grabbing a bottle of Hennessey off the bar. "Follow me. There's an office here somewhere. Let's hope none of Karabian's butt boys are back there playing leap frog.

"Felix, you make it so Phil and his fat friend get that curtain put back before the cops come by and give the girls a ticket for flashing rasty poon tang in front of the almighty public."

Lujack followed Hotel into the office at the back of the club. It was strange that Hotel had come in just after the fight. It was strange that Hotel had wanted to meet him at Salome's in the first place.

"So what gives, Hiram?"

"What're you talking, my man? You called me. Said you were a little heavy on the Steelers and the Jets and wanted to throw some of it my way."

"You can take it?"

Hotel swirled the brandy in his bar glass.

"How much you got?"

"Twenty-five thousand on the Steelers at minus four. Twenty thousand on the Jets at plus five."

Hotel swirled the numbers as he did the brandy. "Steelers minus five, Jets plus four and a half," Hotel offered.

"Steelers minus four and a half," Lujack countered.

"You got it." Hotel laughed richly. "Now tell me why you're doing it."

"New policy. We're pulling in a little of our exposure."

"Tommy's getting nervous, eh? Fuckin' Chinaman. Not like you to pull anything."

Hotel was enjoying having him on the spot. Lujack had expected it.

"We took a thrashing on the Series."

"That's the trouble with you local boys. When the home team wins, you get killed. I told you three years ago, you should spread your action around. The people on the East Coast were dying to lay off their Yankee bets."

"We haven't been doing great on football either."

"Who has? Bettors must be getting smarter, or the handicappers are getting lazy. Ernie don't like it when the handicappers get lazy."

Lujack could imagine.

"'Course, you and Tommy have all those uptown clients. Movie stars and what have you. I take care of the working man. When I have a bad week, it's like doing social service."

"Yeah. You and Ernie. Just like the Salvation Army, aren't you? Like those girls out here dancing. If they weren't working for you, they'd probably be whores and junkies."

"Chances are," Hiram agreed.

"So what are Phil Karabian and his pet water buffalo doing here tonight?" Lujack asked. "I thought we were friends."

"Hey, my man. I didn't know you and Karabian weren't cool. I brought you down here so none of your players would know we were talking. I was trying to do you a favor, man."

Lujack took a sip of his brandy. "You're right. I shouldn't be so jumpy. Tommy's got me uptight."

"Hey—in this business, you got to expect a down year. What you're doing is right. Lay off when you're going bad. Play the percent for a while. Be cool until the bowl games, then sit back and rake it in. You stay with Hiram, things'll turn around for you."

"There's gotta be a better way to make a living than

having to worry about the L.A. Marlins falling on their kisser every Sunday afternoon."

Hiram snorted derisively. "Fleet White, the Marlins' wide out, told me Phyllis came to training camp this summer wearing a white robe and a pyramid hat. I hear she's really got the hots for this pyramid minister."

"Not as hot as somebody made it for her stepson last night."

"You got that right." Hiram laughed. If Hiram knew anything about Kurt's murder, he didn't let it show. "That kid was as lame as Phyllis. Remember when he used to be the Marlins' water boy, and you, Marty, and me used to pour beer on him and his old man when they ran out of the Coliseum tunnel?"

"I don't remember pouring anything on the Randolfs, but I do remember you drooling over the Marlin Girls."

"You weren't exactly fingering your rosary beads, my man."

Lujack laughed. They had been good times. In those days, Hiram was manager of the Pearl, a classy black nightclub on the Strip. He hadn't known why a cool brother like Hotel would want to hang out with two Hollywood beat cops. When he finally found out, it was too late.

"I heard an interesting story the other day about old Charlie," Lujack said offhandedly. "Word is that he used to get down big on the pros, sometimes even against his own team."

"That don't surprise me. Charlie Randolf would bet against his own mother if there was money to be made."

"I heard he put a lot of money with Frank Nimmo."

"Hey, I thought you were out of the cops," Hotel said with a broad smile. "And anyway, what should I know about money with Nimmo? You know Ernie and I don't have anything to do with the Vegas scene. Sure, we lay off some action with Frank, but Ernie don't like getting too close to Frank and his Chicago friends."

"So—Charlie never got down here in town. Not even at the Lido?"

This time, there was less than full value to the smile. Hotel took another sip of brandy. It was obvious he wasn't going to say any more until Lujack told him why he wanted to know. Before Lujack could think of anything to say, there was a loud commotion outside. A man could be heard yelling. Both Hotel and Lujack recognized the voice.

"Fuck, what's that ravioli face doing down here?" Hotel said with exasperation. "Better let me handle this, Jimmy. Strictly a social call, right?"

Lujack wasn't about to argue as the door abruptly swung open and the square form of Ernie Barbagelatta entered the office. Ravioli face—with plenty of marinara sauce—was a fitting description of Ernie. He was a short, thick man with a body still hard for his age. His hair was beginning to recede, but it was still as black as that day in Brooklyn when he had dropped a three-hundred-pound barbell on the throat of a Gambino family henchman, Carlo Benedetti. Hence "Ernie Barbells."

"What's this asshole doing here?" Ernie demanded.

"Jimmy and I are old friends," Hotel said smoothly. "We were catching up on the old days."

"He's shit. He and that fuckin' Chinaman are both shit. I don't want him in any of my clubs."

Lujack thought it was time he paid his respects. "How ya doing, Ernie? Nice place you got here."

"You the one who punched out those Armenian scumpots?"

"They gave me the wrong table."

Ernie's marinara sauce slowly turned an eggplant purple. "And maybe you think you can show me where to sit?"

"Here. Take my chair," Lujack offered, knowing that, besides Felix, Ernie had at least two bodyguards of his own outside. "I was just telling Hiram that I was late for my date."

He was halfway out of his chair when Barbagelatta's hand pushed him back. "What you doin' here, Lujack?"

"Like the man said, we were talking about old times—how we used to piss on Charlie Randolf when he ran through the Coliseum tunnel."

"Lujack, you never had the balls to piss on old Charlie. As for Hiram, he knows better than to piss on rich white folks, don't you, Ram?"

Ernie shot Hiram a hard look. The question wasn't a joke.

"Not unless somebody richer and whiter's payin' me to." Hotel smiled.

Barbagelatta laughed but wasn't amused. Lujack wondered what was going down between them. The two had been together ever since Hotel had helped Barbells move into the top spot of the L.A. crime family in the late seventies. At the time, many people had been surprised that a made mafioso like Barbells would be so closely associated with a black bookmaker, but their collaboration had consolidated much of Southern California's gambling establishment and had made both men a lot of money.

"That's right, you were a friend of Charlie's, weren't you, Ernie? You used to play the horses together at Del Mar . . ."

"That wasn't all we played." Ernie smiled fondly, and Lujack knew he'd guessed right.

"I heard there was one filly, a blonde . . ."

Ernie's eyes squinted suspiciously. The game was over. "Forget it, Lujack. I read the papers."

"I never doubted it."

"Good-bye, Lujack."

Hiram stood up. Lujack followed his lead.

"I'll be back in a minute, boss. Don't want Jimmy to break any more of our property."

"Then we'd have to shoot him," Ernie cackled.

Hotel walked Lujack out past Barbells's phalanx of bodyguards, the always taciturn Felix, the sallow dancing girl, and the rest of the debris in Salome's Lair. The night was still warm. In the background, he could hear a siren. Probably a 211.

"What gives with you and the godfather?"

"Picked up on that, did you?"

"I'm not as dumb as I look. College dropout. Class of '72."

"Sometimes I think you'd have been better off graduatin'," Hiram said as they entered the parking lot.

"Sometimes so do I," Lujack said. "In the meantime, maybe you can do me a favor."

Hotel kept walking. Hiram wasn't one to volunteer.

"Find out the name of the blonde who used to play with Charlie Randolf down at Rancho Verde."

"The man's dead a long time, Jimmy. What do you care?"

"Let's say it's a debt to the family."

"Some debts are better left unpaid. If I remember, you told me that."

"That was when I was a cop."

"You still blame yourself for Anna, don't you?"

Lujack hesitated, watching Hotel's handsome countenance. "Why shouldn't I?"

"Because you're twice the person and twice the cop that Marty ever was."

"Anna didn't think so."

"Maybe she did," Hotel said as they stopped in front of the Mustang.

Lujack suddenly felt the helplessness enveloping him. He wanted to get out. "You'll call when you get the name?"

Hotel smiled, then nodded.

"If I were you, Hiram, I'd stay away from Italian restaurants for a while."

"Since when are you worryin' about my sweet ass?"

"Since I gave you forty-five grand of my action."

"Talk to you Tuesday." Hotel laughed and strolled back into the club.

Lujack sat in the parking lot for a minute before starting the Mustang. Maybe she did?

Chapter 5

LUJACK FORLORNLY POKED AT his chicken chow mein. He'd lost his appetite two days earlier when Mick Mayflower had thrown three touchdown passes in the second half to rally the Marlins to within three points of the heavily favored Cowboys. First beating the Saints, then almost knocking off the Cowboys. Burt Masters and his Hollywood hotline had been right—Mick Mayflower actually could throw a spiral—and Tommy and Lujack were paying to watch him. To the tune of twelve grand that Sunday.

"What's the matter, Jimmy? You look yellower than your partner," Susie Katz said, digging into her second plate of Mu Shu pork. Susie was unorthodox in many ways—one of them being her love for Mu Shu pork.

"Poverty's bad for my digestion."

"Poverty. You and Tommy've made more money than any bookies I've ever worked for. And that includes my late husband, Myron—may he rest in peace."

"I think we'd all be better off moving to Vegas and piggybacking on Irv's action."

"Irving's a wonderful son and the smartest handicapper in the western world, but, believe me, he'd drive you crazy in two hours. He's the only person I've ever heard of who brushes his teeth by the numbers."

Lujack managed a smile as Susie demolished another forkful of pork. Susie wasn't a sixty-five-year-old woman trying to look forty. She was earthy, dignified, a typical Jewish grandmother—who happened to work the phones at the neighborhood bookie joint.

"I think I might have a new player for you."

"Another Lido Club defector?"

"Ever since Lefty Morgenstern got iced and the purple people-eater took over, nothing's been right at the club," Susie said, lamenting again the murder of Lefty Morgenstern six years ago and the subsequent takeover of the Lido Club (Beverly Hills's most popular men's club) by Ernie Barbagelatta.

"This guy's a connoisseur, Jimmy. Ten, fifteen dimes a week. The only problem is he likes to bet before he goes to work. And I'm not taking any action before breakfast for anyone. Not even for a cute bookie like you."

"Tommy's an early riser. If this guy's the player you say he is . . ."

"Have I ever brought you a stiff?"

Lujack didn't have to answer. Susie was responsible for eleven or twelve of the Good Book's best customers. All were serious bettors who used to do business with her late husband. For bringing them into the fold, Susie got a standard fifteen percent of their losses. Lujack knew she picked up nearly twenty grand a year off her clients.

"So when do we meet him?"

"Not today," Susie said, looking past Lujack. Lujack turned to see Lieutenant Kyle Thurgood coming into the restaurant. The beefy homicide detective was, per usual, dressed in an expensive dark suit complete with a handkerchief discreetly tucked in his breast pocket. Thurgood had the appearance and the personality of an Irish pimp who bought his clothes on Savile Row. He stopped briefly to have a word with Tommy, who waved an arm in Lujack's direction.

"I think I'd better be moseying home, Jimmy," Susie said. "I've got a horse going in the fifth at Oak Tree."

"I'll call you when the phone's back on the hook."

Thurgood approached as Susie was getting up. He purposely blocked her exit.

"Long time no see, Susie. You bringing Lujack any luck?"

"Some people don't need luck, Lieutenant," Susie said, looking at Thurgood's ample stomach. "They're just born fat."

"Maybe you won't be so funny if I take you downtown and charge you with bookmaking."

"I'm a seamstress, Lieutenant. My husband was the bookmaker. God rest his soul."

"Save it for the rabbi, Susie."

"Jews don't believe in confession, Lieutenant. We *know* who's guilty."

"What can we do for you, Lieutenant?" Lujack interjected.

"See you later, boys. Jimmy, I'll call you when the silk comes in," Susie said with a wink.

This time Thurgood let Susie pass.

"It's a miracle that broad's never done any time," Thurgood said.

Lujack didn't respond. He was no fan of Kyle Thurgood's.

"I hear you got a new job," Thurgood continued.

"What's it to you?"

"It's my job, too. The chief got a call this morning from the D.A.; Ballard confirmed arson. That means murder. That means me."

"May the best man win."

"That's why I came down here. To wish you luck . . . and to tell you that if I even hear about you poking into places you don't belong, I'll have this Chinese grease factory closed down before you can say health inspector."

"What's the matter, Kyle, can't stand the competition? Afraid someone might have to go to jail this time?"

Thurgood's weary blue eyes pinched in anger.

"I'm not the one who couldn't hack it on the right side of the law, Lujack."

"That's right, Kyle. I got sick of cops who looked the other way for a new set of tires or four season tickets."

"Sometimes I don't know if you're stupid or just dumb."

"Three young boys get murdered, next season you're sitting on the fifty-yard line in the box of one of the suspects. To me, that's simple arithmetic."

Thurgood reached across the table to grab Lujack's throat; he was too slow and too fat. Lujack banged his arm down on the table with a quick, hard chop.

"Shit!" Thurgood yelled. Tommy looked up from the bar. The customers glanced uneasily at Lujack's table. "You broke my fuckin' wrist."

"I doubt it."

Thurgood painfully lifted his wrist off the table and made a motion to get up.

"What I said about the Randolf case—don't even think about it."

"You going to have your friend Sterling cancel my check?"

"Still don't know when to quit, do you, Lujack? No matter who gets hurt."

It was Lujack's turn to get angry. "Meaning?"

"You know damn well who I mean," Thurgood said, shooting an expensive cuff with his good arm. Even in retreat, Kyle played the fat dandy.

Lujack did know who Thurgood meant. During that season of discontent, there was another couple at many of the games with Thurgood in Clark Sterling's box: Marty and Anna. The first time, Lujack thought maybe Marty might have been along for the ride, but later, when he saw Marty joking with Sterling, Lujack began to wonder. He'd never asked Marty about Sterling, but he'd heard that Marty had met the lawyer through Hiram. There was talk of Sterling representing Marty and Thurgood for a television show about the two cops' adventures. After Marty killed himself, the word was the sponsors lost interest.

"Kyle didn't look very happy," Tommy said, sitting next to him.

"It must have been something I ate."

"I keep telling you, Chinese food is unhealthy, stunts your growth, turns your skin yellow."

Lujack took a bite of cold noodles.

"Lane Randolf called while you were schmoozing with Thurgood," Tommy said. "She'll pick you up at five-thirty . . . and don't be late," he added, doing a decent imitation of Lane's patrician accent.

"She's a paying client, Tom. Fifty thousand dollars, half of which goes to the business."

"She's a rich and beautiful woman. My uncle says, 'Woman wash laundry. Men wash money.'"

"This money-laundering uncle of yours, is he any relation to the gambling uncle that was in the coma?"

"The Chins are a very big family."

"I know. I've read about them in the phone book."

Chapter 6

DRIVING DOWN SUNSET BOULEVARD in a Rolls Royce convertible with a woman like Lane Randolf made living hard to resist. The American dream was still shimmering . . . at least for the moment. Lane had insisted on taking her car to the NFL charities party Phyllis was giving at the Randolf mansion. The party would give Lujack a good chance to observe the respectable suspects on Kurt's list: NFL Commissioner Dick Pressley, Dr. Paul Makaris, L. Clark Sterling, the Reverend Billy Moore, and, of course, Phyllis herself.

After his friendly chat with Kyle Thurgood and the meeting the day before with Lane and L. Clark Sterling, Lujack knew he was going to have to find the man or men who had killed Kurt Randolf and his family. Maybe if he were lucky, he would find out why. That was the difference between vice and homicide. In vice, nobody asked why . . . only how much.

Lane's long brown arms turned the wheel effortlessly through the gates leading to the Randolf mansion. Her posture even when driving was relaxed and alluring. She was wearing a dark green summer dress that matched the color of the grounds. An emerald bracelet completed the picture.

In addition to the Marlins, Phyllis had inherited the thirty-room mansion. Whatever the tax benefits in the inheritance sweepstakes between Phyllis and Charlie's two children, Stepmom Phyllis had undoubtedly come out a winner. Lujack guessed about sixty million for Phyllis as opposed to forty million split between the two kids. The house and grounds were supposedly worth ten million dollars, and as Lujack rode up the seemingly endless driveway toward the Georgian mansion, he didn't doubt it.

"Daddy always wanted to own the most spectacular home in Bel Air," Lane either explained or apologized, "and when the Litton property came up for sale, he couldn't resist."

"This place makes Pickfair look like God's Little Acre."

"Do you know Dr. Buss?"

"Probably not as well as you do. We've spoken on the phone."

Lane let that sleeping innuendo lie, for which Lujack was thankful.

There were probably two hundred guests milling about between the pool and a large, colorful circus tent.

"The only backyard I've seen bigger than this was at Versailles."

"For an ex-cop, you seem to get around." Lane smiled.

"U.C. Berkeley student exchange program. *Parlez vous français?*"

"Seulement en lit."

Lujack smiled dumbly, and Lane's magical eyebrows arched seductively. He made a mental note to find out what the hell she'd said.

"Let's find Phyllis. It shouldn't be too hard."

They slowly made their way through the crowd. NFL heroes from the past and the present were on hand plus a goodly number of Hollywood celebrities, some of whom were Good Book customers. The way Lujack saw it, the producers were trying to get tips from the athletes, and the ex-athletes were trying to get jobs from the producers. Burt Masters was standing at one of the bars with Aaron Spelling, Jim Garner, and Joe Theisman. Masters did a double take when he saw Lujack wending his way through the crowd with Lane.

"What are you doing here, Jimmy?" Masters asked, breaking away from the bar. "In your business, you don't need any deductions."

"You've been winning so much money lately, I had to find out where you're getting your information. Now I know."

"Theisman? Are you kidding?" Masters laughed. "I asked him how his knee was after the Giants game, and he gave me a lecture on the patella, the tibia, and the fibula. I thought he was talking about the 1949 Fordham backfield."

"Burt, this is Lane Randolf."

"Nice to meet you, Miss Randolf. I was very sorry to hear about your brother and his family."

"It's nice to know someone is, Mr. Masters," Lane said, glancing around the premises.

The only reminder of Kurt's death Lujack could see was the Marlins team flag at half-mast.

Burt quickly excused himself as Lujack heard a rustling behind him.

"Lane, darling, there you are," said the friendly voice of Phyllis Randolf, president and owner of the Los Angeles Marlins.

Lane may have been more beautiful than her pictures, but Phyllis was certainly more dramatic. Her white floor-length hostess gown had a plunging neckline more reminiscent of Hedy Lamarr than Vanna White. Phyllis was rumored to be in her early fifties, even though she listed her age as forty-two in the Marlins press book. Whatever her age, Lujack had to admit she was quite attractive.

She looked just like the kind of broad an aging tycoon would marry the third time around—which was pretty close to how it happened. Her figure was firm, and Lujack didn't doubt that she could still make a few laps around the roller rink. "Phyllis Berry, the darling of Gary." The first girl to ever skate through the Playboy headquarters in Chicago. She did it as a publicity stunt, and Hugh Hefner had immediately offered her a centerfold, but Phyllis wouldn't take her skates off. It wasn't until she met Charles Randolf at one of Hefner's parties that she unlaced them. Hefner moved out to Los Angeles before Phyllis, but the joke was she got the better mansion. Lujack had to agree.

"This is James Lujack. I told you about him on the phone," Lane said with formality.

"How do you do, Mr. Lujack?" Phyllis greeted him with a handshake more roller derby than socialite. "Naturally, I'll help in whatever way I can. Kurt and Kathy were such nice people. And the two little girls . . . my little treasures."

Phyllis's voice cracked, and for a second Lujack thought she was going to cry.

"I'm sure you can console her without my help," Lane said and headed for the bar.

Lujack stood awkwardly in front of the Marlins owner. He wasn't sure she'd heard Lane's remark. The tears, however, did not appear. Instead, Phyllis pursed her lips in what Lujack took to be disapproval.

"Where I come from, manners are taught before reading and writing," she said with an unmistakable Midwest twang. "Do you like football, Mr. Lujack?"

"I've watched a few games."

"Most men have watched more than a few. Charlie told me that if it weren't for football, this country would probably be at war with the Russians. He said football did more to channel men's aggressions than sex."

"I think it has more to do with nuclear bombs than the seventy-yard-pass play variety."

Phyllis appeared to ignore the answer as a waiter brought them two glasses of champagne. She hooked her arm through his and guided him down the steps toward the tent.

"Do you believe in Jesus Christ?" she inquired.

"As much as the next guy."

"Then you've heard of the Reverend Billy Moore?"

"Only by reputation," Lujack answered, refraining from questioning the corollary. He had the feeling Phyllis made up her own conversational agenda, and you either rolled with the non sequiturs or you didn't talk.

"Billy couldn't be here tonight, but one of his miracles is," she whispered conspiratorially.

"Oh, yeah?"

"You know Mick Mayflower? My quarterback?"

"Who doesn't?"

"He's had a shoulder injury for the past year. This summer, he could hardly throw the football."

"I read about it."

"Three weeks ago, Reverend Moore put a few

grains of sand that he brought from Needles into Mick's whirlpool. In the last two games, Mick's thrown five touchdown passes, and his shoulder has never felt better."

"Sand? From Needles? Isn't that like coals from Newcastle?"

"I don't think so. It's from the first Christian pyramid. Reverend Moore thought it fitting that the pyramid be built there. East of the Mojave Desert on the west bank of the Colorado River. Sort of like Giza is east of the Sahara and on the west bank of the Nile."

"If I were you and the reverend, I wouldn't tell the whirlpool company."

"We're not telling anybody yet. Especially the press. They've been horrible about Reverend Billy all season long. I sometimes think sportswriters are the most ungodly group of people on the face of the earth."

"Right up there, anyway."

"The only reason I told you is because you're a private investigator and can keep a secret." The way she looked at him implied future secrets shared.

"Actually, I'm not exactly a private eye."

"It doesn't matter. You're awfully handsome."

Somehow they'd ended up near the photographic session. Press photographers were snapping pictures of different players posing with the three crippled or retarded children especially chosen for the event. One of the children, an Asian girl suffering from muscular dystrophy, couldn't help dribbling on whichever player posed with her. As subtly as possible, the stars involved were lining up to get shot with the leukemic black boy and a pretty blond girl who was mentally retarded.

Without missing a step, Phyllis went over and picked the Asian girl right out of her wheelchair. The girl must have weighed nearly sixty pounds, but Phyllis showed no strain. The photographers went crazy shooting pictures of Phyllis twirling the girl around. She dribbled on Phyllis's shoulder and dress, but the little girl was also smiling for the first time since Lujack had seen her.

He took the opportunity to trade in his champagne for a scotch. During the transaction, he was approached by a tall, tan, gray-haired man dressed in a blue blazer, white shirt, regimental-striped tie. He reeked of money. The man introduced himself as Dr. Paul Makaris.

"She's a remarkable woman, isn't she?" the doctor said of Phyllis.

Lujack mumbled something which could be taken for agreement.

"You're the man who's looking into Kurt's death, aren't you?"

"Word travels fast."

"Clark Sterling told me about you. Said he and Lane signed over a fat check to you yesterday."

Makaris scrutinized him carefully, as if Lujack were applying for a life insurance policy. Lujack noticed a tiny white pyramid with a cross at the apex pinned on the lapel of the blue blazer. The insignia of Reverend Billy Moore's Christian Pyramid Church. The reverend and his mother's grave seemed to be a fast-growing concern among Bel Air's in crowd these days.

"They say you used to be with the police."

"They say right."

"They say you quit before you were fired."

"They say you were Charlie Randolf's personal physician," Lujack interjected. "They also say you happened to be at Rancho Verde the day he died. In fact, they say you were the one who signed the death certificate."

"Not that it's any of your business, but I have an office in Rancho Verde and one in Beverly Hills."

"I don't suppose you know anything about Kurt's investigation into his father's death?"

The well-scrubbed skin pulled tightly in anger. Lujack definitely wasn't going to get the policy.

"Charlie Randolf died from an occlusion of the ventricle, a heart attack in layman's terms. Considering his age and his zest for life, Charlie's passing was most regrettable, but I assure you it was accidental."

"But not unexpected, considering the condition of Charlie's heart."

"As much as I liked Kurt and am shocked and saddened by his passing, I considered his investigation, as you call it, a misguided and somewhat puerile attempt at a postmortem reconciliation with his father. It was no secret that the two men weren't terribly close at the time of Charlie's death."

Lujack was going to keep operating, but Phyllis returned before he could make his next incision. She was out of breath and happy.

"Whew! That dance took it out of me."

"Your partner seemed to enjoy herself," Lujack said.

"Poor little Betsy," she said, tidying up. She seemed far less concerned about the saliva on her elegant dress than any of the players had been about their suits. "We used to visit a lot of hospitals in the roller derby. I always like working with the disabled children. It takes so little to give so much. Of course, it might be easier to realize that when you're getting paid twenty dollars a week to roller skate than when you're paid five thousand a week to play football."

"Come on now, Phyllis," Makaris chided gently. "Dick Pressley and the NFL do a lot for the charities of this country, and you know it. None of these players had to be here tonight."

"Have you seen Mick? I wanted to introduce Mr. Lujack. I told him about Mick's miraculous recovery."

Dr. Makaris frowned at Phyllis's revelation. Lujack didn't think Reverend Moore was accredited by the AMA, but an NFL publicist showed up to take Phyllis away before he could say anything. It was time for the hostess to perform a skit with John Madden.

"John just hated the idea of singing with me," she said happily, "but I promised an exclusive the next time I fire a coach."

"I'm sure Chub Simmons will be pleased to hear that," Lujack said, referring to the current Marlins coach.

Thinking that there were few things in the world that he would enjoy less than watching John Madden sing, Lujack decided to take a tour of the grounds. Lane seemed to be engrossed in a conversation with NFL Commissioner Dick Pressley. The sight of them together triggered something in Lujack's memory. A picture in *People* magazine? He had a recollection that Pressley and Lane were once an item. Maybe they still were. Lane's taste in men wasn't outstanding. Lujack recalled a polo player who drugged his ponies and a movie star who couldn't act.

There was a long white trellised fence covered with bougainvillea stretching out behind the tent. Lujack made his way slowly along the border. The sun was still warm, although it was past six—nearly the end of daylight saving time. Then no more long warm evenings, no more barbecues, no more late swims at the beach. If he ever felt the need for a family, it was at times like this. Moments when he had acute awareness of his own mortality. Worse than birthdays for a true Southern Californian was setting the clock back to standard time.

There was a gazebo at the end of the trellis. Lujack could hear voices.

"I happen to think you're one of the best quarterbacks in NFL history, but that doesn't change things, Mick. Business is business."

"I've got to get back," the other voice said, unhappily conceding the point.

Lujack deliberately kicked his foot on the border lining the pathway. He had recognized one of the voices and didn't want to appear to be eavesdropping.

The faces of both L. Clark Sterling and his client Mick Mayflower looked up in surprise when Lujack walked into the gazebo. Mayflower was almost too handsome for a football player. He had been the best college quarterback of his year and, until a series of injuries two years before, had been on his way to becoming one of the best pros. This was a make-or-break year for Mayflower, trying to lead his team back to the glory years of Charles Randolf's day.

Lujack wondered what "things" weren't changed.

"Ah, Mr. Lujack, patrolling the grounds, are you?" Sterling said with the same air of superiority and hostility which had marked their first meeting the day before. His close-cropped military haircut and muscular frame were indicative of his legendary discipline and stamina—in court battles or in negotiations with NFL owners. After one particularly painful session, a bruised owner moaned, "When Clark Sterling dies, they're going to have to screw him into the ground."

"Certainly don't want any uninvited crippled kids crashing the party."

Sterling grimaced. He had no intention of introducing Mick Mayflower.

"Nice game Sunday. The shoulder getting better?"

Mayflower smiled. "Thanks. Yeah, almost like new."

"The power of sand can never be underestimated."

Mayflower did a double-take, but Sterling was quick to the rescue. "You've been talking to Phyllis."

"She swore me to secrecy."

"I didn't like the idea of letting you sniff around the Marlins organization to begin with, Lujack, and now that I've met you twice, I like it even less. The police will find the man who killed Kurt and his family with or without your help. As far as I'm concerned, you're just another con man who somehow talked Kurt out of fifty thousand dollars."

"Give the guy a break, Clark," Mayflower said uncomfortably.

"You take care of the Giants next Sunday. Let me handle this little matter," Sterling told his client coldly.

"You better get your ten percent back to the party before I make him five percent," Lujack said to the quarterback.

Sterling took a half-step toward Lujack but thought better of it.

"Come on, Clark, let it alone," said Mayflower.

"I've seen guys like you my whole life, Lujack," Sterling said, getting angrier. "Losers who've watched too many late movies. You used to be a cop. Now you're a bag man for a chink bookie, and a second-rate extortionist. The next stop is jail, pal, and we both know it."

Lujack weighed the advantages and disadvantages of kicking Clark Sterling's butt. On the one hand, it would make him feel awfully good, but on the other hand, the legal problems he might incur by punching

out the feisty little lawyer could be troublesome.
Besides, he wanted Sterling cocky and unmarked.

"A hundred bucks you get there first."

"Me?" The lawyer laughed. "What have you been
sniffing, Lujack?"

"I take it you don't want to bet."

"Make it a thousand," the lawyer shot back.

"You're on," Lujack said. "Remember, Counselor,
there's no statute of limitations on murder."

"You're out of your league, Lujack."

"Maybe, maybe not. It's a long season."

"Come on, Clark, I've got a hot date waiting,"
Mayflower said impatiently.

Sterling continued glaring at Lujack. "Let's get
outta here, Mick," he said finally and turned to leave
the gazebo.

Mayflower nodded awkwardly to Lujack and followed the lawyer.

It struck Lujack as very odd that an athlete of Mick
Mayflower's stature would be so obsequious around
his agent. Usually, it was the other way around. Of
course, Clark Sterling was no ordinary agent. He was
part of the new breed of sports-entertainment agent-
lawyer who were sometimes bigger star material than
their clients, if only because they represented the sum
of their clients. Still, there was no mistaking that the
overheard conversation had had a mysterious tension
to it. Everything he'd read about Mick Mayflower—
the beautiful women, the beach house, the commer-
cials—had given him the impression that Mayflower
was a decent if pampered guy. Why get mixed up with
a barracuda like Sterling?

Lujack watched silently as Lane Randolf approached. Coming down the garden path, she looked
like a modern-day Persephone.

"Back from Hades, are you?"

"I assume you're referring to Dick Pressley."

"You know your mythology."

"The schools I went to were very big on mythology, etiquette, French, and horseback riding."

"Tools for everyday living."

"What did you say to Clark? He was seething."

"We made a bet on who would end up in jail first."

"Wonderful. I thought you were supposed to be trying to find my brother's murderer."

"I am. What's the story on Mick Mayflower? He seems too civilized to be hanging around with Sterling."

"Sterling's a good agent. Mick's shy and greedy."

One of the things he liked about Lane. She was succinct.

The crippled children had gone home. Most of the jocks had left too. The younger ones first; they didn't need to kiss up to the producers because their knees were still good and their paychecks fat. The older players, the Miller beer commercial crowd, had formed a circle at the bar telling stories about the good old days when a player didn't need an accountant to tell him how good he was. They should be so lucky.

Lujack was slowly nursing his third scotch and watching Phyllis Randolf doting over her star player and lobbying the NFL commissioner about Mayflower —as if she thought Pressley was responsible for selecting the All-Pro team.

"You know, when he's healthy, there's no better quarterback than my Mick," she said, giving the embarrassed Mayflower a kiss on the cheek. "And now, thanks to Jesus, he's never been healthier."

"Mick's a great one, nobody can doubt that," said the slightly bemused commissioner.

Pressley was a smooth, articulate, uptown New Yorker whose charm and cool were only equaled by his ambition and ego. He had been the NFL commissioner since the late 1960s, a tenure which paralleled the rise of pro football as America's number one sport. It was no coincidence.

In fifteen years, the most serious threat to his leadership had come from Charles Randolf. Shortly before his death, Charles had proposed setting up his own cable TV network in the Los Angeles area and other interested markets—a clear violation of the NFL–major network TV contracts. It was the last of a series of proposals Randolf had put forth to undermine Pressley's leadership. More than any rival football league or the NFL Players Association, it had been Randolf who threatened Pressley's hold over the NFL. Now, with Randolf gone, Pressley again enjoyed unchallenged power. He could afford to humor Phyllis and her quarterback.

"I hope you don't mind, Mr. Commissioner, but I've written a little poem. I was hoping ABC would let me recite it on our next Monday night game, but Frank says they can't use original material on the air."

"He's proof of that," Pressley joked.

Without registering, Phyllis launched into her poem, "Song of the Marlin":

> "I sleep by the open sea, waiting.
> Will he return to me?
> Love is cold, but I am bold.
> Time like the doldrums,
> Air of despair.
> While the world is turning,
> I am burning.
> Walk to the sand, the waves caress my lap,
> The moment is near, my Marlin is here."

Dick Pressley chewed nervously on an ice cube. Mick Mayflower, apparently moved by the poem, clapped softly. Lujack took a large gulp of scotch, hoping it would sober him. Or get him drunk. Anything but his current condition.

"Thank you, Mick," Phyllis said. "You know I'm working on a poem about you, but it's not ready for public consumption."

"Thank God," Pressley murmured.

"Pardon, Mr. Commissioner?"

"That's a shame, Phyllis."

"I'm thinking of putting 'Song of the Marlin' in next year's press guide. You know we're going to win the Super Bowl next year. Reverend Moore told me."

The NFL commissioner, for one of the few times in his career, was speechless.

"Do you like poetry, Mr. Lujack?"

"Only when it's in motion, Mrs. Randolf."

Phyllis struggled with that one, then decided it was harmless. Taking Mayflower's arm—he had, after all, clapped for her poetry and was on the Marlin payroll —she announced she was in the mood to dance.

Lujack was left standing next to Dick Pressley. Pressley smiled graciously, the way the famous and powerful acknowledge the existence of others put close by social circumstance.

"I don't think Elizabeth Browning has much to worry about," Pressley remarked.

"Bukowski might be in trouble, though," Lujack answered.

"Phyllis is a piece of work, isn't she?" Pressley chuckled, deciding Lujack was all right. "What do you do, Mr. Lujack?"

"I was an acquaintance of Kurt Randolf's, and I've been asked by the family to look into his murder."

The commissioner hesitated, then nodded. Objection sustained. "A horrible tragedy. I'd known young Kurt since he was this high," Pressley said, lifting his hand waist-high off the patio floor. "Before I became commissioner, I used to work for the Giants. Wellington Mara and Charles Randolf were best of friends, and every time the Giants would come out to the Coast, we would get together with Charles and his family."

Lujack had visions of Pressley eyeing Lane as a teenager and muttering impassioned vows in the Randolf poolhouse.

"As you know, Kurt was very upset about his father's death and the disposition of the team."

Pressley nodded again. "The estate taxes in this country are ridiculous. I know many families who've had that problem."

"Kurt told me that he'd come to see you a few months ago with information about his father's betting."

This time the objection was overruled. The commissioner's eyes locked in disapproval. "I'm not sure what tack you're pursuing, Mr. Lujack, but whatever conversations Kurt and I had about Charles's gambling activities are none of your business. And, believe me, you don't want to make it your business."

"Possibly not, but I'm sure those activities might be of interest to Sam Ballard of the arson squad. Also Lieutenant Kyle Thurgood of robbery-homicide. In some circles, such knowledge might be considered a motive for murder."

"Wait a minute, friend!" Pressley hissed. "If you want to take Randolf's money, that's their business, but you don't threaten me, and you don't talk around town about Charles Randolf's gambling. The police know the facts. You don't know shit. If I hear about you spreading gambling rumors concerning any NFL owner or player, I'll have you in court faster than you can duck."

"Mmm. Sounds like I'm just in time," Lane said, coming out of the house with a champagne glass grasped precariously between her fingers. Paul Makaris was walking next to her protectively.

"The commissioner was just explaining the finer points of libel," Lujack said.

"Oh. Dick knows all about libel. It rhymes with Bible," Lane said, smiling hazily at Pressley.

"Another poet," Lujack commented, steadying Lane with his hand.

Lujack hadn't noticed her getting swacked. But even with her hair a little mussed and a slight tilt of her lovely head, she was still the best-looking broad in L.A.

"Mr. Lujack, perhaps you should be taking Lane home," Dr. Makaris suggested.

"You took the order right out of my mouth."

Neither Makaris nor Dick Pressley reacted. Nor did they say goodbye. All in all, Lujack hadn't proved too popular. Except possibly with Phyllis. Of course, with her, it was hard to tell if you were coming or going. Lujack figured he'd insulted or offended three of the most powerful men in the city. The thought satisfied him.

The parking attendant drove Lane's car to the porte cochere in front of the mansion. Lujack had made an attempt to find Phyllis, but she was nowhere to be found. Probably practicing center snaps with Mick Mayflower.

"This way," Lujack said, deftly taking Lane by one lovely arm and depositing her in the passenger seat. "I'm driving. You're getting the fresh air."

"Take me to the Polo Grounds," she commanded as the Rolls slid into the cool Bel Air night.

"Polo Grounds? I think you may have the wrong city, the wrong decade, and the wrong sport."

"Just keep going on Sunset. I'll tell you when to stop."

Lujack drove toward the beach. The half-moon was at their backs. He was in no rush to get away from Lane, no matter how plastered she was. Indeed, he wasn't sure she was all that drunk. Her eyes had focused easily when they left the party—and she'd managed the stairs without help. For all he knew, the tipsy act could have been a ruse to leave the party— also fine with him.

"Hard-boiled."

"Beg your pardon?"

"People like you are hard-boiled. That's what it says on the book jacket."

"I'd rather be deviled."

Lane nodded. She might even have smiled. Lujack couldn't tell. They kept driving west on Sunset. Their voices were loud over the traffic.

"What do you think of the family?"

Family was underlined.

"You mean Phyllis?" Lujack asked. "She's charming."

Lane laughed sarcastically.

"About as charming as frostbite," she said, and Lujack knew whatever she was, it wasn't drunk. "Do you know what she told a *Sports Illustrated* reporter the day she fired Kurt?"

Lujack shook his head.

"She said my father told her, quote, 'If the little bastard gives you any trouble, fire him.'"

Lujack couldn't help chuckling. Lane didn't like it. They drove the next two miles in silence.

"Turn up here," Lane told him when they came to the entrance of Will Rogers State Park. Lujack followed the road up through the eucalyptus trees until they came to a metal gate across the road. Lane jumped out of the car and unlocked the gate with a key from her purse. Lujack drove the Rolls past Lane, and she jumped back into the car.

At the top of the rise, they came to a large clearing. The moonlight silhouetted the white rail around the huge polo field. Lujack had been to the park before but never at night. With the stars and the night-blooming jasmine and the white railings and huge dark infield—it was an overpowering experience.

"If you close your eyes and listen, you can hear the horses," she said, getting out of the car and walking up to the railing.

Lujack didn't want to close his eyes. He had everything he wanted. He was next to her near the rail. Almost touching and very aware of the body next to his, he felt himself falling for her. She was arrogant and beautiful and spoiled and rich, but she was also pretty damn smart and, if his instincts were right, noble. He had never known a woman like her. She had married jerks, but she herself wasn't a jerk. Maybe it was one of the penalties for being beautiful and rich.

His large hand covered hers on the wall. The moon caressed her hair. He very much wanted to kiss her but couldn't bring himself to do it. Jimmy Lujack, the Lothario of Los Angeles, paralyzed on the rail.

Lane Randolf smiled, as if she were coaxing a young boy on his first date. It was she who kissed him. Gently, carefully. When he tried for more, she moved slightly away. The smile was still there.

"It's a shame you were born rich," he told her.

"Don't flatter yourself. If I were poor, you wouldn't have a chance."

Chapter 7

THE THING LUJACK LIKED best about Las Vegas was
that it made Los Angeles seem normal. Las Vegas was,
in Lujack's opinion, the only city in the world that
must appear the same to both animal and man. A Gila
monster or a coyote or a human being all must have
the same reaction on coming out of the Nevada desert
and arriving at Highway 91, aka the Strip.

The neon oasis. Lujack knew better than to think it
was run on solar power. That was another thing he
liked about Vegas. It was oblivious to progress. People
thought of it as America's most modern, streamlined
city. A desert community of five hundred thousand
existing in the artifice of air-conditioned technology
similar to a lunar community of the twenty-first
century. But in reality, Las Vegas was a garish monu-
ment to postwar America. The casinos of Atlantic
City had seriously cut into the business of the casinos
of Las Vegas, as had the proliferation of bookies like

Lujack himself. Also, the country had changed since Ben Siegal had built the Flamingo Hotel in 1946. The allure of girls, sun, and money which had for many years jerked America's middle-aged middle-class success stories across the desert to its bright lights did not offer as much to America's new generation of exercise-conscious, computer-oriented, fiber-eating winners. But Vegas wouldn't change. In some future years, man or Gila monster would wander down Highway 91 to find a row of tall buildings with burned-out lights and empty swimming pools, with sage brush rolling snake eyes across the green felt, and would wonder.

"As usual, you look like the runner-up in a Joe Palooka contest," said a familiar voice as Lujack walked out of the terminal into the dry heat.

"And you look like the captain of a Mogen David team on College Bowl," Lujack said, greeting Irv Katz, oldest son of Myron and Susie Katz and owner-operator of Bet the Farm Sports Pix, the best tout service in America.

"What took you so long? I've been waiting out here a minute and thirteen seconds."

"I was admiring the artwork of the local children along the wall. How come all the kids here draw their airplanes with three insignias on them? Although I admit it's not a bad idea—Jackpot Airways."

"Kids," Irv said in astonishment. "What kids? I've been here seven years and haven't seen one."

"Your mother sends her love. She also sent along two jars of gefilte fish and some matzoh ball soup. Here."

"Momma doesn't believe there are any synagogues in Las Vegas."

"I don't blame her. It may be in the middle of the desert, but it's not exactly the Holy Land."

"Vegas is the only city in America where instead of times for Sunday masses or Sabbath services, they list odds on redemption. From what I hear, the Hindus are a good bet."

They picked up the luggage and walked out to the loading zone.

"Is this *yours?*" Lujack said as Irv steered him to what must have been a twenty-five-foot-long Cadillac parked in front.

"I told you, tout sheets are where the money is. And it's legitimate. I got a business license, the whole schmeer. The Las Vegas Chamber of Commerce is giving me an award next month. Businessman of the Year."

"Who'd you beat out? Frankie Carbo?" Lujack laughed as they got into the air-conditioned, chauffeur-driven Cadillac.

"Where do you want to go, Jimmy?" Irv asked once they were settled.

"1214 Virginia. I think it's off Charleston Boulevard."

Irv gave the chauffeur the address and, while he was on the phone, decided to get the latest movement on the pro lines. He'd put out Washington minus five at Dallas as his pick of the week and wanted to know how much the spread had dropped at the Super Bowl Sports Book. Bet the Farm's key release had gone out by one-day mail to Irv's fifteen thousand subscribers yesterday morning, and he was proud to tell Jimmy the spread was now Washington plus two, the money bet by Irv's customers having driven the betting line down three points.

"Not bad for a day's work," Lujack said, genuinely impressed. "What does it come to, about two mil?" he asked, referring to the amount bet by Irv's subscribers.

"About two million here in Nevada and probably another three million dollars from the rest of the country," Irv said, talking about the money bet legally in Las Vegas and Reno and the money bet illegally with bookies all around the country. "One thing about our boy Nimmo, his betting line always shows *all* the action."

"Speaking of the devil, did you get me an appointment?"

"Better than that. I got you an invitation to his birthday party."

"Birthday party? He had a mother?"

"I'm not so sure about that. Anyway, the party's at the Ritz Vegas and starts in about two hours. It's supposed to be a barbecue. Indoors, of course."

"Of course," Lujack said, looking out the tinted windows as they drove past the shimmering bric-a-brac of real estate between the airport and the Sahara Hotel. Every gasoline, motel, and fast-food chain in America seemed to be represented on the Strip. There were literally hundreds and hundreds of signs on the wide four-lane highway.

"Wasn't it thoughtful of the city fathers to put the telephone lines underground along here?" Katz remarked, watching Lujack. "I mean, they didn't want the place to look cluttered."

Lujack just shook his head.

There was a patch of green between the Strip and the old downtown area of Las Vegas. Rumor had it there were even homes tucked under the trees.

They turned east on Charleston until they came to Virginia Street. The houses were one-storied, and there were trees, palms, and other desert varieties, along with little gardens and picket fences. An older woman in a soft cotton dress was out weeding her garden.

"That's the first woman over fifty I've ever seen in this town not playing a slot machine," Irv said as the chauffeur stopped in front of a house next to the woman's.

"Take your time, Jimmy. I've brought my work with me," he went on, pushing a button on the leather console between them. A small computer screen appeared where the top of the console used to be. "These portable computers are a handicapper's dream. Injury reports, trend analysis, every statistic on record—all right at my fingertips."

"No wonder bookies are losing money. What happened to betting your instincts?"

"Animals have instincts, Jimmy. Handicappers have probability equations."

Jimmy pushed open the picket gate and walked up to the porch of the house. The screen door was closed, but the front door was open. He could hear a television set; the local news was beginning the early-evening narration of grease fires, supermarket openings, murders, and other noteworthy events in and around Clark County.

Phil Muscagy was in no hurry to get to the door. When he finally made it, Lujack found himself facing a fit-looking man in his early fifties whose eyes immediately went to the black limousine parked out front.

"Mr. Muscagy, I'm James Lujack. We talked on the phone."

"I told you I've nothing to say," the former FBI agent said gruffly, making no move to open the screen door. Lujack knew the type—bristle clean, no nonsense.

"You had a lot to say to Kurt Randolf, enough to get him murdered."

Muscagy's expression hardened, but he opened the screen door. Lujack walked into a simple but comfortably furnished room. A woman he assumed was Mrs. Muscagy was lying on the couch watching television and barely looked up. Muscagy took Lujack into his air-conditioned study.

"She likes the heat," he said.

The study, like the man, was neat. Everything in its place. Shelves of books covered the walls. There were no pictures or newspaper clippings. Phil Muscagy had evidently retired with his pride and not a whole lot else.

"You said on the phone you were working for Kurt's sister. She must have you on a pretty nice expense account."

"The limo belongs to a friend. Not that it's any of your business."

"I did a little checking on you, Lujack. I didn't like what I found. I invited you in because I didn't want my wife to hear what I was going to say."

"Your wife wouldn't have cared even if she did hear. You invited me in because you want to tell me something about Kurt Randolf or his father, and you wanted to make sure no one was aiming a shotgun mike at us."

Muscagy nodded in approval.

"You're not dumb. That's a plus. You also aren't crooked. Which is what I found on my *second* call to Los Angeles. The unofficial one."

"You mean there's somebody left in the department who still likes me? Give me the name, and I'll put him on my Christmas list."

Muscagy ignored Lujack's attempt at self-effacement or whatever.

"About six months ago," Muscagy began, "Bill Jenkins, a sportswriter for the *Las Vegas Sun,* told me he'd received a call from Charlie Randolf's kid. Jenkins and Charlie go back ten years or so to when

Bill was working in L.A. for the old *Herald*. Anyway, the kid thought that Bill might be able to help him with his 'investigation' of his father's death. Bill couldn't help him: he thought it was a little strange that the kid was still nosing around two years after his old man's death, no matter how bad the stepmother screwed up the team. So, one afternoon after we played golf, he just happened to mention it. I didn't say anything to Bill, but the kid's call interested me because of a bookmaking investigation the bureau had been doing on Frank Nimmo when I was there."

Muscagy paused to let the irony of "bookmaking investigation" sink in. Lujack had gotten used to such pauses.

"The Nimmo investigation had always stuck in my craw. It was the reason I quit the bureau. The last straw, so to speak. It was also the reason I finally wrote to the kid. I was hoping that he might make it hot for some people. I never in my life thought I was making it hot for him."

Lujack thought it uncanny how FBI agents always managed to choose the wrong word. He pulled Muscagy's letter out of his coat pocket. "You wrote Kurt his old man was a large bettor on Marlins games and he used Ernie Barbells. Was there anything solid on Nimmo or Ernie?"

"The phones we had belonged to Johnny Stella, Nimmo's gofer. There was a bank of three pay phones outside the Italian restaurant where Stella ate. We had a tap on all three."

"So you never had Nimmo's voice on the wire?"

Muscagy shook his head.

"Stella was responsible for taking outside action at the Super Bowl Sports Book. Strictly pass-along stuff. Very big, a hundred, two hundred fat ones a day."

"From Ernie B.?"

"Actually, from Ernie's spade, Hiram Hotel. Hotel and Stella would occasionally comment on the bets. I guess Hotel liked dropping names. One of the names was Charles Randolf. He and Stella once talked about Charlie betting against his own team, saying they should report it to the commissioner. You know— hood jokes."

"How did Randolf do?"

"The Marlins were a good team then. NFC champs that year, so they were always giving points. From what I remember, Charlie usually won, even when he was betting against the Marlins."

"That doesn't surprise me. I assume the action Hiram was laying off came from the Lido Club."

"That's the assumption we were working on," Muscagy said, shaking his head. "One day Quentin Rule, the special agent in charge, came into the office and told us to close down the operation. He said something about the deputy attorney general not wanting to waste time frying the small fish while the big ones swam away."

"But you didn't buy it?"

"At the time, I thought he might have something else going. Rule's ambitious, and he certainly knows which way the wind blows inside the bureau, but he's a good agent. You know how tricky it is to turn grunts like Johnny Stella—we pick him up and he's a dead man. But then something happened. I figured Nimmo had simply gotten word of the wiretap and pulled a few strings. Goddamn ropes is what he must have pulled."

"I know the feeling."

"The bottom copy is we end up with nothing. That's when I decided to retire. Twenty-five years in the Feebs, and I took a look around the Vegas office and knew I didn't really trust five of the ten agents I worked with. Half of them ate at the casinos more nights than they ate at home."

"I gather it wasn't the first time your office had had a problem."

Muscagy laughed. "Once we had a phone wired that belonged to a girl Nimmo was hosing. A broad that worked in the revue at the Ritz. Two days we have the wire grooved, he's talking to Stella about business. How much on this game, spread changes, etc., hood code but relaxed. We think we might be getting close to a major screwup. All of a sudden, on the third day, he starts talking about what is he going to buy his mother for her birthday. Five days we sit there listening to the biggest hood in the country talk to Stella about a birthday gift for his mother."

"Did you ever come across a hood by the name of Michael Largomasino?"

"Matches Largomasino?" Muscagy smiled. "Sure, he's a Chicago boy. Buddy of Nimmo's when they were both in Chi, before Frank made it to the big time."

"A friend of mine in the arson squad called me before I left L.A. today and told me Matches and another guy from Chicago, Pete Liccata, were at the Marlins-Dallas game last Sunday."

"Your contacts pretty good then?"

"Some."

"Matches has to be your prime candidate for the Randolf fire. Though I'll be damned why a man like Frank Nimmo would bother with Kurt Randolf. The kid was nice enough and not stupid, but once I'd talked to him I knew he wasn't going to be putting anybody in jail."

"That's been bothering me too. If the fire was connected to the kid's investigation, which I think it was, then it's a good bet that Charlie's death was no accident. But why would a guy like Frank Nimmo, or Ernie for that matter, want to take out Charlie Randolf? His gambling wouldn't have hurt them much. Hell, to have an owner as a client is a sign of status."

"Frank Nimmo is one smart hood," the FBI man said somberly. "He's got brains, and he's got class. Sometimes you forget he killed six people to make his bones with the Chicago family."

"I'm going to his birthday party tonight."

"That's your problem, not mine," Muscagy said with a dour smile.

"Thanks for your help."

"You know I'm going to have to make a report to Rule. Even retired personnel are required to."

"Write slowly then, will ya?"

"Hell, it'll take me a coupla days to find my pen."

Lujack shook hands with the agent. It occurred to him that the only men he seemed to feel affinity with these days were ex-cops and small-time hoods.

Chapter 8

THE RITZ VEGAS WAS the only high-rise luxury hotel in downtown Las Vegas, or "Casino Center" as the Chamber of Commerce called the area. The best name for the old downtown section along Fremont Street was given it by the locals: "Glitter Gulch." Distinct from the newer, more glamorous Las Vegas along the Strip, Glitter Gulch was where the more serious gamblers lived and almost breathed. The hard-core players who didn't need or want the facade of golf courses, tennis courts, swimming pools, and elaborate entertainment to remind them why they were in Las Vegas. The only reminder they needed was the arm of the slot machine, the feel of the dice, or the unmistakable sound of poker chips on green velvet. The three blocks along Fremont have more gambling establishments, pawn shops, bright lights, and hard-luck stories than any in America—and nobody is about to quit, not as long as there's a dollar in their pocket and eleven still comes after seven.

In the mid-1970s, the Chicago mob, with a generous loan from the Teamsters, decided—after constructing numerous hotels along the Strip—that it was time to do something "nice" downtown. It was also fitting that they decided to build their hotel on the site of the old Las Vegas train station, where, in 1905, Senator William Clark and his San Pedro, Los Angeles, and Salt Lake railroad friends auctioned off lots to create the city. The man they chose to run their nice hotel was Frank Nimmo, a man who'd never been west of La Salle Street and whose qualifications for the job consisted of loansharking, bookmaking, breaking legs, and the execution of enemies on command for the Chicago mob since he was fourteen years old.

Lujack was invited to Frank Nimmo's birthday party at the Ritz Vegas, home of the famous Super Bowl Sports Book, the largest legal sports book in the United States, because he was a friend of Irv Katz. It was Irv, with two other handicappers, who put together the betting lines for the coming week's pro games every Sunday night at the Ritz. Frank Nimmo would release those betting lines to his best customers—the cream of professional sports bettors—and, depending on how the bettors reacted, the lines would be adjusted. When bookies like Lujack, newspapers, and other subscribers received their lines from Nevada One on Monday morning, it was the betting line set by Katz and company and adjusted by the big sports bettors. On Wednesday, after closely studying those betting lines that he had helped create, Irv would pick one or two games in which he thought the lines were off. Those picks would go out to his Bet the Farm subscribers as a key release. Twice a year (usually one regular and one playoff game), Irv would give his subscribers his Bet the Farm special. Over the past four years, Katz was eight for eight on the specials, the envy of the profession. His key-release record was somewhere near seventy percent—also very impressive.

As Irv explained to Jimmy on their way to the hotel, "How can I miss? I get paid to set the line, then I get paid to beat it."

"Isn't that a conflict of interest?" Lujack asked.

"There's no such thing as a conflict of interest in Las Vegas if you get paid for it," Katz answered.

When they were a block from the Ritz, Irv put a hand on Lujack's arm. "It's none of my business or anything, Jimmy," Irv said carefully, "but . . ."

"What do I want with Frank Nimmo?"

"The guy's bad news, Jimmy."

"Tell ya the truth, I'm not sure what I want with him. I think there's a connection between him and the murder of Kurt Randolf, maybe the murder of Kurt's father, Charlie."

"You think the mob wants their own football team?"

"It's a possibility." Lujack smiled. Irv always found an angle.

"From what I've heard about Phyllis Randolf, they couldn't have found a better front."

Lujack wondered if there were something to it. But why kill Kurt if Phyllis was already in place? Because the kid was making trouble? Asking questions? He wondered then if he was next on the list . . . or could it be Lane?

The party was being held in the Sports Room. Irv said it was Frank Nimmo's pride and joy. Lujack had to admit it was impressive. And, just as Irv had promised, it was a western-style barbecue—indoors. The guests' attire ranged from designer suits to designer cowboy clothes, with a generous sprinkling of leather vests and chaps worn by some local talent.

"Have you noticed what's under those chaps, pardner?" Irv said to Lujack.

"From what I can see, not a whole lot," Lujack commented, watching one of the nicest fannies imaginable drift past him.

"I think I know the ranch where Frank got these cowgirls."

"Mustang?"

"Bingo."

A particularly fetching cowgirl, the rounded curve of her breast only partially covered by her leather vest, came over and planted a kiss on Irv's cheek.

"Hi, Katzy-Watzy."

"Good evening, Denise," Irv said, only slightly embarrassed.

"Isn't this a fun Bar Bee Q? And it's so nice and cool in here."

Denise gave Lujack a quick once-over. "Who's this one?" she asked with showgirl directness.

"This is Jimmy Lujack, a good friend of mine from Los Angeles."

"Oh, Los Angeles!" she said enthusiastically.

Lujack waited, but there was no payoff. "Where's the birthday boy?"

"Guess he's still up in his penthouse," Irv said.

"They had to turn all the smoke alarms off," Denise said brightly. "Too much smoke, I guess. Luckily, the fire chief is a friend of Frank's."

"Luckily," Irv agreed.

"One of your subscribers?" Lujack teased.

"Something like that." Irv laughed. "I see Johnny Stella over there. Let's see what we can do about getting you an audience with the star."

Johnny Stella was Frank Nimmo's "director of operations." It was a sign of the times that hoods now had titles like corporate executives. In reality, Stella was one of Nimmo's gofers. Lujack had run into Stella once before in Los Angeles at a nightclub on Sunset. Lujack had ended Stella's particular party with a haymaker.

"What's he doing here?" Stella barked, motioning toward Lujack.

"He's my guest. He wants to talk to Frank," Irv said with more moxie than Lujack expected. There had been a time when Irv was obliging to the point of obsequiousness with men like Stella. That's what eight out of eight can do for you in Las Vegas.

Stella regarded Lujack hostilely. Stella was a small man, balding, and he looked ridiculous in his western garb.

"Frank don't see no assholes on his birthday."

"If I needed a proctologist, I would have stayed in L.A. Just tell the man I'm down here and would like to see him."

Two cowboys stepped closer. They resembled the Dallas Cowboys in size.

"If you got some business you want to lay off, small time, you do it with me. You wanna do it privately, come to my office."

"Come on, Johnny, don't be difficult," Irv said impatiently.

Stella's black eyes glared at Irv. "For a Jew boy with no muscle, you sure are talking a lot, Katz."

"For a guinea with no brains, you're not doing so bad yourself," Lujack said, stepping in front of Katz. The conversation wasn't going in the direction he had hoped, but then conversations with jerks like Stella seldom did.

"Throw him out," Stella ordered his two muscle-bound cowboys.

Lujack wasn't stronger, but he figured he was quicker and smarter than Stella's associates. He knew his best chance was inside the casino—no telling what goodies the two men had under their vests. Lujack knew enough about casino security police to know that once he got out of public view, the marquis of Queensbury wouldn't be watching.

One cowboy tried to grab his left arm, and Lujack hit him hard in the midsection. He doubled up, and Lujack hit him with a half-punch, half-karate chop to the back of the head, sending him into a plate of marinating ribs standing next to the open pit. Juice and ribs spilled onto the fire, and flames and smoke shot up a makeshift draft. The second cowboy was momentarily stopped by the fire, and Lujack hit him directly on the jaw, sending him flying into the potato salad.

Amid the chaos, Johnny Stella stood coughing, pointing at Lujack and motioning for him to be thrown out. Three more steroid cowboys appeared from nowhere, while cowboy number one was licking barbecue sauce off his hands and cowboy number two was wiping off potato salad. Suddenly, Lujack found himself facing seven hundred pounds of beef, not including the ribs.

"I think maybe we should punt," Irv suggested.

"I'm afraid it's even too late for a quick kick," Lujack told him.

"Take him out, and make it so he can't come back in," Stella ordered.

"Hold it, Johnny," came a rough but calm voice from behind the crowd of spectators. Everyone in the room recognized the voice, and the cowboys stopped in their tracks. The guests stepped backward and made a path for Frank Nimmo. As usual, Nimmo was impeccably tailored, his trim figure fit snugly into a custom-made suit. Stories about Nimmo's fastidious dressing habits abounded—Italian tailors and shoe-makers flown to Las Vegas, shirt makers brought over from Los Angeles. No cowboy duds for Frank. His cuffs were calculated to the centimeter, and his gold stick pin was perfectly calibrated. The hair, done daily by his barber, was perfectly coiffed and still plentiful. At forty-two, he looked more like Frankie Avalon than Frank Nitti.

"Frank, this is nothing for you to be involved with," Stella said, "I was just escorting this riffraff out the door."

"Mr. Katz is hardly riffraff, Johnny," Nimmo said warmly, shaking Irv's hand. "It's men like Irv who make this town go."

"Happy birthday, Frank," Irv said with undisguised relief. "This is a friend of mine, Jimmy Lujack, from L.A. I told you about him on the phone."

"Sure, sure." Nimmo smiled, extending his hand. Lujack wasn't sure if Nimmo wanted him to kiss his ring or shake his hand. "Follow me, Mr. Lujack," Nimmo said, then announced, "The rest of you—live it up, that's what birthdays are for."

Johnny Stella, still seething, took a step backward to let them pass. Implicit in Nimmo's comments was that the meeting be private. A chorus of "Happy birthdays" followed as Lujack and Nimmo made their way out of the Sports Room.

Up on stage, a master of ceremonies was announcing the greased-pig contest, but, instead of a pig, they were using a particularly lithe chorus girl wearing knee pads. The roped-off area in the center of the room was going to be the corral. There didn't seem to be any lack of competitors as the contest put the party back on the fun track.

Nimmo's private office was just off the Sports Room. There were pictures of Frank Nimmo with America's film and sports celebrities—many of them taken in the hotel, some on the golf course. Lujack noticed a picture of Nimmo and Charlie Randolf. They were laughing. A bored-looking Lane was in the background.

"What the fuck do you want?" Nimmo asked suddenly before Lujack had a chance to sit down.

"I want to know why you ordered Michael Largomasino to burn down Kurt Randolf's house," Lujack said, deciding honesty was as good a policy as any other.

"I heard you were a little crazy. Now I know better. A cop who becomes a bookie? That's crazy. A bookie who comes into my hotel on my birthday and accuses me of murder? That's stupid."

"You used to handle Charlie's bets via Ernie B. and the Lido Club. The FBI was all over you then and had both Johnny Stella and Hiram Hotel on wiretape discussing Charlie's bets. You were afraid that the Feebs might get to Randolf, so you got to him first. I don't know how you found out about his heart condition, but the NFL owners' meeting was the perfect place to kill him. Half the owners plus the commissioner hated Randolf's guts, and the rest wanted nothing to do with the police. You knew Phyllis wouldn't be a problem—you might have even made a deal with her—maybe she was the one who told you about Charlie's weak heart. You get rid of Charlie, and you and your friends in Chicago get a piece of an NFL team . . ."

Nimmo's Roman jaw fell open.

"Everything would have been all right except for Kurt," Lujack continued. "You figured when Phyllis fired the kid from Dad's team, he'd fade away. But Kurt was more like old Charlie than anyone thought. He knew his father was murdered and set out to prove it. He found a witness who saw a blond woman leave Charlie's suite shortly before he died. He found two other witnesses who said there was a suspicious gash on Charlie's head. A gash evidently missed by Phyllis's good friend Dr. Makaris when Makaris examined him. And finally, he discovered evidence of Charlie's gambling, more importantly the FBI's knowledge of that gambling. Of course, nobody seemed interested in the results of Kurt's investigation, not the San Diego D.A., not the NFL commissioner. There's a good chance that in time he would have given up. But, of course, you couldn't take that chance, so you called Matches."

Nimmo had seemed intrigued, maybe even impressed, until Lujack mentioned the FBI. It was then that Nimmo's expression dropped to freezing—as in deep freezing. "You know, Lujack, there's no reason I shouldn't have you killed for what you just said. If I don't, it's because I know you're never going to say it again. To anyone, ever."

Nimmo smiled. His white teeth gleamed. Frank Nimmo not only enjoyed violence, he enjoyed the anticipation of violence. Lujack knew because he had more than a little of that quality himself.

"I won't be as easy to get rid of as Kurt and his family. Whoever you send better be good."

"You must *want* to die."

"I want the truth."

"The truth." Nimmo laughed scornfully. "You want a better lie. Something to make it worth dying for."

Just like Phil Muscagy had said, Frank Nimmo wasn't stupid.

"I hate martyrs, Lujack. They're messy, bad for business. This Sunday, the Marlins are playing the Giants. I'm going to give you a birthday present." He laughed. "What's the spread on the Marlins game in L.A.?

"The Marlins are favored by four."

"Put every cent you can find against L.A. Better yet"—the gangster scribbled a note—"go down to the cage and get fifty-five thousand dollars. When you get back to L.A., call the Lido Club and put it against the Marlins. If you lose, you lose nothing. If you win, you pick up fifty grand."

Lujack looked at the note Nimmo had given him. If he hadn't been sure about the gangster's interest in the Marlins before, he was now. Nimmo had just as much as told him the game was fixed.

Lujack crumpled up the note and threw it on Nimmo's desk.

"Have it your way." Nimmo smiled.

Chapter 9

THERE WERE TWO MESSAGES waiting for Lujack when he arrived at his office Friday morning. The first was from Sam Ballard. Matches Largomasino was still at large. The second was from Hiram Hotel.

"We in business this week?" Hotel's smooth voice inquired.

"Damn right. I'll call you tomorrow with the final totals. Right now, we're heavy against the Marlins at minus four versus the Giants."

"How heavy?"

"Thirty-five big ones and climbing," Lujack said, studying the figures Tommy had left on his desk. They had dropped the spread two and a half points in the last two days, and money still kept coming in against the Marlins. It seemed that Frank Nimmo's hot tip was hardly exclusive. Burt Masters alone had put down ten thousand dollars.

"Tell me about it," Hiram concurred. "A lot of our big players have been loading up against L.A. too."

"One of those players wouldn't be Clark Sterling, would it?"

There was hesitation on the other end. "You know I can't tell you something like that," Hotel chided.

"That's not what Johnny Stella told me. He said you and he used to talk about Charlie Randolf's plays all the time."

"I heard you were in Vegas. Still snooping around on that Randolf thing, huh?"

"It's getting more interesting every day."

Again, a hesitation on the other end. "That favor you wanted?"

"Yeah."

"If you talk to this broad and she tells you that Charlie was smiling and happy when she left his suite—will you let this thing drop?"

"There sure are a lot of people who want me to stop asking questions about a dead man's heart attack two years ago."

"This ain't no nickel-and-dime game on the West Side, Jimmy, and you ain't no cop," Hotel said angrily. "People been giving you and Tommy slack in this town for some time. Don't blow it for some society cunt."

"What's the girl's name?" Lujack asked patiently.

"Alabama Starr. She's occasionally a masseuse at Rancho Verde. Lives in Carlsbad."

"Alabama Starr? Sounds too good to be true."

"Alabama's for real all right. She was a favorite of Charlie's. You know he always was partial to those Bear Bryant players."

"I don't suppose you care to tell me where you got this information?"

"You talk to Alabama, she'll set you straight. Maybe you'll get out of this mess after all."

"I'll call you tomorrow with the final plays."

"I'll be around," Hiram said and rang off.

Lujack dialed Lane's number, but the maid said she was in Santa Barbara for the day. More polo, Lujack surmised. He shouldn't expect her social calendar to be inconvenienced by his investigation—even if her life was in danger. He opened the bottom drawer of his desk and reached for a holstered gun. The four-inch .38 Special felt comfortable in his hand. Not surprising considering all the years he had used it. Marty used to tell him it was too heavy for an undercover gun, but Lujack had spent many long hours making the four-inch Smith and Wesson .38 as natural as the standard two-inch version. When it came to a shoot-out, he knew firepower was sometimes more important than speed. So, finally, had Marty.

He strapped the holster over his shirt and put on his windbreaker. The strap felt awkward—so had his conversation with Hiram. There was a lot of money suddenly going against the Marlins—smart money. If Nimmo did have a player on the Marlins, obviously it would have to be at a skill position: Mick Mayflower, the quarterback; Fleet White, the star receiver; Tim Woodard, the leading rusher. But why would a player making nearly a million dollars a year get mixed up with a man like Frank Nimmo? No matter what Nimmo's relationship was with Phyllis Randolf, it wasn't the kind of partnership that could ever be made public—even to her players. In the meantime, Lujack had to find the only witness he had. The blonde with the breakaway name.

The usual crowd was sitting at the bar when Lujack

sauntered out. Pete Colima looked particularly happy, which wasn't a good omen.

"Guess who's having lunch here today?" Pete asked him slyly.

"Madame Chiang Kai-shek."

Pete was unfazed. "Mr. Dodger Blue himself. Look over there in the booth by the squid tank."

"I thought he only ate Italian," Lujack said, recognizing the fattest Dodger of them all, Tommy Lasorda.

"It's a bet he made with the team hypnotist," Lujack's partner said disgustedly at his shoulder. "If the Dodgers won the series and Steve Sax didn't make any throwing errors, Lasorda promised Dr. Ming he'd eat Chinese for a week."

"It's going to take more than a week's lunches to make back that two hundred grand we lost."

"The lunches are free. I owe Dr. Ming a great debt for curing my sister of shingles."

"You knew the goddamn Dodger team hypnotist and you didn't try to get to him? He could have put half the team to sleep."

Tommy frowned. "Dr. Ming is my uncle. He is an honorable man. It would be unacceptable to involve him in gambling."

"Far be it from me to involve one of your uncles in gambling," Lujack said with a straight face.

"How was Las Vegas?"

"I went to Frank Nimmo's birthday party. Great crowd. Irv said they should have been handing out plaques of the fifth amendment as door prizes."

Tommy wasn't laughing. "You talked to Hiram?"

"Yeah. Told him we'd give him the final figures tomorrow. He says he's heavy against the Marlins too, but they can handle all our action."

Tommy nodded.

"What would you say if I told you Frank Nimmo gave me fifty-five big ones to bet against the Marlins? Provided I bet it through the Lido Club."

Tommy's brown eyes opened wide. "No strings? You win, you collect? You lose, you walk away?"

Lujack nodded.

"I'd say you were hallucinating."

"But if I weren't?"

"I'd say he was offering you a bribe—provided the Marlins don't cover."

"I guess we'll have to wait until Sunday, eh?"

"Did you take the money?"

"No."

"Then you might not have to wait as long as you think."

Lujack couldn't argue with Tommy's logic. "I'm going out for a while. I should be back by seven or eight. Susie can hold down the fort."

"Jimmy, be careful. You're the only partner I've ever had."

Lujack pulled the Mustang into the diagonal parking slot off little Santa Monica Boulevard. Morris Breen's offices were located on the most expensive real estate in California, downtown Beverly Hills. Breen's specialties, probate and divorce, were hardly the only entrees on Morris's menu. His greatest assets in the gaudy world of the Beverly Hills bar were his connections. If Morris Breen didn't know who you were, three to one you weren't anybody.

The full-figured redhead with prescription hose was reluctant even to ring Breen's private secretary. "Lujack, Jimmy Lujack. It's Polish."

"But you don't have an appointment."

"I don't have much time either," Lujack said, walking past the receptionist.

The redhead looked flustered, then pleased. Beverly Hills receptionists understood power.

"Jimmy," Morris said, jumping back from the shoulder of an attractive blonde. "What a pleasant surprise! Debby and I were just going over some preliminary evidence."

Lujack could see enough flesh in the pictures on the desk to guess it must have been one of Morris's quickie divorce cases. The husband settles quickly when Morris shows him the compromising pictures.

"That'll be all for now, Debby."

The secretary gave Lujack a game smile and left. Morris sheepishly put the pictures back in the envelope.

"Somebody's got to do it," the lawyer said.

"Better you than Marvin Michelson."

Breen smiled. "I hear you're working for Lane Randolf."

Lujack threw an envelope on the desk. In it was twenty-five hundred dollars. Ten percent of Lujack's advance on the Randolf case. Morris's usual finder's fee.

"I'll get you the rest when I find out who killed our client."

"Damn shame. I liked the kid. Don't blame yourself, Jimmy."

Lujack let the remark pass. "You also represent Lane, don't you?"

"Best-looking woman in Beverly Hills. And she's not even in the movies."

"What were the terms of Charlie's will? I know the kids got the property and Phyllis got the house and team, but if anything should happen to Phyllis, or if she should remarry?"

"Charlie didn't like the idea of Phyllis's marrying anyone." Breen smiled. "As I remember, there was a stipulation in his will that if she remarried within five years of his death, she would lose everything. Also, if she predeceases either of the children, the team goes to Charlie's heirs. Well now, obviously it can only go to Lane."

"And what happens if both Randolf children predecease her?"

"I assume the team would go to their heirs. But of course, Lane doesn't have any kids, and Kurt's family . . . I guess the team would go to Phyllis or her family. I'd have to check with Clark Sterling. He was Charlie's lawyer," Breen said. "What are you getting at, Jimmy?"

"I think Lane might be in danger. Do you have a number for her in Santa Barbara?"

"I might."

Breen buzzed Debby. "See if we have the number of Lane Randolf in Santa Barbara. Thank you."

Debby gave Breen the number. Lujack dialed. A very old, very English voice answered. It was the butler, Kensington. He said Miss Lane was playing polo and wouldn't be back until later. Lujack said he'd call back.

"Why do you think Lane is in danger? She wasn't the one investigating her father's death. Lane's a lovely woman, but she wasn't exactly overcome with grief when her father died."

"I think Phyllis may have taken on some partners. The kind of partners who don't believe in loose ends."

Breen knew better than to ask who those partners were. Lujack stood up. He had a lot of driving ahead of him—ninety miles south to Carlsbad, then two hundred miles north to Santa Barbara.

Morris Breen handed the envelope back as he stood up in turn. "Why don't you let this ride on the Giants Sunday? The line is still Marlins plus four, right?"

Lujack took the envelope. "What's going on, Morris? When people like Burt Masters, Clark Sterling, and you make big bets on a game, they know something. What do you know?"

"A rumor. All I know is a rumor," Breen said. "You won't move the line if I tell you?"

"You're down on the Giants at plus four."

"I heard from a friend that Tim Woodard's leg has been tender all week. They didn't put that on the injury report because Simmons and the team trainer thought he'd work it out."

"But he hasn't."

"My source says he could barely get out of his car yesterday at practice."

"The Marlins have covered two weeks in a row. The Giants are slumping. Woodard is a great back, but the way Mayflower's throwing . . ."

"Jimmy, you know as well as I do, a back favors a leg, the other team knows it. Linebackers sense leg injuries like sharks sense chum. They tackle the ball, one, two fumbles a game—that's worth points, big points."

"Call me after you talk to Sterling, okay? About that will."

"Sure, buddy. And Jimmy, say hello to her for me," Breen said with a smile. "Santa Barbara is nice this time of year."

"Somebody's got to do it," Lujack said as he walked out.

Chapter 10

CARLSBAD WAS ONE TOWN past Oceanside at the south end of Camp Pendleton. The best weather in the world was said to be along the coast of northern San Diego County. If October 22 were any indication, Lujack had to agree. The temperature was around seventy degrees. It was clear and dry with just enough breeze off the Pacific to keep your deodorant from being tested. The Mustang eased down Interstate 5 through Camp Pendleton at a comfortable ninety miles an hour. The CHP didn't like giving tickets on the nineteen-mile stretch through the Marine base, figuring the Marines got enough discipline in the barracks.

Lujack took the first Carlsbad exit. He pulled up in front of a fast-food stand. There were two Marines sitting at an outdoor table. One black, one white. The black Marine was wearing a T-shirt. A picture of what looked like the bombing of Libya was silk-screened on the front. Above the explosions were the words, "Kill 'em all," below the wreckage the words, "Let God sort 'em out." Morale was high with the troops.

"Your car's a classic," the white Marine said as Lujack got out. "What's it do?"

"'Bout one fifty-five."

"You wouldn't be interested in selling, would you?"

"Not on your paycheck, I wouldn't," Lujack said, and the two Marines laughed.

A fortyish blonde sat behind the counter, reading a copy of *People* magazine. She was in no hurry to look up.

"Excuse me. I'm looking for Ocean Street. 211 Ocean Street."

The woman gave Lujack a long look. "Hungry?"

"No. Just lost."

"Too bad."

Lujack gathered the woman was available for more than short-order cooking.

"Two blocks down, take a right on Grand at the Rotary Park. You can't miss Ocean. It's right on the ocean." She giggled at her discovery.

"Is there a phone around?"

"You makin' a local call?" she asked hopefully.

"No, L.A."

"Around back, next to the gas station," she said, returning to her *People*.

Lujack called Tommy. His partner had already heard about the Woodard injury from one of his sources and had dropped the line to Marlins minus three and a half.

"Hate to give up a fat middle like that," Lujack said, referring to the bettors who would now go the other way, taking the Giants at the new line of plus three and a half. All bettors dreamed of bracketing a middle number like three or four, which gave them a chance to win both ends of a bet while risking only the five percent vigorish.

"I can circle it if you want," Tommy suggested, which would take the game off the board.

"No, leave it up. Bettors hate it when the local team is circled. We'll just lay everything off with Hiram."

"Guess your friend Nimmo has some juice with the Marlins trainer," said Tommy.

"The trainer doesn't carry the ball."

"You still think there's something going on?"

"I'll know soon enough."

Tommy hung up. One warning was all Lujack got.

Number 211 Ocean Street was a quaint wooden house backing on the Carlsbad boardwalk which ran along the beach. Before the real estate boom of the late '70s, such houses were used only in the summer or occupied by bohemian types for a nominal rent. But with the growing population surge in Southern California, there was very little beach frontage between Santa Barbara and Tijuana that hadn't become prime property.

In front of the house was a maroon Volkswagen Rabbit convertible. The license plate read "Bama Girl" and had a bumper sticker which read "Masseuses Do It with Their Fingers." It seemed Miss Alabama Starr was home.

As Lujack approached the open front door, he made a silent wish that Alabama Starr lived alone. All he needed was to tangle with Alabama's boyfriend, probably a former Crimson Tide tackle. Lujack reflected that he'd been in more fights since getting mixed up with the Randolf family than he had in the past four years.

"Hello. Hello. Is anybody home?"

"Come on in," came a decidedly Southern female voice. "Through the sittin' room and to your right."

Lujack cautiously entered the living room. It had that unmistakable beach-cottage smell. The music was Deep South, Jim Croce singing "Big Bad Leroy Brown." There was a large poster on the wall of a wholesome-looking blonde with a highly leavened body in an Alabama cheerleader uniform.

The real Alabama was doing Nautilus exercises in the day room which had been converted into a small gymnasium. She was lither, more muscular than in her college days, but still beautiful. She filled out her Dance Fever leotard in all the right places.

"How are you today?" she said with friendly Southern charm.

"That machine is hardly a match for you."

"Are you a Nautilus buff too?"

"Unfortunately, the most exercise I've been getting lately is chasing tennis balls."

"Tennis can give you a decent workout, if you're any good."

"I usually win, but I'm not very good."

She liked that answer and did ten quick pec decks to show her appreciation. Lujack tried hard not to stare.

"My name is James Lujack. My friends call me Jimmy."

"Alabama Starr. My friends call me Bama," she said, untangling herself from the pulleys and giving Lujack a hearty handshake. Lujack didn't put her much past twenty-four or twenty-five, but there was more in those blue eyes than Gatorade and pompoms. Her nose turned up slightly, and her cheeks were flushed from the workout. She didn't strike Lujack as a hooker, but she didn't strike him as a housewife either.

"Lujack and Starr. Couple of pretty good quarterbacks," Bama said with a smile.

"You know your football, Miss Starr. Are you related?"

"My father always told me we were. But I met Bart Starr two years ago at a golf tournament, and he said he didn't recollect having any kin by the name of Tom Starr. 'Course, I never would say anything to Daddy. Alabama football is his whole life."

"According to my father, I'm Johnny Lujack's third cousin. At home there was a picture of my father standing next to Johnny in the Coliseum when Notre Dame came to Los Angeles in 1947 and mauled S.C. thirty-eight to six."

Lujack abruptly stopped himself. It was remarkable that in only two minutes this girl had him telling her his family history. She had a disarming naturalness. She wasn't naive or innocent, but he knew what men saw in her. She was a Southern ingenue.

"What can I do for you, Mr. Lujack? Most of my clients meet me at the salon."

"I'm not a customer, although what brought me down here is a former customer of yours. Charles Randolf."

"You a friend of Charlie's?" she said warmly, toweling off a seductive line of moisture making its way down her neck toward her cleavage. If the ghost of Charlie Randolf was haunting her, she didn't show it.

"Actually, I'm a friend of his son's, Kurt . . ."

Alabama frowned. "That was a terrible thing that happened to him and his family. I'm sorry. Charlie always spoke so well of Kurt."

"I'm not sure if you're aware of it, but Kurt was investigating his father's death. He never thought Charlie's death was accidental."

"What are you backing up to, Mr. Lujack?"

"A mutual friend of ours told me you used to give Charlie a rubdown when he was in the area."

"A mutual friend?"

"Hiram Hotel."

"That bootblack is no friend of mine," she said hotly. "This part of Alabama is still segregated when it comes to the likes of Hiram Hotel."

"Did you see Charlie on the afternoon he died, Miss Starr?" Lujack persisted.

"No, I did not," she said emphatically.

"But you usually saw him when he was staying at the hotel?"

"Usually, yes. But the day he died, no. I wasn't feeling well that day and had to cancel all my appointments."

"Did Charlie ever say anything to you about his heart condition?"

She laughed. "I was the one who told him to lay off the red meats, cheeses, salt, and scotch, or he'd never see another Super Bowl. But nobody could make Charlie stop living the way he wanted to live."

"How did you know Charlie's heart was bad? I've been told that very few people knew, not even his children."

"Health and physical condition are my business, Mr. Lujack," she said, going back to her workout. "Charlie was sixty-three years old, overweight, under a great deal of stress, performed very little if any exercise, and had an atrocious diet. You didn't have to be a heart specialist to know that his time was coming."

"You'd think a man with the brains he had would be smart enough to try to live for another ten or twenty years."

"Men of his generation tend not to believe in

nutrition and exercise . . . until they have their first heart attack. Unfortunately for Charlie, his first one was also his last one."

Straddling the exercise mat, Alabama began to swing her arms back and forth, touching her toes. Lujack, in his years in the department, had questioned a lot of different people and had always thought he was pretty good at reading witnesses—and suspects. With Alabama Starr, he didn't know if he was coming or going.

"You liked Charlie, didn't you?"

"Like? *Like* isn't the kind of word that applied to Charlie," she said, her ponytail bobbing back and forth from toe to toe. "I respected him. Charlie Randolf was a man's man. You don't see many of them anymore. Especially in California."

"I'm sorry to hear that."

She stopped her toe touches and looked up.

"You strike me as a man's man, Mr. Lujack. Even if you are a bit sneaky."

"I'm afraid I'm sneakier than you think. I talked to a friend at Rancho Verde, and he told me Charlie Randolf helped you buy this house and arranged the business loan you needed to start your exercise salon."

The Southern hospitality evaporated from Alabama's blue eyes.

"You scum-suckin' Yankee blackmailer! I earned every square foot of this property, and I'm not afraid who knows it. And that includes Miss Big-Shot Roller Derby!"

"I'm not here to blackmail you, Miss Starr. All I'm here to do is find out what happened to Charlie Randolf. Whether he was cooked in a sauna, beat up by professional killers, or stimulated to death by your loving touch. I aim to find out what happened to him, because the people who murdered Charlie also murdered his son and his son's family."

"In my part of the country, strangers don't come into people's homes and accuse them of murder," she said indignantly. "You better be on your way, Mr. Lujack, or I'll be calling Sheriff Langston."

She was trying hard to be tough but couldn't quite pull it off. Alabama had something she wanted to say.

"I don't know how much you know, Miss Starr, but the simple fact that Hiram gave me your name tells me that you're in danger. You've become a chit in a very high-stakes game. The only way you can help yourself is to tell me what you know. That way, your value is reduced, and I have a chance to find out who's behind this."

"What are you? A cop?"

"I used to be a cop. LAPD. Now I'm just helping a friend. But I still know a few people in law enforcement who might be able to help you."

She exhaled slowly, as if she'd made a decision. "I could go to jail," she said solemnly.

"Jail is the least of your troubles now."

"I didn't kill him," she said suddenly. "I didn't even know it could kill him until later."

"You didn't know *what* could kill him?"

"Cocaine. Charlie liked to snort a few lines before . . . before his rubdown. He said it got his blood circulating. I never knew cocaine could kill him. Then, this summer, when I heard about what happened to those two colored boys—I mean, they were in the prime of their careers—that's when I figured . . ."

"When you figured the heart attack might not have been an accident."

She nodded. Tears began to stream down her cheeks. She was crying for her old client, and maybe for herself.

"Bama, who was it that gave Charlie the coke?"

"It was Paul, Paul Makaris," she said through the tears.

"The good doctor," Lujack mused, fitting another piece into the puzzle. For medicinal purposes only, to get Charlie's blood pumping.

"I called him when Charlie had the seizure. I was so scared. It was awful. We were . . ."

"So Makaris dragged his body into the sauna, got rid of the coke, and called the police."

"I don't know what he did. I skedaddled after Paul came. The next I heard was on the radio when they said Charlie died of a heart attack. Later, Paul told me if I wanted any more clients at Rancho Verde, I was to shut up about what happened. He said it was an accident, but some people might not see it that way."

Lujack could name a whole list of law enforcement agencies who might not see it that way. He also knew that two years ago, coke wouldn't have been looked for in the autopsy of a sixty-year-old man. Dr. Makaris had committed an almost perfect murder. But why?

"Bama, I think it'd be a good idea for you to visit your dad for a while. Just until I can sort a few things out. The Crimson Tide has a pretty good team this year; you and he can take in a few games, see some old friends down in Birmingham."

"You mean you're not going to the police?" she asked, loosening the rubber band around her ponytail. When she shook her hair free, she became prettier, softer. She didn't seem frightened anymore.

"I don't think there's any reason to. Not until I talk to a few more people."

"I hope you don't get the wrong impression about me," she said, her body language making sure he couldn't. She seemed to have recovered from her emotional outburst. "Charlie was a bastard, but he was a generous bastard. I wouldn't have let him do that stuff . . . if I'd known. I hate drugs myself, don't you?"

She kissed him before he could answer. She tasted like salt and vitamins. They both sank to their knees, still kissing. Lujack's big hands cupped the breasts he'd been transfixed by for the last ten minutes. They were as firm and supple as he'd imagined. She was pulling at his windbreaker as he pulled her leotard down off her shoulder. She started wrestling with his holster, but he was more concerned about his zipper. His gun dropped heavily to the mat as his hands grabbed at the remainder of her tights. Their passion had suddenly developed a frenzied heat.

Surprisingly, the thought of Lane flashed through his mind. Not that fidelity had ever been one of his long suits.

"You must really wallop those tennis balls," Alabama said, running her hands over his bare chest.

"I use a heavy racket," Lujack answered, dropping his hands to her buttocks and picking her up while she nimbly swung her legs around him.

He laid her gently on the mat. She looked like a *Playboy* centerfold without the staple. He was kneeling above her now, helping her hands undo his belt.

"Pants I can handle," she said, pushing his hands away. "It's guns that give me trouble."

The realization didn't come all at once. It's hard to notice little things like sounds and shadows when a gorgeous woman is lying underneath you, pulling at your pants as if she were opening a Christmas present. It was a time-released action, the creaking of a floorboard, Alabama's hands freezing on his crotch, her eyes looking at the door instead of him. It was the blue eyes, brimming with the shock of her own death, that saved him.

He fell to his side as the bullet hit Alabama near the left ear. Grabbing his .38 Special, he rolled toward the doorway, surprising the killer, who had expected him to roll away. Lujack blindly kicked upward. His foot hit the killer's gun just enough to deflect the second bullet, which missed Lujack's head by six inches. That was all the time necessary for Lujack to deposit a .38 slug under the man's chin, jerking his head back violently and sending him through the door.

Lujack crouched behind the doorjamb. He assumed that there was another man. He also assumed that the man he had just shot—judging from the nose, the black, balding hairline, and the pointed Italian shoes —was either Matches Largomasino or Pete Liccata.

He had been set up. Set up by Hiram or through Hiram? The answer to that question would have to wait.

The killer had been stupid, shooting Alabama first. Lujack looked at her magnificent, lifeless body. No more touchdowns, no more massages, no more extras. What a waste.

"Pete! What the fuck's happening?"

The voice was East Coast hood. Maybe Chicago. It sounded scared.

"Pete's dead. You're next, Matches."

Two wild shots struck the doorjamb. They came from the front porch. Another stupid move. When it came to burning up sleeping children, Largomasino was efficient, but he was out of his league now. Lujack knew his best move was to play on Matches's fear. Keep him off balance.

The sun room was exposed to the north side of the

house. The door from the sun room to the outside was open. Luckily, Alabama had liked fresh air. Lujack needed some. Still crouching, staying lower than the windows in case there was even a third man, Lujack crossed the room to the door.

There was movement from the street or the boardwalk. Lujack carefully pushed the door open and stepped onto the sand and the iceplant along the side of the house. Next to the door was an old wooden beach chair, circa 1900s. Alabama's bikini barely covered one of the arms. Lujack slowly started toward the front of the house.

An elderly couple strolled by on the boardwalk. The sight of Lujack half-naked, holding a gun in one hand, didn't seem to faze them. Lujack motioned them to turn around so they wouldn't get in his line of fire. Amazingly, the old man politely turned his wife around, and they headed back in the direction from which they had come. Therein lay the secret of survival and marriage.

He wasn't quite to the front of the house when he smelled gasoline. Matches was resorting to the tactic he knew best. The smell of gasoline set something off inside Lujack. It was the helpless feeling. The despairing part of his nature.

"Ready to die, Matches?" he said, stepping out from the side of the house.

The stunned killer, slightly off balance because of the gasoline can in his hand, hastily fired a shot in Lujack's direction. It wasn't close. There was no second shot from Matches. A .38 Special in the chest from eight feet usually doesn't require an encore, but Lujack couldn't help himself. He wanted to see if blood mixed with gasoline. It didn't.

Chapter 11

EVERYONE IN THE OCEANSIDE jail was an ex-Marine —the sheriff, two deputies, and four of the inmates, including a hooker, who kept telling the jailer that she was suffering from delayed stress syndrome.

"You keep copping guys in the laundromat, Charity, and Sheriff Langston is gonna delay your butt right outta town."

"I told ya, Ken. I was giving the guy change."

"On your knees?" The deputy grinned.

Charity gave a look of embarrassment toward Lujack and the other prisoners. "The boy dropped something. I was trying to find it."

"He dropped his trou, and you found his pecker," a gravely voice laughed, coming into the lockup. The voice belonged to Sheriff Hugo Langston. Lujack had spent a good piece of the past four hours in Langston's company. The experience had been less than gratifying. Langston obviously considered law enforcement a step down from soldiering. Lujack, an ex-cop, was a step down from that.

Langston was followed by a taller, younger man in a suit Don Johnson wouldn't use to buff his Ferrari. The man, in his early forties, looked directly at Lujack.

"Got a visitor, Lujack," Langston said with enough enthusiasm to tell Lujack that Langston considered the visit to be of an unsympathetic nature. The sheriff, despite confirming the identities of Largomasino and Liccata, had still refused to release Lujack on his own recognizance because of Lujack's lapsed gun permit.

"Hello, Mr. Lujack. I'm Quentin Rule."

Lujack looked at Rule's shoes. Brown. He should have known the guy was a Feeb.

"Sheriff Langston has kindly offered me his office so you and I can have a little talk."

Langston's puffy pink hand swung open the cell door. He reached for his cuffs as Lujack walked through.

"That won't be necessary, Sheriff," Rule said, anticipating Lujack's protest.

"He's a mean one," Langston said.

"I'm sure Mr. Lujack has killed enough people today," Rule said smoothly.

Lujack followed the FBI agent into the sheriff's office. Rule took the sheriff's chair and offered Lujack the chair facing. The office had more military memorabilia than a VFW post.

"You and the sheriff don't seem to be hitting it off."

"The sheriff is more interested in killing Communists than catching murderers."

"Is that what you did, Mr. Lujack? Catch a couple of murderers?"

"Largomasino and his buddy burned up a family, including two little girls. They also shot a very pretty young woman in the head. And that's just since they've been in California. If it offends your sense of justice that I had to kill them, maybe you should think of going to law school and letting somebody else wear the Sears suits."

"Lieutenant Thurgood told me you didn't know when to stop."

"He should know."

"He also said you were a good cop."

Lujack shrugged.

"That's why, after we finish our little chat, I'm going to call the San Diego County D.A.'s office and recommend you be released. Unless you like it here."

"Always happy to help the bureau."

Rule hesitated but decided that was as straight as Lujack could get.

"Last Wednesday, you flew to Las Vegas on Northwest Airlines Flight 567. You were picked up by a Mr. Irv Katz—a professional sports bettor and the son of Mrs. Susie Katz, the lady who operates the phones for your and Tommy Chin's L.A. bookie operation, aka the Good Book. You were driven to the home of former agent Phil Muscagy. Muscagy gave you certain information concerning the Las Vegas office's investigation of Charles Randolf and Frank Nimmo, among others. How'm I doing?"

"A for presentation, C-minus for content. Susie Katz is a seamstress who imports silk from one of Tommy's relatives in Hong Kong."

"Muscagy told you that we had certain information concerning Charles Randolf's betting habits but that I shut the operation down when we couldn't get anything on Nimmo."

"Because somebody in the Vegas office kept tipping Frank."

"That's what Muscagy told you?"

"Is that a question? You're the one with all the answers."

"No, Lujack. You're the smart one. You're the one who went barging into Nimmo's office last Wednesday accusing him of murder."

This time, Lujack was impressed. "Are you telling me that you've got Nimmo's office bugged?"

"Nimmo can smell a wire from forty thousand feet."

"Then you've got a guy inside."

Rule smiled. "Let's say we have an informed source. Like they do in Washington."

Things were starting to make sense.

"A source that you almost blew out of the water by barging into Nimmo's office last week on your Kurt Randolf crusade," Rule continued.

"You never dropped the Nimmo case?"

"I knew you'd connect the dots sooner or later. We never could get Nimmo on the wire, but Charles Randolf was willing to try to get him for us . . . in return for certain considerations."

"But Nimmo found out about it and had him killed."

"Randolf insisted on placing his bets directly with Nimmo, which would have been an interstate bust. Nimmo was too smart. Then Randolf said he might have some information about certain players that could interest Nimmo. Unfortunately, Randolf died before that meeting could take place."

"You mean he was murdered before that meeting could take place, murdered because Nimmo either guessed or was tipped that Randolf was rolling over?"

"We think he was tipped."

"By Phil Muscagy," Lujack said, not feeling as smart as he had.

"Muscagy's been on Nimmo's payroll for years. His

wife's a manic depressive. There have been a lot of money pressures . . . Phil got mixed up with one of the girls from the Ritz . . ."

"That's why Muscagy got in touch with Kurt. Not to help, but to find out how much he knew. And you let him. You wanted Kurt to keep digging into his father's death, didn't you, Rule? You wanted him to force Nimmo's hand, because then you could get your precious case back on track. A man had his family burned alive so you and your boys in brown could nab the killers and make a case against Nimmo, but I ruined your dirty little scenario by killing them."

Rule shook his head in disgust. "You don't make it easy on the facts, do you, Lujack? We never knew anything about Kurt Randolf's conversation with Muscagy. We thought the kid had given up. In fact, we did everything we could to steer him away from the truth about what happened to his father."

"Then you did know Charlie was murdered?"

"I told you. We suspected it, but it would have been impossible to prove."

Lujack had to agree. Even with Alabama's testimony, Makaris had constructed a guilt-proof crime.

"Before we continue, I think you should realize the only reason you and your chink partner stay open is because certain people think you're more valuable as a gangster than a cop. What I've told you is privileged departmental information . . ."

"The reason Tommy and I stay open is because it would cost the city of Los Angeles more time and money to shut us down than we're worth," Lujack said, wondering who those "certain people" might be and whose side they might be on.

"I'm not here to argue the economics of busting small-time bookies, Lujack. I'm here to tell you that from this day forward, you're to stay away from Frank Nimmo. You've already ignored Lieutenant Thurgood's warning, and it damn near got you killed. Ignore my warning, and I'll guarantee you'll wish you had been."

"So—I'm supposed to think that you and the other Buster Browns are going to take care of Nimmo. Just like you did the last time."

"Think what you want, but don't say, don't even hint, that we've ever talked. Collect your check from Miss Randolf, and go back to your egg foo yung."

"The bureau has spoken. To live and die in Oceanside."

Rule shook his head like a disapproving schoolmaster.

"You Feebs are all alike. Always the same look. Do the priests teach you that at Loyola, or do you learn it at Quantico?"

"I was prepared not to like you," Rule said, finally giving way to the anger which he'd thus far been able to keep below his Adam's apple, "but you've far exceeded my expectations."

"My pleasure."

Rule stood up. He was about the same height as Lujack but a good thirty pounds lighter. Clean living and calisthenics, Lujack supposed. Rule didn't have to tell Lujack the deal with the San Diego D.A. was off. He could smell it through the FBI man's aftershave.

"Has it ever occurred to you that Nimmo might be getting the information that Charlie promised him? From the new owner of the Marlins?"

Rule hesitated. Lujack kept talking.

"I guess your so-called source didn't tell you that Nimmo offered me fifty-five thousand dollars."

"To do what?"

"To bet against the Marlins in this weekend's game."

"You think Nimmo's got a Marlins player?"

"I think Phyllis Randolf and Frank Nimmo *both* had a lot to gain when Charlie Randolf snorted his way to oblivion."

"Owners don't fix games, players do."

"I can see why they put you in charge."

"Cut the crap, Lujack. What's your play?"

"Phyllis wasn't exactly choked up when she heard about Kurt and his family. With Kurt and his sister out of the way, Phyllis gets the team with no strings attached."

"You think Phyllis and Nimmo are business partners?"

"You said yourself Frank Nimmo would love to have his own professional football team. The league would never let him own one himself, but if he controlled an owner, an eccentric owner . . ."

"Have you told Lane Randolf about your theory?"

"Not yet," Lujack answered.

"It still doesn't explain why Nimmo offered you fifty-five thousand to bet on the Marlins. Unless he was paying you off and you're trying to cover your ass."

"Paying me off for what?"

"You tell me. Maybe you had to take care of some loose ends for him."

Lujack laughed. He knew those loose ends Rule was talking about were Matches and Liccata.

"Just when I thought we were getting along, you go and insinuate I'm a professional killer."

"Not that professional. You didn't take Nimmo's money."

"What makes you so sure?"

124

"People like you don't like being paid twice for the same job. It offends your sense of ethics. Besides, what happens if the Marlins cover and Frank Nimmo wants his money back?"

Now the Feeb was getting closer to the mark. It hadn't been Lujack's ethics that had kept him from picking up that money from Nimmo's gambling cage. It was his keen sense of survival. Whether the Marlins covered or not, it wasn't worth owing Frank Nimmo.

There was a knock on the door, then Langston's head popped in.

"There's a chink out here for Lujack. Says Lujack's lawyer has talked to a judge, and we have to release him or get the D.A. to charge him on the 2214."

"We'll be finished here in a few minutes, Sheriff."

"You mean we aren't going to charge him?"

"That's what I mean, Sheriff."

Langston looked like he'd been denied dessert for a week.

"Is there anything else?" Rule asked the sheriff.

Langston regretfully shook his head and slowly closed the door. Rule turned back to Lujack.

"Just so we understand each other. When you walk out of here today . . ."

"I never talked to you."

"*And* stay away from Frank Nimmo. I'll look into your theory about Phyllis Randolf. If there's something to it, I'll be in touch."

"Before or after Lane is killed?"

"Before, hopefully." Rule smiled.

Tommy drove Lujack back to Alabama's to pick up the Mustang. There were still cop cars and cop tape around the beach house. A body was being loaded into the coroner's van when they drove up.

"You were lucky," Tommy commented, watching the body slide into the van.

"Probably."

"They knew you were coming . . ."

"Maybe," Lujack said, not sure he was ready to deal with the fact that Hiram had set him up. Matches and his friend could have followed him from Breen's office, but that was a long shot.

"Is it over now? This Randolf business?"

"Probably."

"We have made good money, Jimmy, the last few years."

Lujack let out a deep breath. Tommy stopped the car in front of the Mustang. Lujack made no move to get out.

"You found the men who killed her brother. What else is there?" Tommy asked.

"The man who ordered it."

"You don't want any part of him."

"That's what the Feeb said."

"The Feeb is smart."

"He also said you and I run an illegal bookmaking operation."

Tommy raised a black eyebrow.

"First Thurgood, now Agent Rule," Lujack continued. "If I didn't know better, I'd think what we're doing is legal."

"They must want something."

"Damned if I know what it is."

"We could close down."

"Down two hundred grand for the season? I'd rather take a bust than close down now. You know what players think of bookies who pass out during the season."

"I know what cops think of bookies who don't take hints," Tommy said.

"If they wanted us, they would have taken us. Let's just let it ride and hope for the best."

Lujack opened the door of Tommy's Cadillac. "Don't look so glum. I could be dead."

Tommy almost smiled as the Caddy peeled out.

Lujack stopped at his new favorite fast-food stand on the way out of town. The cook was new, but the magazine was the same. He dialed Lane's Santa Barbara number. The English butler answered. He said Miss Randolf had returned to Los Angeles. The way he pronounced "Los Angeles" made it clear he disapproved of anything south of Montecito.

Chapter 12

WHAT CAN I DO for you, Jimmy?" asked Burt Masters on the other end of the line.

"I need a favor," Lujack told him.

"I'm still here."

"I need to get into the Lido Club. Tonight."

"I should be able to handle that."

"I want to surprise someone. Could you leave a name at the door?"

"What kind of name? How about Hugh Winterbottom? They'll think you're one of those English producers with ermine-lined pockets."

"James Lujack, Esquire, should do the trick," Lujack said blandly.

"I'll call Arthur." Masters laughed. "Are you still taking money against the Marlins at minus three and a half?"

"I knew you'd make me pay. How much?"

"Another five thou."

A quick tally told Lujack that he and Tommy were sixty thousand dollars heavy against the Marlins. That was on a total Sunday volume of a hundred twenty thousand. Amazing, considering the Marlins were the local hometown favorites.

"Tim Woodard's sore leg is stirring up a lot of money," Lujack said to stir something up of his own.

"You heard, huh?"

"Yeah, but I don't believe everything I hear."

"Who believes, Jimmy? It's the hoping that keeps you alive," the actor said.

For a gambling junkie, Burt Masters never seemed to lose his perspective.

"By the way," Masters continued, "now that this Iran arms-for-hostages thing has come out, do you think the Union Plaza will change the odds on the Iran-Iraq war?"

"You bet on the Iran–Iraq war?"

"I bet Iran as a two-to-one underdog. I'm hoping now I can get an even-money middle."

"Jesus. What was the over-under? Six hundred thousand killed and injured?"

Masters chuckled. "That's a good question," he said and hung up.

So much for Masters's perspective.

He called Lane's apartment again. The maid said she was out for the evening. Lujack left his name. The maid didn't recognize it. He hoped he wasn't trying to convince himself that Lane was in danger. Quentin Rule hadn't seemed too concerned about her future. And now that Lujack had taken care of her brother's murderers, there would be little reason to keep on seeing her. Only the memory of a kiss.

Next he talked to Tommy. The Oceanside shooting had made the local news. Kyle Thurgood had given reporters the Chin Up as Lujack's office number.

Lujack didn't doubt that Quentin Rule had been behind that ploy—a way to keep Lujack off the streets. Tommy wasn't happy at having to explain Lujack's official duties as the vice-president of East-West Enterprises. Lujack told his partner to stick with "Pacific Rim entrepreneur" until he had a chance to read the fabric brochures Tommy had given him.

"If I'm going to be a fabric importer, I'd better start knowing what I'm talking about," Lujack added. Tommy mumbled an indecipherable Chinese curse.

The Lido Club was located on Wilshire, down a block from Trader Vic's in the heart of Beverly Hills. It was a very private, very altruistic community service club. Started in the thirties by Hollywood's biggest stars as a way to raise money for Los Angeles area boys' clubs, it was the unofficial show business club of Los Angeles. The industry's most famous and illustrious performers, from vaudevillians to movie and sports personalities, were its members. Each year, the club put on a famous Christmas party where underprivileged boys were entertained and presented with gifts. The club was said to have realized more money for charities than any other service club in the state. Its famous celebrity roasts were known throughout the country.

To most people in the country, the Lido Club was synonymous with show business largesse. To its members and to those few locals like Lujack who knew their way around town, the Lido was the apex of Southern California gambling. The place where rich men went to play cards and drink whiskey and place bets on their favorite teams. There was even a miniature casino set up in the basement, originally to accommodate "friendly" games of backgammon and gin rummy. Since the death of Lefty Morgenstern and the arrival of Ernie Barbagelatta, it now hosted some of the most serious games of hold' em and draw poker west of Las Vegas.

How could Hollywood's favorite philanthropic club be home to L.A.'s biggest illegal gambling operation? Lujack had once asked his LAPD captain the same question. "Ask Frank Sinatra," the captain had answered.

The parking valet wasn't old enough to appreciate Lujack's Mustang, but the doorman gave him a wide smile. The Lido doorman was none other than Hector "The Hammer" Lara, a former lightweight contender out of East Los Angeles. Hector was a favorite of Ernie B.'s, some say because of the seventh-round left he took from Roberto Duran in 1978. Hector went down like a bag of wet cement. Duran went on to win, then to lose, the two most lucrative fights in lightweight history. Ernie B. was said to have nodded in his seat when Duran told Sugar Ray Leonard, *"No mas."*

"Lookin' good, Hector," Jimmy said, giving the boxer a playful jab.

"Been a while, Jimmy. Where you been hiding?"

"Under the covers, when I can."

"I hear that," Hector said, opening the ornate door of the Lido.

Lujack slid Hector a fiver as he walked into the club.

Everything about the Lido, from the marble floors to the crystal chandeliers, was exquisite and exclusive. The tall balding man behind the desk fit right in with the environment. Even though the impeccably tailored club manager had seen Lujack five or six times, he looked at Lujack as though he had just wandered out of a Beirut refugee camp.

"James Lujack. I'm a guest of Burt Masters."

Arthur checked his list. Lujack knew there were

maybe five names on the guest list, but Arthur was in no hurry.

"Of course. Welcome to the Lido, Mr. Lujack. Will you be dining with us this evening?"

"No, thanks, I had a late lunch in Oceanside."

Arthur gave Lujack the tightest of half-smiles.

"Has Mr. Hotel been in tonight, Arthur?" Lujack asked innocently, knowing how much it pained the Lido Club's stuffy manager to report the comings and goings of a black hoodlum.

"I don't believe so, sir," Arthur said stiffly.

"If he does come in, will you tell him I'm in the bar?"

The club manager bowed ever so slightly.

Lujack had been hoping to catch Hiram off guard amidst the Beverly Hills high rollers who frequented the Lido. He would hang out around the bar and see what he could shake loose. If Hiram had set him up, which he still couldn't believe, then he wouldn't have a long wait.

"Scotch and water, please," Lujack said to the bartender.

The bar was almost empty. Lujack recognized three of the four other customers. Two were Hall of Fame comedians, Hollywood legends who came to the Lido to tell stories about the days when radio was funny and movies were family affairs. The third man, sitting at the far end of the bar with a spicy Latin lady, Lujack knew as his own customer. He was one of Hollywood's hottest stars. A generation younger than Burt Masters, Paul De Vris was a moody, handsome New York actor whose full lips, tight ass, and pronounced Adam's apple got him a lot of parts where towel scenes were *de rigueur*.

The waiter came back with Lujack's scotch.

"Courtesy of Mr. De Vris," the bartender said.

Lujack nodded to the actor. De Vris motioned Lujack to come over.

"What are you doing in this neck of the jungle?"

"Looking for Hiram. Seen him?"

"Last night he was around. He usually doesn't come in on poker night."

"I thought every night was poker night at the Lido," Lujack said.

"Friday nights are for the heavyweight players."

"Like you, Paul."

"No way, Lujack. Those guys down there play for keeps. I'm a poor boy from the Bronx."

"What's it cost to get into this game?"

"Twenty thousand on the table and *cojones* bigger than basketballs."

"Who might I run into in this game?"

De Vris named one of Hollywood's biggest producers, a studio executive who had been at the same business address for the last ten years, and a prominent Los Angeles attorney. It was the last name that got Lujack's attention. Clark Sterling.

"Is Sterling down there tonight?"

"Don't know. Haven't been down yet. Joy and I are here to have dinner."

Lujack nodded to Joy. She wasn't sure if he was important or not, so she smiled, just in case.

Lujack finished his scotch and debated about going downstairs. The only way to get down to the Lido Club basement was by elevator. After what had happened that afternoon in Oceanside, Lujack wasn't looking forward to a ride in one of Ernie Barbagelatta's elevator shafts. Finally, he decided to push the button and take his chances.

The door opened, and Lujack stepped onto the thick green carpet. Two sturdy-looking boys, who Lujack recognized from Salome's a few nights before, stood in front of the large oak door that led to the Lido Club game room.

"Mr. Hotel isn't here," the more intelligent-looking bodyguard said.

"I'm not looking for Hiram," Lujack said.

"This room is private. Members only."

"That's all right, Barry," came a voice behind Lujack. He didn't have to turn around to recognize the voice.

"Sure thing, Mr. Sterling," the other bodyguard said, opening the door.

Lujack nodded at the crewcut lawyer. Sterling was in his Carroll and Company finery. His gray eyes, the color of a Nazi uniform, matched his Italian shoes. Like most members, he had come in through the private garage.

"Did you come to collect, Mr. Lujack, or pay out?" the lawyer asked as they entered the room, which looked more like a small Las Vegas casino, except that there were no slot machines, old ladies, or hookers. There were six or seven tables. Everyone played with chips. Waiters were busy bringing drinks to the tables.

"That depends on how my luck is running."

"From what I heard on the radio tonight, your luck's been pretty good today."

"Never know who you're going to run into," Lujack said, volunteering nothing.

"Why don't you drop around my office Monday? We'll finish our business."

"I'd like to talk to Lane first."

"I think I might be able to arrange that," Sterling said with a curious smile.

"I can make my own arrangements."

Lujack didn't finish his statement. He didn't have to. There, at a rear table, holding her cards like Doc

Holliday, looking like Persephone, was Lane Randolf. From the number of chips in front of her, she wasn't doing too badly.

"Never know who you're going to run into," Sterling said blandly.

Lane looked up. She was expecting Sterling, but Lujack was a surprise. "What are you doing here?" she asked more casually than Lujack would have liked. She was dressed in black, no jewels. Elegant, simple.

"I was going to ask you the same thing."

"I'm a regular. Been playing cards at the Lido since I was in pigtails."

"Put up or shut up, Lane," Delbert Stanley goaded gently. Lujack knew the white-haired producer was a man who rarely lost—at anything.

Lane threw three blue chips on the table. Lujack assumed the blues were a thousand, the reds five hundred, and the whites one hundred. Like De Vris said, this was a serious game. There was easily ten thousand dollars on the table already.

The producer looked at his cards, then at Lane, then back at his cards. The game was draw poker, and the producer figured Lane was for real. He folded his manicured nails over his cards and tossed them in the center of the table. Jim Frank, a studio president, was the next bettor. You don't head up a major Hollywood studio for twelve years and not know when to run a pretty girl's bluff. He threw in three blue ones.

"And five more," he said, flashing a boyish smile that reminded Lujack of Frank's father, an old Hollywood cowboy actor.

Lane winked at Lujack. Lujack didn't know if it was for his benefit or Frank's. The last man at the table, Carl Schulte, a Hollywood attorney who specialized in labor relations, took a long puff on his cigar, exhaled, and folded. Leaving Lane and the studio head.

"I'll see your five, Jim, and bump you another five," Lane said calmly.

"That's it. Last bump," Stanley said.

Lujack made a rough count of twenty-one thousand dollars lying on the table.

"You only drew one card, darling," the studio head said, as much to himself as to those at the table. "But there's no way in hell you can beat me."

"You're going to have to go there to find out," she said coolly.

"Not tonight, I'm not," the studio head said, throwing in his cards.

Lane carefully put her cards down on the felt and pulled the chips toward her. Lujack could sense her relief—or was it exhilaration? Maybe the ambivalence was why she won. Delbert Stanley picked up the cards and began shuffling.

"Sit down, Clark. Lane's streak is coming to an end."

"Who's banking?" Sterling asked.

"I am," the studio head said without noticeable enjoyment. "But buy from Lane. She's got all the chips."

Sterling wrote a check to Lane, and she pushed across five thousand in whites, five thousand in reds, and ten thousand in blues. Lujack felt stupid, powerless, resentful, standing in back of this table of super-wealthy people who played single card games for what would have been for him, and not long ago, a year's salary. Lujack liked being a bookie. He liked the power of handling hundreds of thousands of dollars in bets per week, but he had never lost his work ethic or his basic respect for money. It was that respect that made him a bad gambler but a good bookie.

"Are you going to buy in or just stare at Lane?" the white-haired man said with some acerbity.

"'Fraid this game is a little rich for me."

"Come on, Lujack, don't mind him. Sit by me," Lane said, and Lujack found himself sitting next to her.

"Mr. Lujack has been very busy today, Lane," Sterling said.

"Oh, really?"

"I found Matches and his sidekick."

"You found Kurt's murderers! You're sure?"

"The police seem to be sure," Sterling said, "but Matches and his crony are in no position to confess."

Lane grabbed Lujack's elbow. She didn't need Sterling's remark explained. Neither did the others at the table, who suddenly looked at Lujack with more respect. Stanley suddenly seemed in no hurry to deal. He shuffled the deck, quickly, evenly. Lane looked at Lujack with those dark, arresting eyes. She seemed frightened, excited.

"Is there a place we can talk?"

"Of course. Let's get out of here," Lane said, pushing away from the table. "Jim, be a dear and cash me out."

"It's not even ten o'clock. You have to give us a chance to win our money back."

"I'll be back next Friday. I promise not to spend it all."

Jim Frank reluctantly counted out Lane's winnings. He obviously didn't like losing, but he wasn't going to pressure her to stay. Delbert Stanley began to deal a new game.

"Texas hold 'em."

Lane took a check from the studio chief before the up cards were dealt. Lujack imagined the evening's losses would have to be folded into the studio's advertising budget for its next big hit.

"See you Monday," Sterling said to both of them.

"I'll call you, Clark," Lane said, taking Lujack's arm.

"Your luck is still running." Sterling smiled at Lujack.

"So is yours," Lujack said.

"How's that?" the lawyer asked.

"You're still out of jail."

Lujack followed Lane's Rolls down Wilshire past the Los Angeles Country Club. She lived in one of those petro-dollar palaces in Westwood where the doormen wore more gold than the residents. The last person he had expected to run into at the Lido was Lane Randolf, although, when he thought about it, it shouldn't have been surprising. After all, Lane was the daughter of one of the Lido's highest rollers. Why shouldn't the daughter have a little of Papa in her?

"My father used to take me with him to the Friday night games," she said, bringing Lujack a scotch out on the balcony. Lane lived on the fourteenth floor. The balcony overlooked the Mormon temple on Santa Monica.

"It was my happiest time with him. With Kurt, it was always football, throwing the ball outside, talking about which play to run. He was even a water boy for the Marlins. I hated football. I'm not sure why—maybe because my mother never liked it, maybe because I thought Daddy liked it too much." She laughed to herself. "Of course, Daddy never liked horses. And he was always so busy with traveling, business, football, so the only real time we had together was when I went with him to Friday night poker at the Lido." She paused, remembering. "They never let children or women downstairs when I first started going. But Daddy made sure I was an exception."

Lujack had never seen the little girl in Lane. The prodigal daughter of the powerful daddy, all alone atop Los Angeles.

"I guess I still play because it makes my memories of him so vivid."

"If what I saw tonight is any indication, your father's friends could do with a little less paternal sentiment."

"I do enjoy beating those smug bastards, that's sure enough. I also like being one of the boys."

"You're hardly one of the boys."

"You know what I mean. With men like that. They have their precious wives at home, their mistresses on this bed, their secretaries at that typewriter . . . every woman in her cubicle. Men are such cowards. The only way they'll treat you with any respect is if you refuse to be pushed into one of their holes."

"Is that why you're not married?"

"Because I refuse to be put in a cubicle?"

"Something like that."

"Believe me, all the men at that table tonight have tried."

"To make you their secretary?"

"You're pretty funny, Lujack."

"For a cop."

"For an ex-cop," she said and sipped at her drink, looking out at the Mormon temple. "The men I married—I guess you could say I was the one who did the pushing."

"And they didn't like being pushed."

"The first one didn't like it. The last two liked it too much."

"Sounds like you should have stayed with the first one."

"Men," she said. "They're all so romantic. The *sturm und drang* of romance."

Lujack knew all about the *sturm und drang;* he wondered if Lane did. Everything about her was so right. She was effortlessly sexy, intelligent, independent, feminine. He guessed she could be vulnerable and merciless without changing expression.

"What is it, Lujack? You don't like Wagner?"

"Wagner was German. I like Poles."

"Because you're Polish."

"It shows, eh?"

"Only when you make coffee."

Lane did a sudden pirouette off the patio, leaving Lujack with the scent of an expensive perfume. He followed her back into the living room. Lane's condominium was a study in casual elegance. There was a Leroy Neiman drawing of one of her husbands on a polo pony, a Picasso drawing of a young woman, a bookcase full of compact discs, comfortable overstuffed furniture upholstered in a French toile.

Lane dallied by the C.D. player. Lujack waited by the couch. He knew she wanted to ask him. He was content to watch her shuffle boxes. She looked awesome in black.

"I'm afraid my jazz collection is no better than my Wagner. I think I might have an old Miles Davis, but not in C.D."

"The older the better."

He recognized the cover. *Sketches in Spain.* The album started—"The Pan Piper." She came back to the couch.

"Good choice."

"Kurt gave it to me. He liked jazz too."

Their eyes touched briefly, then she looked away.

"So—it's over."

"I'm not sure."

She looked blank.

"You did kill those . . . men?"

"Yeah, I killed 'em."

"And Inspector Ballard says they're the men who . . ."

"They did it. For a price."

"And you know who paid them?"

"I have a pretty good idea. A man by the name of Frank Nimmo."

She nodded.

"You know him?"

"No. But I know of him."

"Before my little get-together with Matches and his sidekick, I talked to a girl who was with your father before he died."

"You found the blond girl Kurt was talking about? What did she say?"

"She said your father died from an overdose of cocaine."

"Cocaine? Daddy never used cocaine."

"According to Alabama, he did. It helped him, well . . ." Lujack paused. "Alabama said he did a few lines before they would . . ."

"I think I get the picture," Lane said softly. "And you believe this Alabama?"

"She had no reason to lie. If it means anything, she liked your father."

"I'm sure she did. Why else would she have killed him?"

"Alabama didn't give your father the cocaine. Paul Makaris did."

"Paul Makaris?" she said, this time truly surprised. "Why would he? This is crazy. Paul has been Daddy's doctor for years. He and Phyllis—" She caught the gist of what Lujack was trying to say. "You don't think that Phyllis and Paul . . ."

"It's a possibility. I've been doing some checking on Paul Makaris. His association with Rancho Verde is a very lucrative one. It seems he has an exclusive deal with the Rancho Verde management. I don't have to tell you who runs Rancho Verde."

"The bad guys."

"Frank Nimmo and his friends in Chicago, with help from other investors in Miami, New Orleans, and New York."

"And they were afraid Daddy was going to make trouble for Nimmo?"

"Nimmo knew he was going to make trouble. Nimmo had a man in the Vegas FBI office," Lujack said.

"But what does all this have to do with Phyllis?"

"I'm not sure. I think she and Frank Nimmo may have hit on an arrangement that would be mutually beneficial, but the only way I could prove it is through Makaris."

"Which means you have to make Alabama testify in court?"

"Unfortunately, the only testifying Alabama's going to be doing from now on is at Judgment Day."

Lane gave an involuntary shudder. "It doesn't stop, does it?" she asked.

"What doesn't stop?" Lujack asked, already knowing.

"The killing. First Daddy, then Kurt and his family, now this woman."

"For men like Frank Nimmo, it doesn't stop. No."

"And for you?"

"I don't enjoy it, if that's what you mean. I don't make my living at it either."

"I'm sorry. That was unfair. I'm the one who got you into this."

She reached over and put her hand on his. Her touch made a difference. He put his free hand on top of hers. He wanted to protect her, even though he knew she could take care of herself.

"Before I went down to Carlsbad, I went by Morris Breen's office. According to your father's will, if Phyllis remarries within five years of your father's death, the team goes to you and Kurt or your heirs."

"I remember something like that. Daddy wasn't a complete fool. But you can't think Phyllis would risk everything for one of those bozos she goes out with. I mean, the lady is hardly a firm believer in marriage before sex. Besides, Daddy's been dead almost three years. If she's so hot to get married, I'm sure she can wait another couple of years."

"Maybe one of the boyfriends couldn't wait."

"You mean Paul Makaris?"

"Or Frank Nimmo. Or both. Or somebody else."

Lane shook her head. She was confused. For the first time, he realized she felt she was in over her head.

"It's all so complicated. I just can't think that Phyllis—she loved those little girls. Really."

"Once forces start in motion, forces like Frank Nimmo, there's not much one can do. I'm not trying to scare you." He hesitated. "Well, maybe I am a little."

"You've succeeded."

Before he could finish his thoughts, he was doing what he had wanted to do ever since he saw her holding those five cards in front of her chin two hours before. His mouth coupled with hers. The last time he had kissed a beautiful woman, it had nearly cost him his life. There are some women who are worth the risk. Lane Randolf was one of them.

He drew her down on the couch. She was as impatient as he and started helping with his tie. Setting a new indoor record, he got out of his sport coat and shirt. She stood up and let her evening dress fall to the floor. Her body was every bit as inspiring as he'd hoped.

"Is there a bedroom around here?"

She nodded past the mirrored bar. He picked her up and carried her toward the bedroom. She stuck her tongue in his ear, and he almost dropped her. The bed was big enough for five. He laid her on the comforter and fumbled with his belt. She unhooked her bra and smiled.

"There's always such a hurry the first time," she said.

Lujack wanted to say, yeah, but there wasn't enough time.

Lujack spent most of the next twelve hours in and around Lane Randolf's imperial-size bed. She gave new meaning to F. Scott Fitzgerald's premise that the rich are different. If Tommy hadn't tracked him down the next morning, he might never have left.

"When can I see you again?"

Lane gave him a bemused smile as she pulled on her polo breeches. Lujack knew how Lane's horse must feel—tired but happy.

"Sorry. I've always been pushy."

"I'm busy tonight. Maybe tomorrow."

"Tomorrow I'm booked," Lujack said.

"Bookie business?"

"Sort of," Lujack told her, mulling over Hiram's cryptic message to Tommy: "Tell Lujack, the Pearl after the game. No traffic."

Tomorrow was the Marlins–Giants game at the Coliseum. Lujack planned to watch it on television.

Tommy said Hiram had covered the sixty thousand dollars on the Giants without flinching. The purpose of the meeting was his trip to Carlsbad, not bookie business. Hiram would either have found out who ordered Lujack killed or try it again himself. Lujack had to find out. "The Pearl" was Hiram's old nightclub. "No traffic" meant that he expected Lujack to be followed.

Lane poured him a second cup of coffee on the balcony. The Mormon temple was still there. So was a layer of smog. It was already in the low seventies.

"Who's Anna?" Lane asked, pulling on a riding boot.

The question hit like a two-hundred-forty-pound linebacker from the blind side.

"What do you know about Anna?"

"Nothing. Except that you said her name last night."

"I did?"

"In your sleep."

Lujack couldn't remember dreaming about Anna last night. For the first time in a long time, he couldn't remember even thinking about her.

"She was my wife."

"You're divorced?"

"Five years in January."

"Did she remarry?"

"I guess Clark Sterling didn't tell you."

"Didn't tell me what?"

"About Anna and my partner, Marty Kildare."

"Your partner? Your wife left you for your partner?"

"She left me because of me. Although it took me a while to admit that to myself."

Lane left her other riding boot off. Lujack wasn't sure he wanted to tell her about Anna.

"We met during my second year on the force. Anna was a waitress at a trendy restaurant on the Santa Monica Pier. You know—everybody wore draw string pants and Guatemalan shirts."

"The Yardarm," Lane said, and Lujack nodded.

"I used to go there after work. There were always lots of cute girls, and in those days not all of them needed a gram of coke to be friendly. Anna was always friendly. Always in a good mood, no matter what kind of mood I was in. She was very pretty and a little lost. She'd left home when she was seventeen."

Lujack sipped at his coffee. Lane watched him carefully. Her dark eyes transmitted an empathy he had never noticed.

"We got married after my third year on the force. Two years later, I was transferred to Hollywood. That's when I met Marty. We used to go out a lot with Marty and his girlfriend, Sandy—football games, camping trips, skiing. But Marty wasn't the marrying kind, and Sandy was replaced by a string of girls. Anna never liked any of them after Sandy, and she stopped coming with us."

"But you kept going? With Marty and his dates, and maybe his dates' friends?"

"Sometimes. It was a way to relax. Being a cop—it's not the kind of job you can go home after and mow the lawn or play Scrabble. I needed action, but the more action I needed, the more we grew apart. Then Anna got pregnant. It was right after Marty and I got transferred to vice."

Lujack found himself looking again at the Mormon temple. If he had been a Mormon, his life would have been much simpler. No drinking, no gambling, as many wives as he wanted.

"Working vice in Hollywood"—Lujack shook his head—"you can make a hundred good busts a week and you're lucky to be treading water. After a while, you start getting a little crazy. The pimps, the hookers, the transvestites, the chicken hawks, the street people, the runaways. You can go home and take a shower, but you can't wash it off. I tried to wash it down. One night, I came home late, after three. I was better than half-drunk. Marty and I had been out in the marina with a couple of Delta cabin crews. Anna was in bed; she'd had a miscarriage. The doctor had been there, said she'd be fine, those things happen—the usual pap. But after that, things were different. I tried to be home more; sometimes Marty would come with me. Marty and Anna had a certain *simpático,* something I couldn't share. But it never bothered me. Maybe that was part of the problem. Finally, after the Temple Arms murders, it all came apart."

"I don't know about the Temple Arms murders."

"January 12, 1982. It was about a year after I'd made detective. I was working downtown vice. Rumor was I was in line for homicide. That's what I found on January 12 in Room 206. A triple homicide. Three nameless Latino boys, couldn't have been more than thirteen. They were stacked in the corner of this dingy apartment like eucalyptus branches. Seeing those boys set something off inside me. Maybe it was the frustration of my life. I found their pimp and beat him up pretty bad. The next day, I was suspended. A week later, Anna left me."

"I'm sorry," Lane said.

"I don't think she ever loved Marty, but I do believe she hated me."

"Are they still together?"

Lujack shook his head. "Marty killed himself eight months later."

"And your wife?"

"She hasn't spoken to me since."

"But you still say her name in your sleep."

"If you say so."

Lane pulled on her other boot. She was pissed. Lujack didn't blame her. She went back into the apartment. Lujack found himself alone with the Mormon temple. He'd never had good luck with temples. Ever since his first girlfriend in junior high, Amy Brief, had tricked him into thinking that synagogues were places where people went to watch other people sin.

Chapter 13

ALTHOUGH TOMMY PRIDED HIMSELF on the fact that he had never attended a pro football game in his life, he rarely missed watching parts of every game his satellite transmitter could pick up. Tommy was fooling with the transmitter when Lujack arrived at the Chin Up. Ever since he'd bought the contraption last summer, Tommy spent most of his spare time fooling with the angle of his satellite dish, much to the dismay of his bar customers, who would rather watch one game all the way through than hopscotch the country getting bits and pieces of every game.

"Tommy, they give the scores every ten minutes," Sid Green said for what Lujack guessed was the fifth time that morning, as Tommy left the Eagles–Redskins game and tuned in the Buffalo-Miami tilt.

"The weather is better in Miami. So is the reception."

"But the Eagles were driving. I have roots in Philadelphia," Sid protested.

"Your father was born in Warsaw." Tommy scowled.

Tommy never liked it when his Jewish neighbors pretended to be more American than he was. Without comment, he handed Lujack the betting sheets. They had ended up seventy thousand dollars heavy on the Giants. The line was still three and a half. There had been no mention of Tim Woodard's sore leg in the morning paper. Even Jimmy the Greek had picked the Giants, usually a sure sign the betting would shift to the Marlins, but there had been no shift. It was going to be an interesting game.

"What do you think?" Tommy asked.

"I think if the Marlins don't cover, somebody's going to be out a lot of money."

"Hiram."

"Not Hiram. Maybe Ernie."

Tommy nodded.

"Any more reporters call?" Lujack asked, remembering the story in yesterday's paper. "Ex-cop in Shoot-out with Ex-cons. A textile importer, Jimmy Lujack, a former Los Angeles vice detective, was involved in a bloody shoot-out Friday, killing two Chicago men, Michael 'Matches' Largomasino and Pete Liccata . . ."

"I told them you were on a buying trip."

"I keep getting all this publicity, I'm going to have to go to Hong Kong."

"You keep getting publicity, Jimmy, we'll both be going to San Quentin."

"Hey, Jimmy, good shooting, my man."

Lujack turned to see Lionel Chin, Tommy's thirteen-year-old son, behind him.

As usual, Lionel was dressed like a Ninja, black hair slicked back, black jacket, black pants.

"That's Mr. Lujack to you, Lionel," Tommy told his number one son.

"It's cool, ain't it, Mr. L.?"

"How ya doing, Lionel?"

"'Isn't it, Mr. Lujack,'" Tommy corrected. "Now, what are you doing here?"

"There's a new movie opening at the Rio. Kim and I—"

Tommy reached into his pocket and peeled off ten dollars.

"I don't want you going to any of those devil cult movies."

"*Sword of Samson* is no cult movie," Lionel said defensively, wielding his imaginary sword like a nun chook stick.

"Too bad I didn't have one of those with me in Carlsbad," Lujack said.

"Next time maybe you can take me with you, eh, Mr. L.?" Lionel said, deftly grabbing the ten spot with a karatelike motion and heading for the door.

"And no fighting in the theater," Tommy yelled after him.

"Great kid," said Lujack.

"You encourage him. I told his mother not to show him that story about you."

"At least he can read."

A cheer went up from in front of the television set.

"Hey, Tommy, the Dolphins scored. Marino to Duper," Davey Rosenbloom announced.

"So what else is new? You didn't bet the Dolphins."

"I got family in Miami."

Tommy grunted and began searching the heavens for the Bears–Lions.

"I'm going up to see Susie," Lujack said.

Susie was on the phone when Lujack walked in. Most of the Good Book clients got down early, but there was always a flurry of action after the early games. The rotary phone allowed Susie to keep up with the last-second betting.

"Three and a half. I know they were minus four yesterday. Today they're at three and a half," Susie repeated to a customer.

"Two thousand on the Giants, plus three and a half. Got it," Susie said, writing down the number. "Five hundred on Seattle plus one. Got it."

Susie hung up. Jimmy looked at the numbers.

"Another seven thousand on the Giants?"

"They're coming out of the woodwork to play this game," Susie said and smiled. "Congratulations. I hear you're up for DOA Arsonist of the Month Award."

"The way we're strung out on the Giants–Marlins game, we might need a little fire right here," Lujack said, figuring that he and Tommy were now on the hook for seventeen thousand dollars of the bets on the Giants, having only laid off sixty thousand with Hiram.

"You know what I heard, Jimmy?" Susie asked confidentially. "I heard that maybe Frank Nimmo might like to broaden his horizons. I also heard that he's got the clearance from Chicago and New York."

"Since when did you start dating the *capo di tutti capi?*"

"I've got my sources."

"Irv."

Susie laughed. "Irving's business is numbers, not gangsters. You know that. The word is Ernie's getting nervous, really nervous. As they say in show biz, nobody's returning his calls."

It made sense, all of it. The bet Nimmo offered him—if placed at the Lido. All the heavy action against the Marlins, most of it picked up by Hiram, Lujack guessed. Nimmo was trying to squeeze Ernie out without having to fire a shot. If the Marlins didn't cover today, Lujack's rough guess was that Ernie B. would be minus a couple of million dollars. Usually, that kind of action would be covered by arrangements made with East Coast books or with Frank Nimmo himself. But if the word was out from both the New York and Chicago families that Frank had the okay to move into L.A., Ernie was by himself. Ernie was a rich man, but he couldn't keep dishing out two or three million dollars a weekend and stay in business long, not with Frank Nimmo's garlic breath hot on his neck, not with his right hand, Hiram Hotel, dealing behind his back. Lujack wondered if Quentin Rule's source was as good as Susie's. He doubted it.

The bar had grown more crowded for the Giants-Marlins kickoff. Tommy had the TVs going at both ends of the bar. Lujack took his usual seat under the smaller screen. He didn't feel like eating or drinking, so he ordered a Bloody Mary. Tommy made a great Bloody Mary.

"I have a bad feeling about this game," Lujack said as Tommy shoved a celery stick under his nose.

"I have a bad feeling about this year."

"I know, your despondent uncle."

"February 24," Tommy said knowingly.

"What about February 24?"

"Chinese New Year, 4356. Start year of Tiger. Tigers very powerful. They will kill the Ox."

"I just hope we can hang on."

A cheer went up as the Giants place kicker booted the ball toward the Marlins goal line. Fleet White, the Marlins wide receiver and kickoff specialist, gathered the ball in at the three-yard line and followed the wedge of blockers forward up the field. He was hit by one, then by a second blue Giant. The first stood him up, the second cracked him backward three yards— sending the ball up into the air. Larry Trumpy, the Giants' All-Pro linebacker, picked the ball out of the air and carried it into the Marlins end zone in front of eighty thousand stunned Marlins fans.

Tommy looked mournfully at Lujack. "I have a bad feeling about this game," he said.

The camera panned to Phyllis Randolf's box. Phyllis was wearing a pretty white summer dress which made her look almost innocent. The camera pulled back and showed her standing next to the Reverend Billy Moore, the jut-jawed preacher, who was also in white. Lujack saw that both wore golden triangles above their hearts. The two together looked like Jim and Tammy Bakker just discovering the Easter collection baskets had been stolen. Phyllis tugged on the reverend's shoulder, unable to watch the extra point. Lujack wondered if she was a better actress than Tammy Faye; he would have bet a good portion of the Coliseum gate that she was. Moore, for his part, nodded acceptance of the extra point as the ball sailed through the uprights. A veteran of the Southern California evangelical battlefield for the past twenty years, Moore knew the game wasn't over until the last check was cashed.

Susie came downstairs for the second quarter. By then, the Marlins, behind the running of Tim Woodard, the catching of Fleet White, and, last but not least, the regilded arm of Mick Mayflower, had rallied for a fourteen-to-ten lead. Mayflower had hit six out of six passes in a furious two-minute drill to close out the half. The final completion was a touchdown to Fleet White in the corner of the end zone.

"For those of you who thought the new Mick Mayflower wasn't for real," Brent Musburger declaimed at halftime, "fans, you gotta believe after that last two minutes. If Mick's not all the way back, he's getting there pretty quick."

"Why do sports announcers always have to mangle the English language when they get excited?" Susie said.

"Some mangle it because they don't know any other way."

"Not Brent. He only mangles it when he's on a roll."

"You should write him a letter. Ask him to set a better example for our youth."

"I think it's a macho thing. Myron used to do it. The game would get tense, and he'd start swearing in English and Yiddish in equal parts."

"I'll have to remember that. The next time I get excited."

"You're not the excitable type, Jimmy."

Tommy brought over another Bloody Mary. "What do you think?" he asked.

"I think, except for that opening fumble, White's playing damn good. Woodard hasn't missed the hole all afternoon, and Mayflower looks like the second coming of Joe Namath."

"So it's not a bad day after all," Tommy said hopefully.

"Not a bad first half," Lujack qualified. "My gut and Susie's inside info tell me our points won't stand up."

The Marlins started the second half where they ended the first. Their defense held the Giants to three plays and a punt. On the second play of the ensuing possession, Mayflower hit White for a seventy-five-yard pass play.

Boom, twenty-one to ten. When the Marlins scored again on a touchdown coming from a forty-four-yard tackle-breaking run by Woodard, Lujack began to wonder if perhaps he was wrong—about the game being fixed, about Nimmo making a move on Ernie B., about the link between Nimmo and Phyllis, about everything. Even when the Marlins missed the extra point he couldn't smile.

"What's the matter, Jimmy? You look like they just bounced your social security check," Susie said.

"This source of yours?"

Susie gave him a motherly pat. Lujack sometimes thought she cared more about him than she did her own son. Irv was a wizard, but Susie and Lujack were just people. Most people had to win or lose. Not Susie and Lujack; with them, the pass line was gray.

"I've never known you to ask so many questions."

"Not since the cops."

"You never asked questions with the cops. You followed answers. That's what good cops do."

"But I'm not a cop anymore. Maybe it's good that I start asking more questions."

"Maybe it is," she said. She finished her cocktail and looked at the regulars down the bar—Sid, Davey, Pete. Lujack knew she was thinking of Myron. "If you find any answers you like, let me in on them. Meanwhile, stop worrying. The Marlins won't cover."

Susie waved goodbye. Tommy was waiting for Lujack when he turned around.

"What does she mean, don't worry, the Marlins won't cover? We're out seventeen thousand dollars if they don't cover. Not to mention the sixty thousand we put with Hiram. You know Ernie's not going to like that." Tommy looked up at the screen. The Marlins kickoff was deep, out of the end zone.

"That's the way to kick that leather turd," Tommy cheered.

"Susie told me something very interesting," Lujack said.

Tommy looked at his customers, then leaned closer. There was no need. The Chin Up regulars were the original hear-no-evil monkeys.

"Frank Nimmo and his friends in Chicago have the nod from New York to move in on the Los Angeles betting scene. Evidently, the New York families haven't been too happy with Ernie's performance the last few years. And with the number that wop U.S. attorney is doing on them, they need all the cash they can muster. The plan is to break Ernie's bank, with help from the Marlins."

"But why bring in Nimmo and the Chicago crowd? Why not get their own guy?"

"Ernie B.'s not going to roll over for just anyone. They can't promote Hiram; he's the wrong color. And there's no one else who could make it work. Hell, we both know Nimmo could take two, three times more money out of this area than Ernie does. There must be close to a billion dollars a year bet in L.A."

"Yeah, if he starts to get rid of the small guys like us," Tommy said soberly.

The bar erupted again. The Marlins had just intercepted on the Giants' thirty-three.

Tommy yelled. He turned to Lujack. "Your hypothesis is intriguing but lacking in reality."

Lujack smiled. "That's sort of what I told Susie."

"What'd she say?"

Lujack watched Mick Mayflower throw deep out to Fleet White. The pass was perfect, but the timing was a split second off. Homer Sayers stepped in front of White and ran seventy-eight yards for a Giants touchdown.

Tommy ran his hand through his thick black hair.

"She said it wasn't like me to ask so many questions."

Tommy nodded, looking resigned. "I never should have told that one to wait."

"What are you talking about?"

"The rich one."

"Kurt Randolf."

Tommy nodded.

"We have a lot of rich customers. Richer than Kurt Randolf."

"They're players. Rich I like, rich people I don't. They make me nervous; they think their problems are more important than anyone else's."

"Your Hong Kong cousin is one of the richest men in the world. Does he make you nervous?"

"My cousin is Chinese. In China, money is honorable. In America, it is a sin that all men wish to have forgiven."

Lujack thought of an old prayer: "Forgive me, Father, for I have sinned." The beginning of the Act of Contrition. It had been a long time since Lujack had said those words. He wondered if Kurt Randolf had needed such absolution. He was certain Lane didn't.

The Marlins started the fourth quarter with a good-looking drive that stalled on the Giants' thirty. On fourth and two, Coach Chub Simmons brought in Rafael Caesaro for a forty-seven-yard field-goal attempt. Simmons could never be accused of being one of the smartest coaches in the league, and he wasn't risking that reputation by bringing in Caesaro midway through the fourth quarter when a thirteen-point lead was not much safer than a ten-point lead. The smallish Caesaro, known in the league as the barefoot Chihuahua, was better known for clutch short-range accuracy than for his midfield range. The snap was low, and Caesaro's kick didn't get past the line of scrimmage before being smothered by the Giants' massive tackle, Deacon Long. The Giants' star safety, Homer Sayers, scooped up the pigskin and delivered it into the end zone.

The camera again panned to Phyllis, who was still clutching Reverend Moore's white sleeve. The Marlins were winning, but as every self-respecting gambler knew, it's not whether a team wins or loses, it's whether they cover the spread. After the extra point, the Marlins weren't covering.

"Have you put Chub on your list of candidates?" Tommy asked, bringing Lujack his third Bloody Mary.

"If I were going to fix a game, the last guy I'd talk to is the coach. Anybody who works that hard to win a game—no matter how dumb he looks doing it—will have trouble losing one on purpose."

Tommy's private phone rang. Tommy grunted and handed the receiver to Lujack.

"Is this a bad time?" came Lane's soft voice.

"You're not watching the game?"

"No, I'm out at the stables. Should I be?"

"Your stepmother's team is hanging on to a three-point lead, and she's hanging on to Billy Moore."

"Sometimes I think she really believes in those triangles."

Lujack wondered if Moore knew that Frank Nimmo was the third angle.

"I wanted to thank you for the other night . . . and the next day."

"I should be thanking you," Lujack said, smiling like an idiot into the phone. It had been a long time since a woman had made Lujack so self-conscious. "Maybe we could get together later. I could thank you in person."

"I thought you were busy. Bookie business."

"Oh, yeah," Lujack said, remembering his appointment with Hiram. What the hell, Hiram had only tried to get him killed three days ago. "Maybe after. It shouldn't take long."

"You know where I live," Lane said and hung up.

"Do I ever," Lujack said fervently, but into an empty line.

When his brain refocused, he saw Mick Mayflower underthrow an open Fleet White. The Marlins were forced to punt. Four plays later, the Giants were on the Marlins' thirty with four seconds left to play. The Giants coach chose to go for the tie and send the game into sudden death. Jack Martinelli, the last of the straight NFL kickers, waddled out onto the field. His attempt hit the left upright and bounced harmlessly back onto the Coliseum turf. The Marlins won, but those who had bet on them had lost.

Lujack wasn't sure which Marlin was on Frank Nimmo's payroll, but if he had to guess, the golden arm of Mick Mayflower, perfect all day except for two slightly underthrown passes, seemed a more likely suspect than Tim Woodard's sore leg.

Chapter 14

DURING THE SEVENTIES, THE Pearl had been the in nightclub on the Strip. It was where Smokey Robinson and Marvin Gaye had entertained L.A.'s hippest producers and hottest stars. The up-by-the-bootstraps neighborhood guys who came from the Apple and Philly and Chi, who, between toots in the bathroom, said they hated L.A. because it didn't have any soul. Hiram gave them all the soul and, Lujack always guessed, all the drugs and women they needed. Lujack and Marty used to come in around one-thirty A.M. Hiram liked having the uniforms around when he was closing and counting the night's receipts. Their reward was free booze and an at-bat with the Pearl's cocktail waitresses. The rigors of the night patrol in Hollywood.

Since Hiram had gone to work for Ernie B., the Pearl had lost much of its personality. Hiram was too busy booking bets and laundering money to have time to table hop with the rubber-faced movie crowd. The lounge area had been converted into a dining room. Hiram had gone to New Orleans and hired the best Cajun chef in the bayou country. Hiram, showing Las Vegas savvy, decided on Cajun food because its heavy seasonings made the customers drink more. The Pearl was now an overpriced, understaffed restaurant whose main attraction was the chance of having a movie star sit next to you.

Felix, Hiram's bodyguard, was waiting outside when Lujack pulled up. Seeing Felix, Lujack was glad that Sheriff Langston had let him keep his gun.

"The boss is up in his office," the chauffeur said.

"How'd you like the game today, Felix?"

"What game?" Felix asked, glaring at him.

There were a few men Lujack knew he was afraid of. The five-foot, four-inch bodyguard was one of them. Lujack knew Felix's lethal feet were of the black-belt variety.

"If I were you, James, I wouldn't tease Felix," Hiram said, coming out of the Pearl's main entrance.

"You're supposed to be up in your office."

"After what happened to you last week, I thought you might have gotten the wrong idea." Hiram smiled. "No need for us to take any chances."

The two friends faced each other under the portico. Hiram always could make confrontation into reunion.

"I can't say you didn't cross my mind."

A horn sounded in the driveway. Lujack recognized the driver of the Mercedes 450 as the white husband of one of the Supremes.

"No tell Hotel," the driver yelled.

"Let's go upstairs quick," Hiram said under his breath, saluting the customer.

Lujack followed Hiram into the Pearl. The stairway

to the office was just to the right of the entrance, enabling Hiram to get in and out without being seen. Lujack followed him up the stairs.

"That's the kind of guy who gives Jewish producers a bad name," Hiram said.

"I think he's a little late for that," Lujack observed.

The stairs were dark, but Lujack knew the way. Hiram's office was on the mezzanine. He'd had it built when he and Ernie bought the building. The door was locked; Hiram jiggled his key in the lock and opened the door. Felix stayed outside.

This was Hiram's favorite room in the world. Very few people got to see it. The furniture was antique, the floors hardwood, the lighting subdued, the couches upholstered in a sophisticated print. There was a picture of Hiram with Bill Cosby, another with Frank and Sammy, another with Wilt. The only personal picture was of Hiram standing with an erect black lady in front of a one-story wooden house. Hiram's mother had been a teacher at Dorsey High during the Watts riots. Hiram stole a TV, and she beat him. He was proud of that.

Hiram walked over to the Vegas-style one-way window, from where he could watch the bar, most of the tables, and the entrance to the club. Lujack stood next to him. The place was active for a Sunday in October. The crowd was heavy, and Lujack recognized quite a few NFL players. The Pearl offered the right atmosphere for ex-jocks—well-to-do sports fans who bought the former players drinks, hung on their every memory, and more often than not also bought what the jocks were now selling.

"I've got some Glenlivet in the cabinet," Hiram said.

"Don't mind if I do."

Hiram handed Jimmy his scotch.

"We lost again," Hiram said, sitting down at his desk after taking another quick glance at the crowd.

"Did we?" Lujack asked.

Hiram sensed the sarcasm in Lujack's answer. He cut to the chase. "So you did have a chance to talk to Alabama?"

"We had a nice chat . . . before Frank's friends showed up."

"What did she tell you?"

"She called you a bootblack."

"The black man hath no greater enemy than a Southern white girl turned hooker."

"Turns out Charlie needed a little boost to get it up. A regular Peruvian popsicle."

"Not exactly what the doctor ordered on a bad ticker."

"But exactly what Dr. Makaris ordered."

Hiram frowned.

"You know the good doctor?"

"I've seen him around. Hangs out his shingle down at Rancho Verde and over on Beverly Boulevard. A real credit to the Hippocratic oath."

"He doesn't operate for Frank Nimmo, does he?"

"I told you, James, I didn't know anything about Nimmo or his goons."

"I wanted to believe that, Hiram. But I heard something this afternoon that makes me wonder. I heard that Frank Nimmo is making a move on Ernie B.'s territory. I heard he's got the blessing of the families in New York."

"Where'd you hear that?"

"It doesn't matter. What matters is if it's true. It makes sense that Frank would need someone on the inside of Ernie B.'s operation, somebody ambitious, somebody smart."

Hiram's pink gums shone in Lujack's direction.

"I always said you were too smart to be a cop."

"I always thought you were too close a friend to set me up."

Hiram shook his head. "I'm no all-American hero, but I'd never set up a friend. I don't have enough friends to start feeding them to Frank Nimmo's piranhas. I knew Alabama used to go out with Charlie; if anybody knew the real story, she would be the one. I was hoping once you talked to her you'd find out that Charlie dropped dead in the saddle, and you'd let the whole thing go." Hiram looked out across the Pearl's busy room, then back at Lujack. "So much for the best-laid plans."

Lujack wanted to believe Hiram. It was true; neither one of them had enough friends to waste one.

"Did you tell anyone I was going down there?"

Hotel again shook his head, glancing down at the restaurant. Lujack wondered if Hotel was expecting someone.

"No. Even though you're my friend, I don't make it a point to tell my associates I give you information. It's bad enough we do business."

"Bad enough for Ernie. The Good Book cost him a bundle this week."

"Such are the fortunes of gambling."

"A couple more weeks like this, and Ernie might be broke."

"You can never tell," Hiram said, smiling.

"Ernie gets down four or five million, his New York people will pull the credit string on him. Frank Nimmo comes to the rescue and has all Southern California in his pocket. I hope Nimmo's paying you lots of money, Hiram, because when Ernie finds out his own people sold him out and used you to do it, he's gonna pickle your ass in gasoline."

"By the time Ernie finds out he's been brokered, he

won't have anybody left to pull the trigger. That's what I like about the new breed of Mafia soldiers. They're independent contractors. No pay, no play."

"Everybody's an entrepreneur."

"You got it right, James."

"What about Nimmo? You really think he's gonna let you run all this himself? You don't think he's gonna send your pal Johnny Stella over to make sure the skim machine is working? If both New York and Chicago are agreed that Ernie isn't doing the job, you're gonna have to double the profits the first year."

"I got some pretty good ideas."

"Like taking over the small-time bookies?"

Hiram smiled. "That might be one of them. Better collections might be another."

"You can't break all our legs, Hiram. The reason gamblers stay in business is because they're not messy like drug dealers. They don't leave bodies lying around on the street. You start playing rough, and you'll have every TV station in town on your ass. Where there's TV, there's police. Ask the hookers."

"Take it easy, my man. I'd never go after you and Tommy. 'Sides, I don't want your customers mad at me."

"It sounds like you're ready to strike."

"If you found out, that means others know. That means Ernie will find out. That means the sooner we do it, the better."

"Next Sunday?" Lujack guessed.

"I've told you enough already."

"Nimmo has to have a player on the Marlins. Who is it?"

"I don't know, and if I did I wouldn't tell you. My advice to you, James, is cash your check and cool out. You got the kid's killers, leave it at that. I'm sure Nimmo's not happy about you taking out his boys, but if you walk away now . . . Maybe I can put a word in for you—after things settle down."

"Who should I bet on this week, Hiram? The Marlins are favored by two over the 49ers."

"Where'd you get that line?"

"I phoned Irv after the game. He did it in his head, but he's pretty sure that's what the spread will be. The Marlins are winning, and the game's at home."

Hiram smiled. "I'm not a betting man, but if I were you, I'd take the 49ers."

Hiram opened his desk. He took out a straw manila envelope and pushed it to Lujack. It would contain fifty-four thousand dollars, the sixty thousand wagered minus the ten percent vigorish. He knew that was as much as he was going to get out of Hiram. This week's game would be the big one that pushed Ernie over the edge. If he was going to find out who the Marlins player on Frank Nimmo's payroll was, he had to do it soon. If he was going to tie Phyllis Randolf and/or Paul Makaris to Nimmo, he would have to act fast. Once Ernie B. was out of business and Nimmo and his Vegas crazies had taken over the Southern California gambling scene, Lujack wouldn't have time to play detective.

"You still gonna book our action this week?" Lujack asked.

"If I'm giving you a chance to make a lot of money, James, book it yourself. You know the Marlins won't cover."

"Our big players are all going to bet against the Marlins."

"Then move the line and play the middle."

"That's not a bad idea," Lujack said, picking up the money.

His hand hadn't cleared his coat when he saw Hiram jump back from the window. Suddenly, the glass shattered from a spray of bullets. Both Hiram and Lujack hit the floor. A second later, the door burst open. It was Felix. In his hand was a Smith and Wesson 9 mm. Lujack could hear screams coming from below.

"It's Ernie's boys. One of them has a Mac 10!" Hiram shouted as he pulled open a drawer and grabbed a revolver. Lujack was already over at the shattered window, his own revolver out.

"Felix, keep an eye on the door. I'll see if I can get a shot at the cocksuckers."

"Don't hit the customers. They'll sue," Hiram pleaded.

"Sue what? Your estate? Go over and watch the door with Felix. They aren't going to fly in here."

Lujack didn't wait for Hiram to answer. He threw Hiram's cigar box out of the open window. There was another machine-gun blast. Lujack quickly aimed three shots in the direction of the shooter who was crouched behind the bar. It was Barry, Ernie's chief enforcer. There were more screams as the bullets splintered the bar, and customers, waiters, and bartenders tried to crawl out of range. Out of the corner of his eye, Lujack saw Barry slip from the bar underneath the window. At the same time, another burst of fire came at him from the door to the kitchen. Lujack ducked behind the wall just as Felix began shooting at a third assassin in the hallway.

"There are at least three of them," Lujack said coolly. "What's the police response time around here?"

"Same as it was when you worked this beat. After they finish their coffee and wipe their butts."

"I guess Ernie's sources are better than you thought."

Hiram gave Lujack a strange look.

"This wouldn't be a payback, would it?"

"They're shooting at me too, Tonto."

Before he finished, two gunmen rushed the door, the chilling sound of ten bullets per second tearing into Hiram's office. Felix charged into the line of fire, screaming epithets in Tagalog and firing his 9 mm. With an action almost as quick as the gunfire, Felix kicked the automatic pistol out of the nearest gunman's hand, then fell to the floor. From where Lujack stood, he could see Felix's shoe and the gunman's head. Neither man was moving. The Mac 10 machine pistol lay in the hallway, tantalizingly out of reach.

Lujack took Felix's position on the left side of the door. He thumbed three bullets into the chamber of his gun. He and Hiram heard a man in the hall yell to a man downstairs.

"Forget the window. Rick's been hit. Get your ass up here."

Lujack looked over at Hiram. "I don't suppose there's another way out of here."

"Just down those stairs."

Lujack looked over at what used to be the one-way window. "What say we try a flanking maneuver?"

Hiram pointed his revolver toward Lujack. "You're staying here, James."

Lujack didn't blame Hiram for not trusting him or vice versa, but this was no time for an open forum. "You got a better plan?"

"No."

"Then you'll have to trust me."

Lujack moved slowly over to the window. He wasn't sure who was going to take the next shot at him. Hiram or Ernie's gunsels. He looked down at the floor of the club. It was a jump of fifteen feet, into tables and chairs and broken glasses. The customers and employees were long gone, except for a black bartender who stood behind the bar, drinking from a bottle of Jack Daniel's. Lujack listened for the sound of police sirens, a last-second reprieve.

"Marty always said you were a fool."

"Fools live."

"That's not what I heard."

Lujack tried to land between two tables on the part of the floor with the least broken glass. He only partially succeeded, missing both tables but hitting the leg of an overturned chair. He fell hard against the floor and felt a shard of glass puncture his upper arm. It hurt, but he couldn't cry out.

He quickly made his way through the rubble of what two minutes before had been one of L.A.'s nicer restaurants. He reached the stairs just as both machine pistols opened fire from above.

As Lujack bolted up the stairs, he thought he heard two rounds fired from Hiram's revolver. By the time he got to the top of the stairs, only one man was in the hallway. Lujack dropped him with two shots.

He felt the same familiar surge he'd known four days before. The hunter and the hunted. He was relaxed, knowing he had the stronger position, knowing Barry was trapped. He could hear a siren in the distance. All he had to do was wait for the police.

"Show's over, Barry. Throw that Colombian cherry picker out in the hall."

"You ever want to see your nigger friend again, Lujack, let me walk outta here. Now."

"He means it, James," Hiram echoed.

"I thought you were dead."

"So did I."

"Cut the chatter, assholes!" Barry yelled. "I'm coming out. Make a move, Lujack, and Hotel dies."

Barry stepped into the doorway. He had the Mac 10 aimed at Hiram's head. Hiram didn't look at all comfortable. The two men stepped between the three bodies in the hall.

"Drop the gun, Lujack. Drop the gun, or Hotel dies."

Lujack looked at his .38 Special. No way was he going to give up his gun to this character. "So shoot him. I'm keeping my gun."

"Thanks, James," Hiram said through clenched teeth.

Barry didn't have time to argue. The sirens were getting closer. "Stay in front of us, Lujack. You go down the stairs first."

Lujack backed down the hall to the top of the stairs, holding the Special loosely at his side, ready to snap it toward Barry. He could feel the blood from his cut running down his arm and off the gun. As he took the first step down, one of the bodies moved. It was Ted Smythe, Barry's partner.

"Don't let me die," Smythe moaned.

Barry kept moving, not about to take his eyes off Lujack, his gun still pointed at Hiram's head. "You aren't going to die, Teddy."

"Just spend the rest of your life in jail with four thousand queer niggers," Hiram said.

Lujack recognized the signal. Hiram wanted to take his chances with Lujack rather than wait for the police.

"Shut your fuckin' yap," Barry screamed at Hotel.

"He's right. I'd rather be dead," Smythe groaned, trying to get up on one arm. He'd been gut shot with Lujack's magnum and wasn't going too far.

Barry glanced at his partner, and Hiram made his move. He tried to butt the Mac 10 out of Barry's hands, at the same time pushing Barry back into the wall. Barry was too strong to lose either his gun or his balance, but the maneuver gave Lujack a millisecond to raise his pistol and fire. At less than ten feet, the force of the .38 was enough to knock Barry off balance. The Mac 10 flew out of his hand. The second shot killed him.

"God damn, James. Fools do live," Hiram said with a grateful smile.

The bullet from Felix's 9 mm hit Hiram in the back of the head. It was like his nose exploded, and he fell forward. Only the smile remained.

Lujack put another bullet in Smythe before the man could fall back to the floor.

"Not all fools," Lujack said softly to his dead friend.

The first cop up the stairs was Kyle Thurgood. Thurgood's puffy eyes surveyed the wreckage. Four bodies, at least six quarts of blood, enough guns to start an armory. He didn't seem to need an introduction to any of the victims, although he had to turn Smythe over with the point of his Italian shoe to make the identification.

"I wouldn't want the job of cleaning this carpet."

"They came in shooting. They belong to Ernie B."

"I know who they belong to, Mr. Lujack," he said brusquely.

Chapter 15

THERE ARE PROBABLY LOTS of ways to explain an envelope with fifty-four thousand dollars in cash to the police—with the bodies of four dead gangsters lying within gunshot range. The one Lujack came up with—he had recently sold his late aunt's stamp collection and hadn't yet had a chance to go to the bank—didn't impress Kyle Thurgood. Thurgood confiscated the money "as part of his investigation" of the shooting: "You might get it back in a month." The fact that there had been some fifty witnesses to the attack didn't impress Thurgood either, although he had Lujack released on his own recognizance.

"So what do we do? Tell our clients to pick up their winnings at the police property room?" Tommy said to Lujack later that night over coffee and fortune cookies at the Chin Up.

"I'd rather do that than tell Hiram's mother to pick up her son at the morgue."

"Hiram was a fool to get caught between Ernie and Nimmo."

"Fools live," Lujack said to himself.

"No, Jimmy, fools die. And if you don't make peace with Frank Nimmo, you'll die. You'll die as certainly as Hiram did."

"From what Hiram told me, Nimmo is going to be after both of us soon enough. He's going to be after all the small-time books in L.A. once he breaks Ernie B."

"After tonight, it doesn't seem that Ernie's just going to hand over his territory to Nimmo on a silver platter."

"Ernie's spent a lot of capital. All five of those men were his, even though Hiram and Felix had played out their options. He's going to need to call reinforcement from New York and Atlantic City, but my guess is the new soldiers will take their time getting here."

"Maybe we should help Ernie out?" Tommy suggested.

"Help him out! The guy just tried to have me filleted by three machine guns."

"Frank Nimmo wanted you burned alive."

"You've got a point there."

"I've got a better point, Jimmy. Let's mind our own business and let those two bastards fight it out between themselves."

Lujack didn't argue. Tommy had made his point. Especially when Lujack read his fortune: "You will suffer a financial setback. Think about changing partners."

"I'll call you in the morning," Lujack said, pushing the fortune cookie over to Tommy. "I think this is yours."

Tommy read it. "Too late." He smiled and tore it up.

"I can always dip into the emergency fund," Tommy said. He added, as Lujack was getting up, "I'm sorry about Hiram."

"Yeah," Lujack said, then stopped. "I'm sorry I got us into this. Something tells me if I don't finish it, it'll finish me."

By the time Lujack got to his apartment, it was past ten. He had tried to call Lane after Thurgood cut him loose, but she hadn't been home. So much for their late date. He thought about calling her now but didn't want to be depressed if she wasn't home.

The maid answered on the fourth ring. No, Miss Randolf was not home. No, the maid didn't know where she had gone. Lujack went into the kitchen and opened the cupboard. His hand was halfway to the bottle of Johnnie Walker when he realized what a horrible headache he had, and, as long as he'd been drinking scotch, it did nothing for headaches. His hand went for the bottle of aspirin.

Throwing his clothes onto the dresser, he climbed into bed and flipped on the TV. The pain in his shoulder had settled into a dull throb. The medic had stitched him up and told him not to throw any forearm shivers for the next few weeks. The "Sunday Sports Final" gave the highlights of the game. There was an interview with Mick Mayflower and Chub Simmons—very upbeat—the Marlins were on a roll. The showdown next week with the 49ers could be the game that decided the Western Conference champion. The setup was perfect. Everybody and their mothers were going to bet the Marlins next week against the 49ers. Ernie B. had to take the bets—so did Lujack and Tommy. Too bad the Marlins were going to lose. Hiram had as much as told him so.

"Today is the happiest day of my new life," Phyllis

Randolf was saying to a cluster of reporters. "The Marlins are in a tie for first place, and the man I love has asked me to marry him."

The handsome, cleanshaven face of the Reverend Billy Moore came onto the screen. The reverend was asked if he was a football fan.

"I'm a fan of the Lord," he replied.

"And of mine," Phyllis interjected. The reverend couldn't help but smile.

Lujack tried Lane's number again. There was no answer. Phyllis's engagement would put to an early test Lujack's theory about the five-year waiting period in Charlie's will. Although being engaged wasn't the same as being married, Lujack knew, when it came to Phyllis Berry, the darling of Gary, where there was a will, there was a way. He hoped that way wasn't over Lane's dead body.

Lujack pulled his Mustang into a row of expensive cars and pickup trucks at the Marlins training camp. Like all NFL teams, Marlins players drove according to their race and position. White linebackers drove heavy-suspension pickups, black running backs drove Mercedes 450 convertibles—Lujack didn't have to think hard about who he'd rather ride with. At the end of the row, Lujack saw a 1976 Bentley which he assumed belonged to the Marlins quarterback. Mick Mayflower had always struck him as being a touch out of step with the rest of the NFL.

Paul Makaris's Beverly Hills receptionist said the doctor was at Marlin Park seeing a patient. Lujack knew of Makaris's relationship with Phyllis but didn't know that the doctor was treating any of the players. Getting past the Marlins security guard and into the four-acre park wasn't going to be easy. Lujack was working on a story when Phyllis Randolf and her husband-to-be pulled up in her chauffeur-driven limousine.

"Good morning, Mr. Lujack," Phyllis said brightly, stepping out into the Los Angeles sun.

"Congratulations," Lujack said to her and to her fiancé.

"We should be the ones congratulating you," Phyllis said, "after all you've done for the family. I told Lane last night that hiring you was the smartest thing she could have done. If we had to wait for the police, the men who killed Kurt and his family would never have come to justice."

"It might have taken a little longer," Lujack allowed.

"The young man's right, darling. Justice can be forestalled but never forfeited," Reverend Moore chimed in.

"Don't tell that to my tax accountant," Phyllis said with a pixieish smile. "I don't think you two have been formally introduced. Mr. Lujack, my fiancé, Reverend Billy Moore."

Lujack and the reverend shook hands. Although in his late forties, Moore showed by his grip that there were muscles behind all that rectitude.

"What are you doing here, Mr. Lujack? Going to look at the films of yesterday's games? I should think, after what you've been through the past few days, you'd have seen enough real violence."

"I'm looking for Dr. Makaris. I was told he was out here."

"Let's go inside and find out," Phyllis said cheerfully, leading the way. Lujack followed the Marlins owner and her fiancé into the one-story Marlins headquarters.

"By the way, Billy and I are going to have an engagement party next Sunday in my box at the Coliseum. I'd love you to come. Lane will be there."

Lujack didn't like the way she added Lane's presence, as if to ensure his own.

"Have you set the date yet?" he asked innocently.

The question drew a sharp look from Reverend Moore and a stage laugh from Phyllis. She was a consummate pro—whatever the endeavor.

"I'm afraid you're going to have to wait until after the 49ers game. Just like everybody else," she said coyly.

Lujack wondered if the wedding date depended on the outcome of the game or the outcome of the point spread.

Chub Simmons was walking down the hallway with two of his assistants. When he spotted Phyllis, his cheery mood quickly disappeared.

"Here's my favorite coach," Phyllis said, giving him a kiss.

"How ya doing, Mrs. Randolf. Uh, congratulations to . . . to both of you."

"Phyllis is anxious to see the films of Sunday's game," Reverend Moore told the coach.

"Do you want us to put a triangle above the projector?" Chub asked the reverend.

"We'll do whatever Phyllis wants," the reverend said. "Won't we, Chub?"

Moore easily assumed the role of Phyllis's spokesperson, although Lujack was unsure how much control he had over her. Making Phyllis happy, even getting her to heaven via Needles, that was one thing. Making her rich was another.

"Mr. Lujack is here to talk to Paul. Have you seen him, Chub?" Phyllis asked.

Chub gave Lujack the once-over. He didn't approve, but there was little he could do. "Dr. Makaris is in the whirlpool room, third door on your right."

Lujack thanked Phyllis and continued down the hall. Behind him, he heard the Marlins owner congratulating Chub on a brilliant game plan. Lujack shook his head. One thing bothered him. Phyllis hadn't even asked why he wanted to see Makaris. If she really were involved with Nimmo from the beginning, including the death of her husband, wouldn't she know that Makaris was the link that could bring her down? Phyllis hadn't flinched when Lujack mentioned the doctor's name. Nobody's that cool. Lane was right; it was confusing.

Lujack found the whirlpool room right where Chub Simmons said it would be. Mick Mayflower and a giant lineman, Buddy Bacitich, were getting out when Lujack walked in. Makaris's arm was in the whirlpool bath, taking out a test tube of water which he placed in a container.

"Better leave that in, Doc. Reverend Billy and Phyllis are here."

Makaris gave Lujack a puzzled look, then remembered where he'd seen him before and frowned.

"How's it going, Mick?"

"You tell me, Lujack. You're the one making all the headlines. Must have been pretty exciting at the Pearl the other night."

"Is this the asshole that killed Hiram?" said Bacitich, taking a step toward Lujack.

"Take it easy, Buddy. I'm the asshole that tried to keep Hiram from getting killed."

"You didn't do too good a job," Bacitich said. "I liked Hiram. He used to give me free beers every time I went into the Pearl."

"It's tough to lose a soft touch," Lujack agreed. Pro athletes were so sentimental.

Mayflower ushered his lineman out of the room before Buddy could figure out he was being made fun of.

"What are you doing here, Lujack?" Dr. Makaris said, rolling down the sleeve of his starched shirt.

"I was about to ask you the same thing."

"I'm treating my patient. Not that it's any of your business."

"Mick Mayflower?"

"Phyllis asked me to monitor the progress of Mick's arm."

"By keeping enough sand in his whirlpool?"

"I was testing the water for sodium sulfate," Makaris said testily. "It acts as a muscle relaxer. The sulfate has worked wonders for Mick the last few months."

"And I thought it was the sand and the triangle."

Makaris looked at the triangle hanging from the ceiling. It was clear he didn't think much of Reverend Moore's Christian pyramids but would never say anything that might get back to Phyllis. Makaris put on his sport coat and straightened his tie.

Lujack noticed another small pyramid on his lapel.

"Speaking of working wonders, Doc, I had a talk with a mutual friend of ours the other day. Alabama Starr."

Makaris's elegant head jerked to attention.

"That's right, Doc. Your buddy Nimmo's goons didn't get there till after I talked to her. She told me an interesting story. About you giving Charlie Randolf a gram of cocaine so he could work wonders with his Johnson."

Makaris stared at Lujack.

"Unfortunately, it was what you might call a Pyrrhic victory. He got it up, but his heart gave out before he could use it," Lujack went on.

"I don't know what you're talking about, Lujack. I told you before, Charlie's death was accidental." A smile crossed his thin lips. "And since Miss Starr is no longer with us, I doubt if you can prove otherwise."

"Unless I get a writ of exhumation for Clark's body."

"I doubt if the San Diego D.A. will grant you one."

"But he would grant it to Lane Randolf."

Makaris's dark eyes flickered nervously.

"I did some checking, Doc. Phyllis didn't scrimp on the funeral. Bates casket, the best embalmers. Old Charlie's probably in better shape now than the day he died. Who knows how much of that Colombian love potion he still has in him," Lujack said, pressing his advantage. "Alabama said you came right down to the bungalow. But you got your initials mixed up, didn't you, Doc? Instead of administering CPR, you made sure he was DOA."

Makaris began to look for a way out. There was only one door. Lujack was standing in front of it, and he had no intention of moving.

"How much did Nimmo pay you? Or did you do it for Phyllis? A mercy killing for money, or maybe a few shares of the Marlins."

"I don't have to listen to this," Makaris shouted.

"My God, it wasn't for love, was it? I hope Phyllis didn't promise to marry you, then jilt you for the missionary position."

Makaris's tan was turning purple. Like most doctors, he didn't like it when he wasn't in charge.

"You can tell me what happened, Doc, or you can tell Quentin Rule of the FBI. That's right, Doc. The feds have reopened the case."

It was a lie, but Lujack didn't have much time.

Desperation was creeping into Markaris's eyes; he was about to break. Just then, Lujack felt someone trying the door.

"Paul, are you in there?" a voice asked.

"Yes, I'm here," Makaris said with relief.

Lujack stepped back as the door flew open. If he had remained in front of the door, he would have been sandwich meat. The huge frame of Buddy Bacitich entered the room. Buddy was followed by a smaller man, much smaller but considerably smarter. Clark Sterling. All Sterling had to do was look at the flustered doctor to know what was going on.

"Sorry to interrupt you, Paul, but I heard Mr. Lujack was on the premises."

"That's all right," Makaris said nervously. "I was just leaving."

"Buddy said you two were in here," Sterling explained. "Buddy's one of my clients."

"What shall I do with him, Mr. Sterling?" the lineman said.

"What's the matter, Buddy, didn't you get enough steroids in your breakfast chum?"

This time, Buddy knew he was being insulted, but Sterling gently put his small hand on Buddy's forearm.

"It's all right, Buddy. I'd like to talk to Mr. Lujack alone."

"I was just on my way back to the office," Makaris said gratefully. The doctor wasn't much more comfortable in Sterling's presence than he was in Lujack's.

"Buddy, help Dr. Makaris with his equipment."

Makaris was going to protest but thought better of it. Buddy picked up the doctor's medical bag and the box of chemicals next to the whirlpool.

"Mick's very happy with the solution, Doctor,"

Sterling said to Makaris as he was leaving. The doctor didn't bother to say goodbye to Lujack.

"Paul is a very talented physician. He's done miracles with Mick's arm the past few months," Sterling said when they were alone.

"So I've heard."

"You've been rather busy yourself lately."

"Just trying to stay alive."

Sterling reached into his sport coat. He took out an envelope. "I hear you misplaced some money last weekend." He gave the envelope to Lujack. "This might help ease the pain. It's the remainder of your fee. Twenty-five thousand plus a bonus."

Lujack took the envelope. In it was a check for thirty-five thousand dollars. Sterling was right; he could use the money. He handed the envelope back to Sterling. "The men who torched Kurt's house are dead, but the man who hired them isn't—I'm not finished."

"I don't have time to play games with you," Sterling said with irritation. "Take the money. You're finished. *Comprende?*"

"I was hired by the Randolfs, not by you, Sterling. I work for Lane."

"Whose idea do you think the bonus was?" Sterling laughed. "If it were up to me, I'd have canceled the first check."

Sterling put the envelope on top of the stainless steel rubdown table. "Lane's a very special young woman, Lujack. But she's a bit spoiled. When things are over, they're over. She doesn't like messes. She particularly doesn't like messes with men."

Lujack wanted to punch the spry lawyer through the wall, but the knot in his stomach left him powerless. He'd been trying to reach Lane since the shoot-out at the Pearl on Sunday night. It was now Tuesday, and she still hadn't called him back. Could Sterling be telling the truth? Was she finished with him?

Lujack picked up the envelope and took out the check. It had two signatures, Lane's and Sterling's—something he hadn't noticed before.

Chapter 16

LUJACK FOUND HIMSELF DOING seventy miles an hour going out Sunset toward the stables where Lane kept her horses. He down-shifted the Mustang with dangerous precision as he came to a particularly sharp turn. The rear end swung out over the double divider and then back. The combination of speed and danger helped him focus his thoughts.

The check Clark Sterling had given him was in his shirt pocket. Lujack thought he could feel its warmth next to his heart. The feisty lawyer had caught him off balance. As usual, Sterling's timing had been unfortunate, for a number of reasons. Dr. Makaris was the weak link in whatever chain surrounded the murders of the Randolf family. The doctor had to be involved with either Phyllis or Nimmo or both. There was no other reason for him to help murder Charlie. Was it greed or love or fear which motivated Makaris? Lujack thought he had been close to finding out when

Sterling and Buddy had interrupted his tête-à-tête with Makaris. He doubted Phyllis had time to call Sterling, but the only other way Sterling could have known his whereabouts was if Lujack was either being followed or being bugged.

The Mustang's rear end fishtailed in the gravel as Lujack took a hard right into the entrance of Will Rogers Park. Lane kept her horses at the stables adjacent to the polo field. He accelerated up the hill, then pulled over beneath a huge eucalyptus tree and waited. One, two minutes passed—no other cars came up the hill. From his parked car, he could see Lane's Rolls in front of the white stables. She was riding alone in the fenced-in area next to the building. Starting, stopping—polo exercises. He knew it was her; even from a half-mile away, her "seat" was unmistakable. He could feel the insides of her thighs on the saddle. She had told him a good rider doesn't need to use a whip or the reins to control a horse—she can do it with pressure from the inside of her thighs. He knew the feeling.

She saw him approaching in the Mustang and rode toward the nearest fence. She jumped off her mount and kissed him over the top of the fence. The place smelled like horses, but she smelled like Lane Randolf. "I missed you," she said, out of breath, happy to see him.

"I tried to call Sunday night and yesterday."

"One of my horses, Whirlaway, had a bad case of colic. We didn't know if he was going to make it. Didn't Tommy give you my message?"

"No. I'm sorry about Sunday."

She laughed. He loved watching her laugh—her eyes sparkling, her white teeth shining.

"Jimmy, you don't have to apologize." She shook

her head. "I was sorry to hear about your friend Hiram."

"He was one of a kind."

"So are you."

She gave him another kiss. He tried to put an arm around her, but it wasn't easy through the fence.

"I think I should come over to your side, or you should come over to mine."

"I'll come over to yours," she said, putting her leg over the railing. "It smells better."

"Better not let the horse hear that."

"Citation can handle it. He has a good self-image."

"Did his psychiatrist tell you that?"

"We don't call her a psychiatrist, we call her an equine consultant." She laughed.

"Are all your horses named after famous race horses?"

"Only the best ones."

"How many do you have?"

"Ten here and more than twenty in Santa Barbara. My best horses are up there. That's where the finest West Coast matches are held."

"Do you use all of them? In one game, I mean."

"One, sometimes two, per chukker. There are six seven-minute chukkers in a match."

"That's a lot of horses," Lujack said gamely. He wanted to talk to her about the check, about the case, about Phyllis's upcoming wedding. He also wanted to make love to her.

"Why don't I finish up with Citation and meet you under those trees? It's cooler there," she said, nodding toward a grassy area halfway up the hill. "I'll bring some champagne from the tack room."

Lujack waited up on the hill. He watched her finish her workout. She was the only rider in sight.

* * *

She drove up and pulled a bottle of champagne and a blanket out of the trunk. The champagne was cold, the blanket comfortable. Lujack lay on his side, watching her uncork the bottle. She was sitting with her legs crossed, the bottle between them.

"Do you like Dom Perignon?"

"If you don't have any Cold Duck."

"No Cold Duck. No glasses."

She delicately popped the cork, then tossed back her head, her chestnut hair going obediently over her shoulder. She took the first sip, then passed the bottle to Lujack. Lujack took a swallow; most of it went up his nose. He coughed. She patted him on the back.

"Never drink champagne from the bottle while you're lying down," she told him, offering a kerchief. "My second husband taught me that."

"Better your second husband than the Mexican police."

She didn't understand but didn't ask for an explanation. The champagne had run into his pocket. He pulled out the check. If Lane recognized it, she didn't show it.

"I saw Clark Sterling this morning. He gave me my severance pay. Plus a bonus."

"I went to his office yesterday. We agreed it would be best if . . ."

"If I stopped asking questions."

"I told him what you said about Paul Makaris. He told me that was crazy. Paul thought the world of Daddy; he had no reason to hurt him."

"You heard about your stepmother's wedding plans?"

"A match made in heaven." Lane smiled. "I talked to Clark about that too. He said six months before

Daddy died, he changed the terms of the will. The five-year clause was taken out. She is free to marry whoever she wants, whenever she wants."

"Did Sterling say why the change?"

"He seemed to think Daddy didn't want to look like he was running Phyllis's life from the grave."

"That doesn't sound like your father. Caring how things looked."

"You're right, it doesn't. Daddy did things his way, all the way. But Clark showed me the will, and that's what it said."

"You think you're out of danger then. You don't need a bodyguard anymore?"

"I want us both to be out of danger, Jimmy. That's why I signed the check. I don't want anything to happen to you either."

Lujack didn't have time to sort out the permutations of Charlie Randolf's will. He knew Lane was still in danger, no matter what the disposition of the Marlins and/or Phyllis's marital status. He couldn't explain it to her. He wasn't sure he could explain it to himself. All he knew was that Makaris could give him some of the answers. The doctor was the only connection between Phyllis and Nimmo, other than Charlie himself.

"If you want me to, I'll keep the check," he said. "But I can't cash it. Not until I know this is over."

"When will that be?"

"Soon. After this weekend."

"What happens this weekend?"

"The Marlins play the 49ers."

"What in the world does that have to do with us?"

"I'm not sure."

She brushed her fingers along his cheek. "Can't you

just leave it alone? Then maybe they'll leave you alone."

"I'm afraid it doesn't work that way."

"The other night," she said, watching him carefully with her luxuriant dark eyes. "That kind of thing doesn't happen to me. Not that way."

"It doesn't happen to me either."

"When I came to your apartment the first time, after we talked about Kurt, the last thing in the world I expected was to get involved."

"Is that what we are? Involved?"

"One of us is," she said evenly.

Lujack felt the doubts Sterling had stirred in him evaporate. He wanted her so much he could barely stand it. She wanted him too. He could see it. He could feel it.

"Comprende?" she asked, still caressing his face.

Sterling had asked him the same question. Coming from the lawyer, it had triggered an ugly memory. Coming from Lane, it sounded like entreaty.

"Comprendo," he answered, grabbing her hand and pulling her on top of him. It didn't take long to stop thinking about the uncertain future and concentrate on the sensual present.

"Not here." She laughed as he rolled on top of her. He was acutely aware of her body under him, the smell of the grass and of the woman. He was about to explode.

"Why not?"

"The trainer might drive by."

"That's why we have a blanket," he said, pulling the blanket over them. The ground was cool and hard. All the better.

"You're going to get grass stains on your slacks."

"Not if I take them off I won't," he said, unbuckling his belt.

"This is crazy. What will the stable boys think?"

"I don't see any stable boys. All I see are horses, and they do this kind of thing all the time."

"I thought you didn't know anything about horses," she said and brought him down on top of her. They kissed again.

"What about your boots?"

"We can leave them on. I'm not wearing spurs," she said.

"Ride 'em, cowboy."

The offices of Paul Makaris were on Beverly Boulevard just above Cedars Sinai Hospital. Lujack noticed Makaris's parking space was empty, but doctors were known to have side entrances and more than one parking space. Especially if their field of expertise was making middle-aged rich ladies feel better.

There was no one in Makaris's outer office. A few copies of *Architectural Digest* and *Gourmet* magazines lay on the tables. The receptionist sat behind a low divider. She was a tanned, robust, white-haired lady in her fifties. An advertisement for clean California living. She seemed to be alone in the office.

"Good afternoon," Lujack said pleasantly.

The woman looked up. She seemed perturbed, harried. "Yes?"

"My name is Jack Robinson. I'm a friend of Phyllis Randolf. She suggested I see Dr. Makaris about my shoulder," Lujack responded.

"Are you an athlete, Mr. Robinson?"

"No, I'm a weekend tennis player. At least I was until my shoulder went."

"Please fill out this form. I'll check the book—we can probably fit you in next week."

"I was hoping to see the doctor today."

"So was I. He was supposed to be here by noon, and it's after three."

"Does he usually disappear like this?"

"Not on Tuesdays. Wednesday is his golf day."

Lujack took the form. As with any doctor in Beverly Hills, it wasn't who you knew, it was who you were covered by. The phone rang. Lujack pretended to fill out the form while the receptionist apologized to Mrs. Cribbs.

"I did leave a message with your housekeeper, Mrs. Cribbs. That's why you're calling me.

"I don't know where the doctor is or when he'll be in," she said, growing more exasperated. "I would certainly tell you if I knew."

Lujack studied Makaris's medical certificates on a back wall. A tingle shot up his spine when he saw that Makaris had gone to the University of Chicago Medical School, graduating in 1958. Was this the connection he'd been looking for? Both Makaris and Phyllis had lived in Chicago in the late fifties, early sixties. Makaris was supposed to have been Charlie's doctor, transferring his attentions to Phyllis only after Charlie's death. It was entirely possible that Phyllis and Makaris were old friends.

And, of course, Chicago was the home of another player in Lujack's mystery. Frank Nimmo had been sent out to Las Vegas by the Chicago family in the late seventies to run the Ritz. Nimmo was maybe ten years younger than either Phyllis or the doctor. But since when did a protégé of Dante Caligari, the Chicago *capo,* need a formal introduction to an up-and-coming party girl or an ambitious doctor?

"Mr. Robinson, you haven't filled out your form."

"It's my shoulder. I'm having trouble writing."

She looked at him, making a decision, then took the form. "Maybe I can help you. What's your full name?"

"Dr. Makaris, he's from Chicago?"

"You can read better than you can write."

"I guess he's been out here for quite a while. To have built up a practice like this."

"Mr. Robinson, what makes me think you didn't come here about your shoulder?"

Lujack gave her a found-out look. "I've never been a very good liar, Miss . . ."

"Cook. Constance Cook. Now, why are you really here, Mr. Robinson? If that's your name."

"Actually, my name's Lujack. I was an acquaintance of Alabama Starr's. You may have read about her in the papers."

"Yes. And about you, too."

"Then you know that Dr. Makaris may be in some serious trouble."

"And I suppose you're going to help him?"

"I might be able to."

She looked at him, making another decision. "Something tells me not to believe you."

"You're very protective, Miss Cook."

"That's my job."

"It might interest you to know that the man you're protecting is a murderer."

"Paul is a brilliant doctor. He knows the body as well as anybody alive," she said enigmatically.

"Except for the heart," Lujack said, letting Constance Cook figure out what he meant. It was Lujack's guess that Miss Cook's own heart had not been immune to Dr. Makaris's expertise. If he could only get a look at Makaris's patient files.

"It's been a long day, Mr. Lujack, and I still have

many things to do. If you want to leave me your card, I'll make sure the doctor sees it."

The phone rang again. She picked it up immediately with a look of anticipation. She answered a question with a monosyllabic "yes." Suddenly, her face went pale. "Are you sure? That's impossible!"

Lujack leaned over the divider.

"I can't believe it. Why would . . ."

Her mouth was beginning to quiver. She looked at Lujack. There was a flash of accusation. He knew what had happened.

"Yes, of course. Thank you, officer."

She put down the phone and wept. The years of love and hurt burst out in torrents of tears. Lujack waited, not knowing what else to do. Makaris had been his best hope.

She finally stopped crying. He was still there.

"He's dead, isn't he?" Lujack asked softly.

"They found him in front of a Chinese restaurant. He was propped against a door." She broke down again.

Lujack didn't have to ask the name of the restaurant.

"Paul didn't even like Chinese food," she sobbed.

"Neither does the guy who sells it," Lujack said.

Constance Cook looked up at Lujack in a strange way. Then she looked around the office, at the art, all the memories of unrequited devotion. "I'd better call my husband," she said.

"You're married?"

"Ten years this month," she said.

Chapter 17

PEKING DOC," TOMMY SAID, quoting the sign he had found taped to Paul Makaris's body. The bullet-ridden corpse had been propped against the entrance to the Chin Up.

"Two birds with ten bullets," Lujack said.

"Come again?"

"They get rid of Makaris and give us a very clear message," Lujack explained.

The police weren't letting anyone near the body. And for obvious reasons, the Chin Up wasn't going to be serving dinner. Not with Dr. Makaris's ever-stiffening body guarding the door.

"Davey Rosenbloom thought he was a bum asleep in the street. When was the last time you saw a bum wearing a Sulka tie and a St. Laurent suit?" Tommy laughed.

"Davey's been wearing his own glasses too long."

"The phone's been ringing all day," Tommy said,

looking at the flashing light behind the bar. "I told Susie not to come in. I had the calls rerouted to her home."

The Chin Up was crawling with police. Lujack had noticed Kyle Thurgood outside, talking with two detectives. Then there were at least five patrol units from the West L.A. station, plus the crime lab team to inspect the crime site, the public affairs officer to handle the press, and the coroner's staff to take away the body.

"The way our people have been betting the 49ers, I'm not sure we should stay open. With Hiram gone, we have nowhere to lay off the money," Tommy added.

Lujack had told Tommy about his conversation with Hiram—that Nimmo had a player on the Marlins and most of the smart money in town knew it. The Good Book bettors had already put forty thousand dollars on the 49ers at plus two, and it was only Tuesday.

"We have to take the action. We can't afford not to. A bookie three hundred thousand dollars down for the year who takes a game off the board, a hometown favorite at that, doesn't stay in business long."

"The way things are going, we may not be in business long anyway. We could lose another three hundred thousand this week," Tommy said.

"Or we might win three hundred thousand."

Tommy did a double take. "What are you up to, Jimmy?"

"Before Hiram died, he said this Sunday's game was a chance to make a lot of money. Hiram thought we should move the line and take the middle. I've got a better idea."

"I'm listening."

"The insiders are betting the 49ers because they know the game is fixed. What happens if we unfix it?"

"How do you know how to unfix a game when you don't even know the player?"

"I know the player."

"How can you turn him around? You're a bookie, not a gangster."

"It's going to be a little harder now," Lujack admitted, "especially after he finds out what Nimmo did to his doctor."

"My mother wanted me to be a singer. You know, the Chinese Tony Bennett. Times like this, I wish I'd given it a try," Tommy mused.

A uniformed cop came into the restaurant and told Lujack that Lieutenant Thurgood wanted to talk to him.

"You better call Moe Breen, Tommy, on the off chance that Thurgood tries to put a padlock on this place."

Tommy groaned. He didn't sound like Tony Bennett.

The crime lab crew was working on the remains of Dr. Makaris. The doctor had been Lujack's best chance of bringing down Frank Nimmo, but there was more than one way to skin a bastard.

Thurgood was still talking to the two detectives, but he motioned Lujack to join him.

"Talk to everyone. Some of these old Jews don't remember if it happened half an hour ago or ten years ago. Pin them down. Ask if the sun was shining."

"The sun always shines in L.A., Lieutenant," the younger detective told him.

"Not at night it don't, Sears," Thurgood told him.

The two detectives set out to question the local shopkeepers. Lujack didn't envy them their job.

"Dead bodies like to follow you around, don't they, Lujack?"

"It seems that way."

"Kurt Randolf, Miss Starr, Hiram, and now Makaris. If I were a friend of yours, I'd start wearing a bullet-proof vest."

"Makaris was no friend of mine."

"That's right, he wasn't," Thurgood said. "Matter of fact, I hear you and he had a little argument this morning out at the Marlins training park."

"I wouldn't say that."

"I didn't think you would. But we've talked with two people who will testify differently."

"Let me guess. One of them is Clark Sterling."

Thurgood smiled. "We haven't even talked to Sterling yet."

"You're wasting our time, Lieutenant. I didn't kill Makaris. Hell, I was sitting in his waiting room when you found his body."

"When we found him, he'd been dead for at least three hours. Would you mind telling us where you were from approximately one P.M. to three P.M. this afternoon?"

Lujack didn't need a murder alibi to bring that memory into sharp focus. He could still feel Lane under him on the grass.

"I was . . . I was having lunch with a client."

"What's the name of this client?"

"I don't have to tell you that."

"We don't have to book you for murder one, but we will if you don't come up with a name, and fast," said Quentin Rule from the front seat of an anonymous-looking car which had pulled up behind Lujack.

"That's the quietest GS 13 issue I've ever heard," Lujack said as Rule got out.

"First Lieutenant Thurgood tells you to back off,

then I tell you. Anybody with half a candlepower's worth of intelligence would know that when the LAPD and the FBI tell you to step away, they have a damn good reason."

"You're forgetting, Mr. Rule, that I used to work for the cops, so I know better."

"Are you going to book him?" Rule asked Thurgood, leaving no doubt what the FBI wanted done.

"I was thinking about it," Thurgood said easily.

"I'm having the IRS pull his tax returns for the past four years. It'll be interesting to see how a retired cop living on a pension can play tennis at Riviera and ski at Vail."

Lujack reached into his jacket pocket and pulled out his check.

"See this check, Mr. Rule? It's for services rendered as a security consultant. This money, along with the pension and my interest in East-West Imports, allows me to buy suits that fit and drive a car that I can spot in a parking lot."

Rule looked mad enough to hit him. But before the FBI man could move, Thurgood grabbed Lujack's arms and handcuffed him.

"You have the right to remain silent. You have the right to an attorney . . ."

"What are you doing?" Lujack yelled as Thurgood finished Mirandizing him and patting him down for weapons.

"We've had enough of your bullshit, Lujack. You're going downtown."

"What are you, crazy? I told you, Thurgood, I got a witness. Her name's on this check."

Thurgood took the check out of Lujack's hand-cuffed hand.

"Security consultant, my ass," the lieutenant said, pushing Lujack into the backseat of the squad car.

Quentin Rule watched the proceedings with surprise.

"Do you want me to drive him, Lieutenant?" an officer volunteered.

"I think I can find the way, Crowley," Thurgood said, getting in the front seat.

"See you at the briefing, Quentin," Thurgood said and sped off, leaving Rule standing next to his drab gray car.

Thurgood drove quickly down Pico in the direction of the West L.A. booking station on Purdue Street. When he got to Sepulveda, he took a hard right, sending Lujack into the door.

"Thurgood, you're fucking crazy. Moe Breen will have me back on the street before my fingerprints are dry."

Thurgood swerved over in front of the Club 69, a dingy bar frequented by nobody Lujack had ever heard of. He stopped the car abruptly and got out, came around to the curb side of the street, and opened Lujack's door. "Come on, get out."

Lujack had been a cop too many years to be in any rush to get out of the patrol car. "Oh, no, pal. I'll take my chances in the booking cage, rather than be shot by some cop gone bonkers."

"Shut up and get out. We're going inside for a drink."

Thurgood had the keys to Lujack's handcuffs out. Lujack looked at the dandified homicide man. "What's going on?"

"Nothing. I didn't like the way Rule interrupted our little conversation, so I figured this was as good a way as any for us to talk."

Lujack slowly got out of the car. He wasn't at all sure it was the right thing to do. But as much as he disliked Thurgood, he didn't figure the lieutenant was going to shoot him in the back.

When Lujack was out on the sidewalk, Thurgood unlocked the cuffs.

"You're serious? You wanna have a drink?"

Thurgood didn't answer but walked into the bar, leaving Lujack alone on the sidewalk rubbing his wrists. Lujack followed him inside.

The Club 69 was a no-frills establishment. It was dark enough so you couldn't see the dirt and light enough so the bartender could see your money. Thurgood was sitting on a stool in the middle of the bar. There were two motley-looking longhairs at the end of the bar talking to the bartender. The music on the jukebox matched the bar perfectly—"Who'll Stop the Rain" by Creedence Clearwater.

The bartender came over. She was in her midforties with hair pulled straight back in a bun. Lujack doubted it was for health reasons; it was to highlight the tattoo on her forehead. She regarded Thurgood's tan summer suit with disdain.

"What can I do ya?"

"Two scotches," Thurgood said. "You got anything older than that song?"

"Yeah, me." She laughed and pulled up a bottle of Haig and Haig Pinch. She poured two drinks. "That'll be five dollars."

Lujack pulled out a twenty and laid it on the bar. "We'll run a tab."

The woman nodded and walked back to the regulars.

"I give up, Thurgood. What's going on?" Lujack asked when she left.

Thurgood raised his glass. "To justice."

Lujack hesitated, then picked up his glass and

drank. He wasn't fooled often, but Kyle Thurgood was fooling him. "I take it I'm not under arrest?"

"Not for the murder of Paul Makaris. We know who did that."

"You mind telling me who?"

"Last night, Johnny Stella arrived in town from Vegas. He met two point men from Miami. The Guerrero brothers. They're *cubanos*. Very nasty."

"The Cubans did the doctor?"

"That would be my best guess. Especially after you told me that Clark Sterling had been with you at Marlin Park."

"When did you get interested in Clark Sterling?"

"Stella met with Clark Sterling last night at a little restaurant out in Westchester. The Guerreros came in three hours later from Miami. When Sterling saw you talking to Makaris this morning, he probably called Stella and told him to move up the doctor's operation."

"You're telling me that Clark Sterling works for Nimmo?"

"Let's say they're associates."

"Sterling's one of the most respected attorneys in Los Angeles. My God, he's the fuckin' NFL commissioner's bosom buddy."

Thurgood finished his Pinch and ordered another round.

"And he used to get me and Marty season tickets, even worked to get us a TV show. But that don't mean he ain't a piece of garbage."

"Does Rule know you're telling me this?"

Thurgood smiled. "That's one of the reasons I got you away from him. Rule knows I've suspected Sterling for a while, but being a Feeb, he's a bit . . . reticent about going after guys who eat dinner on a regular basis at 1600 Pennsylvania Avenue. Rule wants Nimmo on his dust jacket, you know, Public Enemy Number One, not a well-connected, politically influential lawyer."

"Does he know that Nimmo is trying to move in on Ernie B.'s gambling operation?" Lujack asked for reasons he wasn't quite sure of.

"After what happened at the Pearl last Sunday night, he'd have to be a fool not to. But Rule and his friends at the bureau tend to see what they want to see. They want Nimmo. Sooner or later, they have to tumble to the fact that the reason Nimmo has gone to all this trouble—getting rid of Charlie, burning up the family, killing Alabama and Makaris—is that he's making a move on Ernie and needs the Marlins to do it."

"How long have you known what Nimmo's been up to?"

"Longer than you," Thurgood said.

Lujack was stunned. Thurgood had always been the enemy. The guy who covered up the Temple Arms murders. The guy who dragged Marty into the sewer. "Why the hell are you telling me this, Thurgood? What's going on?"

"You still don't get it, do you, kid?"

"Get what?"

"Get why I want Clark Sterling almost as much as you do."

Thurgood took another drink, staring into the bar, deciding what he'd already decided. "The night Marty . . . shot himself, I was the first cop on the scene. Marty was in the bedroom, lying on the bed, the Special in his hand, his brains on the pillow. Anna was just staring at the wall; she couldn't stop staring, it seemed like. I took her out to the living room. By that time, the patrol cops had arrived. I went back into the bedroom."

Thurgood took another drink. Lujack could see Marty's apartment in his mind, though he'd never been able to envision Anna in it. Up till now. Now he could see her staring at the wall.

"The way Marty was dressed seemed strange. I mean, he had on his skivvies and a shirt. A guy's gonna kill himself, it's kinda strange he's wearing his underwear. That's when I noticed his closet door is open."

Lujack felt his stomach start to tighten. He didn't want to hear any more of Thurgood's story.

"So I walked into the closet. I mean, Marty and I got to be pretty close after you guys split up. I never had that many friends in the department. I don't have to tell you—Marty was so easygoing, fun-loving."

"Yeah, Marty was fun."

"I don't know why I did it, maybe because I knew someone else was going to. Maybe because of the way he was dressed, or wasn't dressed, I thought there was something wrong. I looked in the closet and saw a coupla centuries on the floor. I reached down to pick up the bills and saw a shoe box next to 'em. I opened the box and found it was full of hundreds."

Thurgood stopped.

"How much?"

"Ninety-one thousand nine hundred."

"Change from a hundred thousand," Lujack said to himself.

A hundred thousand that Clark Sterling had given Marty to make sure Manny Ramos didn't talk about who hired the boys for that party and the man who called Ramos late that night to pick up the bodies.

Lujack finally knew what Kyle Thurgood was trying to tell him. It wasn't only that Clark Sterling had ordered the murder of those three boys. It wasn't only that Sterling had then paid Marty Kildare one hundred thousand dollars to kill the only witness. It was that Anna, his Anna, had found the money in Marty's closet. It was *Anna* who blew Marty's brains out. After she killed him, she could only stare at the wall.

"She killed him, didn't she? Anna found the money, she knew what it was for, then she killed him," Lujack said, repeating his thoughts, hoping they'd sound different coming out of his mouth.

"I don't know what happened that night, Lujack. But, yes, I think she found the money. When they took Marty's body off the bed, there were three hundreds lying under him."

"She must have thrown them at him, then shot him, then . . ." Lujack couldn't finish.

"It took me a while to figure out where Marty got the money. At first, I thought you might have something to do with it."

"She should have called me."

"Then I went back and looked at your file. You had beaten up Ramos pretty bad. He gave you two names. Charlie Randolf and Clark Sterling. Manny was killed before I could ever question either one," Thurgood said. "The only other person who knew those names . . ."

"Was Marty Kildare," Lujack said, remembering that he had told Marty the night after he interrogated Ramos. He'd told him there were two leads. Randolf and Sterling. Marty had told him to cover his ass. Those weren't the kind of people to be involved in a triple homicide without a church full of eyewitnesses saying they were somewhere else.

"Marty must have gone to Sterling. Somehow, Sterling got Marty the same gun that the boys were killed with. Undoubtedly, Ramos killed the boys on

Sterling's orders. Sterling must have set up a meeting with Marty and given him the gun. However it went down, that's the only way Marty Kildare could ever earn a hundred thousand dollars cash."

"Anna must have figured the same thing," Lujack said, understanding the awful truth. What he didn't tell Thurgood was that Anna had left him because of what he did to Manny Ramos. It was the last straw. Then, one night eight months later, Anna had discovered that the man she left Lujack for, his partner, Marty Kildare, had shot Manny Ramos in the head the *same* day that he had comforted her about Lujack's brutality. Lujack knew that the reason Anna had shot Marty wasn't because he was a murderer; it was because of the man she had left. She had loved him, not Marty. That was the tragedy.

Lujack put his head down on the bar. The last five years of his life seemed to drain out of him like blood after sweat. He couldn't breathe.

"What's the matter with your friend, mister?" the bartender asked. "We don't like for guys to nod out at the bar. Maybe you should take him out to the alley before he pukes."

"Maybe you should bring us that bottle and mind your fuckin' business," Thurgood told her.

"Nobody talks to me like that in my own bar, asshole. I don't care how many faggots it took to make your suit."

"If I were you, Slick, I'd be respectful of Marie," one of the longhairs said. "You look too fat to crawl outta here with your tie between your legs."

"I came in here for a drink. Not a Tom Hayden for President rally. Give me the bottle, Marie."

Lujack heard bar stools move backward. When he looked up at the two, he thought they looked more in the Sonny Barger for President category. Both had knives.

"Feel up to having another drink?" Thurgood asked him.

"I'll take the guy in the Willie Nelson headband," Lujack answered.

The two guys were about three feet from Thurgood by the time Lujack and the lieutenant were off their bar stools facing them. Lujack knew the two had expected them to run, and when they didn't, there was a moment of hesitation.

"That's right, assholes, we're not goin' anywhere," Thurgood said as the nearest man plunged at the lieutenant with a five-inch knife. Thurgood deflected the man's arm with a heavy karate chop. Then, with remarkable quickness, he kicked the assailant square in the nuts. The man yelled and bent over in pain, dropping his knife. Thurgood stepped on the blade. The man lay groaning on the floor. The second man came at Lujack in a frenzy, slashing the air with his knife and yelling obscenities. Lujack was in no mood to be cut up by a burned-out hippie. He picked up his drink and threw it in the man's face, then efficiently put him down with a left hook. The two made the right decision and staggered out the back door. Marie brought out the bottle of Pinch and poured two more drinks.

"To protect and serve, right?" she said to Thurgood.

"Something like that," the lieutenant answered. Marie went back to her end of the bar. Lujack's mind went back to Anna.

"After all this time. Why tell me now?"

"It wasn't my idea. It was Chief Bane's."

"What's it matter to him?"

"He doesn't want Frank Nimmo in his city, and he figures the more road blocks he can put up, the better."

"Because I'm a bookie."

Thurgood smiled. "Maybe because he doesn't like what happened to you. You'll have to ask him."

"He could have done something then."

"He wasn't chief then," Thurgood pointed out. Then he continued, "There was another person at Clark Sterling's party that night five years ago. Mick Mayflower."

"So? Mayflower is Sterling's client."

"Not then he wasn't."

Lujack recalled the conversation he'd overheard at Phyllis's party: "You're one of the best quarterbacks in NFL history, Mick, but business is business."

"You think Sterling's blackmailing Mayflower?"

"It's a possibility," Thurgood said.

"Why don't you question Mayflower?"

"He's only the most popular athlete in the city right now. You think he's gonna talk to us about a remote possibility he might be being blackmailed?"

"What do you want from me?"

"I want you to keep the pressure on. Make Sterling show himself."

"You mean I should have a little talk with Mick."

"Whatever it takes," the cop said, pouring another drink for each of them.

"To whatever it takes," Lujack said, raising his glass.

Chapter 18

ESTHER HOTEL STOOD ERECTLY next to a casket in the front of the Bethune Church of Christ. The casket was closed. Lujack fell into the line of mourners going up to pay their respects to Hiram's mother. In front of him was the only athlete he recognized, Kenny Dumas. Dumas had been the greatest running back of his day, a Heisman Trophy winner in his junior year. After four years in the pros, Dumas had discovered crack. He was out of the league a year later, and in and out of jail ever since. Lujack had read that Dumas had brought his Heisman Trophy to court when he was to be sentenced for a breaking-and-entering conviction. He got six months. When he was on the street, Kenny occasionally ran errands for Hiram to make chump change. "He used to carry a football. Now he carries my laundry," Hiram told Lujack. It was sadly fitting that of all Hiram's illustrious friends in sports and show business, only Kenny Dumas came to his funeral.

Lujack looked at the bronze casket. Black churches believed in open caskets, but no mortician's magic could put back Hiram's smile, not with half his face gone.

"Mrs. Hotel, my name's Jimmy Lujack. I was with Hiram the night he died."

Esther Hotel nodded in recognition. "The cop who became a bookie."

"Hiram was a good friend."

"My son used to talk about you. He said if a cop could go bad, anybody could. I told him that most people have a good reason to go bad. That doesn't make it right."

"No, ma'am," Lujack said.

"God bless you, Mr. Lujack." He took the blessing as dismissal.

He followed Kenny Dumas out of the church into the ugly morning. The first storm of the season had arrived in L.A. the night before. Across the street, he saw a dark brown Ford. There were two men in suits sitting in the car. One black, one white. Lujack had no doubt at all that they worked for Quentin Rule. Rule was betting that Lujack was next on Frank Nimmo's hit list, and the FBI wanted to be there when it happened. Knowing Rule, probably right after it happened. Lujack didn't know how much Kyle Thurgood was going to tell Rule about their conversation, likely just enough to keep the FBI from picking him up.

"Hey, Kenny," Lujack said, calling after the man in front of him. "Can I give you a lift?"

The rain was starting again. Dumas turned up his fake fur collar.

"Central and 68th," he said, following Lujack.

"Horrible day for a funeral," Lujack said.

"Don't make no difference to Hiram."

"You got a point there."

Lujack unlocked Kenny's door and ran around to his own. He didn't have to watch the brown Ford to know it would be following.

"I hear you was with him when it happened," Kenny said at the first stop.

"You heard right."

"Hiram should never have gotten mixed up with that guinea bastard. I told him so."

"Hi always thought he could handle anybody. You know that."

"I used to think that too. Till I ran into the pipe." Dumas hesitated. "You're not holding, are ya, Lujack?"

Lujack knew the question was coming. Junkies didn't surprise you. "That's not my style, Kenny. Besides, I got two FBI agents on my ass."

Dumas turned around and saw the brown Ford. "What are they after you for?"

"They think I'm going to be killed."

"Great," Dumas said, slipping down an inch or two in his seat.

"Kenny, you played a couple of games for the Marlins before you got busted, didn't you?"

"Five games. They gave me the ball three times. I fumbled twice."

"Did you get to know Mick Mayflower?"

"Shit, why would I want to know that faggot?"

Lujack laughed. "What makes you think he's a fag? I've read a lot of lines about his girlfriends."

Dumas gave Lujack a sideways look. "Something tells me I'm earning my ride home."

"It might help fix the people who killed Hiram."

Dumas considered the proposition. "Fifty bucks."

"So much for friendship," Lujack said.

"I'm not the one with the FBI on my butt."

Lujack reached into his pocket. He had three twenties. "I don't suppose you have change."

Dumas laughed and grabbed the three twenties. "Mick had a lot of white players fooled, with all his Hollywood starlets jive. But the brothers knew what he was lookin' at in the showers, and he wasn't measuring for shoe sizes."

"Anybody on the team? Were there any rumors?"

"I heard once that Buddy Bacitich was spending a lot of time up at Mayflower's beach house. But that was a coupla years ago."

"Bacitich is married, isn't he?"

"Since when did that stop faggots? What's this got to do with Hiram, anyway? Ram was a man's man."

"Exactly where does Mayflower live?"

"I was only there once," Dumas said, hesitating.

Lujack pulled out another twenty. Dumas took the money.

"By Malibu. There's a gate."

"He lives in the Colony?"

"No, not the Colony, further up," Dumas said. "Past Johnny Carson's house."

"Trancas."

"Yeah, that's it. Trancas."

They were nearing the corner of Central and 68th. The barred storefronts didn't look much different from when Lujack had first patrolled the area nearly fifteen years ago, just after he had graduated from the academy. A group of young blacks stood on the corner. They were wearing blue colors.

"Drop me off on the other side of the street. This here is Crip country."

"What do the Crips have to do with you?" Lujack

asked. He knew about the notorious L.A. street gang which now controlled drugs and murder in ghettos and prisons from Mexico to Canada.

"I buy my rock from the Blood. Crips don't like it."

"The two gangs fight for your celebrity business?"

"There ain't much down here they don't fight for. Not if it's worth havin'."

"I hope the Blood gives you a discount."

"Yeah," Dumas said, getting out of the car. "The first hit's free."

Lujack watched as Dumas disappeared into a storefront. Standing in front of the building were two black teenagers, both wearing red armbands. Blood colors. Lujack figured the eighty dollars he'd given Dumas would keep him high for the better part of the miserable afternoon.

The sun came out as Lujack neared the beach. The FBI tail was keeping a discreet distance behind him. When Lujack disappeared into the tunnel that marked the end of Interstate 10 and the beginning of the Pacific Coast Highway, he floored the Mustang. When he came out of the tunnel onto the highway, he was a good quarter of a mile ahead of the FBI Ford. He ran the light in front of the Jonathan Beach Club and knew that by the time the Feebs got to the Chataqua turnoff, they wouldn't know whether to keep going straight to Malibu or turn back toward Lujack's house. Knowing the FBI, they'd play it by the book.

He waited above the Malibu Canyon Road for ten minutes. There was no sign of Rule's men, no sign of anybody else's either. He pulled back out and followed the highway north. The sky was clear, the ocean blue and white. The storm had blown over, and the

Southern California beaches were never prettier than when a northeast storm cleared the air and sand of smog and tanning lotion.

It was early afternoon, and Lujack knew Mick Mayflower wouldn't be going to Marlin Park until late afternoon. There was a service for Paul Makaris at the Brentwood chapel of the Christian Pyramid. Attendance was supposedly mandatory. Chub Simmons and most of the coaches would be there. The players wouldn't.

Lujack didn't know where Johnny Carson's house was, but he knew enough about Malibu to keep going on the Coast Highway until he got to Trancas Market. He made a left turn across the highway toward the ocean and pulled up to the gate.

There were enough gated communities in Southern California for any self-respecting con man to figure out a variety of ways to get past the guards. Lujack had his own methods, depending on the electronics, the age, and the girth of the security cop. The older, fatter, and more electronically out-of-date the security man, the harder it was to get past him.

"Brad Funston to see Mick Mayflower," Lujack told a pleasant younger guard.

"Is Mr. Mayflower expecting you, sir?"

"He should be if he wants to beat the 49ers this Sunday," Lujack said, tapping a spiral notepad. "I've got the Marlins' game plan with me."

The guard buzzed Mayflower's house. "There's a man here with a notebook from Chub Simmons."

There was a hesitation. Then a voice Lujack recognized came over the speaker. "Send him through."

"Drive right in, sir. Number 198," the guard said, opening the gate.

Lujack was two hundred yards down the private road when he put a face to that voice. Buddy Bacitich.

He pulled the Mustang in front of the shingled carport marked 198. Mayflower's Bentley was in one slot, a Ford Bronco in the other. Neither Mayflower nor Bacitich was expecting the *National Enquirer,* but if there was any hanky panky going on between the two, Lujack knew things would get prickly quick.

While it was true not every gay in the Los Angeles Basin had a leaded-glass front door, Lujack didn't feel like he'd wasted a trip when he knocked on the beveled centerpiece. Judging from the outline behind the door, Lujack wasn't surprised when Buddy answered. The lineman was wearing shorts and a T-shirt that read "CANNES."

"What are you doing here, Lujack?"

"I came by to see Mick, express my condolences about Dr. Makaris."

Lujack stepped inside while Buddy was figuring out what to do next. Once inside, Lujack looked around the interior. Like most of the houses in Trancas, Mayflower's opened on the beach. It was light, not very large, and didn't look like it cost two million dollars.

"Chub didn't send you over here," Mayflower said, coming out of the kitchen. He had a towel wrapped around his waist and was holding a health drink of some kind. "What do you want, Lujack?"

"Every time I see you, you're wearing a towel, Mick."

Another man came out of the kitchen. A very buff, very handsome blond. Mayflower didn't need a crystal ball to know what Lujack was thinking.

"This is my weight trainer, Heinrich," Mayflower said awkwardly. "We're doing my morning calisthenics."

"I thought you liked Mexican boys, Mick."

215

Mayflower's expression froze momentarily. Lujack had hit a nerve.

"I don't know what you're talking about," he said, recovering. "Throw him out, Buddy."

"First I want you to have this, Mick," Lujack said, holding out his hand. Bacitich's hand encircled Lujack's forearm, but Lujack kept his palm open.

"Wait a minute, Buddy," Mayflower ordered and walked toward Lujack. The quarterback's eyes were transfixed by the tiny gold cross in Lujack's hand. With his thumb and index finger, he picked it up.

"Where did you get this?"

"I got it from a young Mexican boy. He came to Los Angeles from Ciudad Obregón about five years ago. He and two friends. They were going to make their fortune in El Norte. Instead, they ran into a man named Manny Ramos. Ramos told them that the best way to make money in the United States was to go to work for a gringo family and learn the language. Ramos said he would introduce them to these rich gringos. He bought them new clothes and found them a place to stay. Then he took them to parties with nice gringo men."

"You don't have to listen to this, Mick," the weight trainer protested.

"Let him talk," Mayflower insisted.

"At first, the boys were ashamed of what the gringo men wanted them to do. They weren't *maricones,* these boys. But Manny gave them pills that made them relax and not care. He said this was how Mexican boys got hired by rich gringos and made their fortune. Besides, if they didn't do what he said, he would call the *migre,* and they would have to go back to Ciudad Obregón. One night, there was a party in the Hollywood Hills. Ramos took the boys there.

The man giving the party was Clark Sterling. There were lots of gringo men who liked young boys. You were there, Mick, weren't you?"

"Mick, don't tell this guy anything. He don't know from nothin'."

"I know there's no statute of limitations on murder," Lujack said, playing his hole card.

Mayflower looked at Lujack. There were five years of anguish in Mayflower's face. Lujack knew the feeling.

"Let me take care of this fuckin' twirp," Buddy said, pulling at Lujack's arm.

"Get your hands off me, Buddy, or I'll break your fuckin' legs. Then you'll never be able to hang out in the locker room again."

For a minute, Lujack thought he was about to be spiked into Mayflower's shining hardwood floor.

"Leave him alone, Buddy. Why don't you and Heinie go for a walk? I want to talk to Mr. Lujack alone."

Buddy released Lujack's arm. He was a good soldier. Lujack understood why Mayflower got sacked so few times. Heinrich didn't follow immediately. The weight trainer looked at Lujack with a flash of jealousy.

"Well, I guess he is kind of cute in a film noir sort of way," he snapped.

"Buddy's waiting, Heinrich."

Heinrich took a sharp breath and left.

"So much for the all-American man," Mick said in a way that was sad, not embarrassed.

"I don't know. I just gave a former Heisman Trophy winner eighty dollars so he could spend the rest of the day trying to remember what he can never forget."

Mayflower nodded. "There's something about the

adulation of athletes in America. It distorts everything. Maybe it's the same with rock stars or movie actors. Except, of course, for the competition."

The last thing Lujack wanted to hear was why an all-American football player had ended up as a faggot. But he had a lot riding on this football player, no matter how much he liked the snap from center.

"What happened that night, Mick?"

"I lost my soul," Mayflower said without expression. He walked into the kitchen, opened the refrigerator, and pulled out a wine cooler. He asked Lujack if he wanted one. Lujack declined, logging another reason, besides AIDS and assholes, why there wasn't much chance of him turning gay in the foreseeable future. Mayflower next grabbed a pack of Benson and Hedges out of a kitchen drawer.

"Marlins break training," Lujack said.

Mayflower didn't smile. He sat down at the kitchen table. Lujack joined him. The view out the window was beautiful, the beach peaceful and clean. Not a Crip or a Blood in sight.

"You know, Lujack, I never really understood until that night. I mean, I knew I wasn't straight. Even when I was in high school. I went out with a lot of girls, but I went out with guys too. I guess I liked the danger, the edge. I always knew I had to be different so I could win.

"It all changed the night of Clark's party. I was pretty fucked up—booze, Quaaludes, it was one of those Hollywood nights. Most of the people, like Charlie Randolf, had gone home when this Ramón Navarro clone showed up with these three Mexican boys. He said he'd bought 'em at an auction in Tijuana. So he held another auction for the night. I think I bought mine for a hundred dollars. We went into one of the bedrooms. The kid was nervous. He didn't speak English." Mayflower looked at the cross. "I tried to be nice. At some point, I passed out. When I woke up, the boy was next to me, groaning. I could see blood everywhere. I couldn't remember anything I'd done. I couldn't remember anything.

"I panicked and started yelling. Sterling came into the room. He was calm, sized up the situation, and said he would take care of everything. His chauffeur drove me home. I left town that night without knowing what happened to the boy. Sterling called me at my parents' in Los Altos a few days later. He said the boy had a very rare blood type, and no match could be found until it was too late. He said there would be no investigation. He knew the doctor and the police wouldn't be a problem either. Nobody asks questions about dead Mexicans who don't speak English. He said nobody ever had to know."

Mayflower took a drag on his cigarette. The wine cooler was untouched.

"Three months later, when Clark said he wanted to start representing athletes as well as entertainers, I became his first sports client. He's always been true to his word. No one ever knew. And then you show up today. I don't know how you found out, but if it's blackmail you're after, Lujack, I'm afraid you're goin' to have to get in line."

Lujack tried to layer the people with their actions and their motives. In Sterling's case, it was a fit. The oldest story in the book, provided Mephistopheles had enough faces. But Mick Mayflower was no devil.

"What was it that you understood that night? What was it that changed you?"

"The rules." Mick laughed. "My rules. You know, good and bad, straight and gay. All the bullshit. All the morality."

"What about the edge?"

"That is the edge, Lujack," he said without irony. "It's not good or bad. It's ugly."

"I don't think so, Mick. You don't either. You wouldn't have looked the way you looked when I showed you that cross if that's how you figured it."

Mayflower's steady gaze measured the words. Then he looked out to the ocean. He was turning the cross over in his fingers.

"The one on the bottom was wearing the cross," Lujack said softly.

Mayflower turned back, listening. "What do you mean, on the bottom?"

"There were three of them. Naked. Each one shot in the back of the head. Piled on top of each other in an apartment on Temple Street. Yours was on the bottom." Lujack took a breath. "It didn't seem right that one of them should be wearing a cross, so I took it off before the coroner came."

"What do you mean, they were shot?"

"I mean they were murdered. Sterling had all of them killed so he could own the best young quarterback in the NFL. I wouldn't be surprised if that son of a bitch didn't drug you with more than Quaaludes to set you up."

"No . . . no . . ." Mayflower said, resisting his worst fears. "It wouldn't be worth it. What kind of a lawyer would risk a triple-murder rap to negotiate a quarterback's contract?"

"A lawyer who works for the mob, a lawyer who knows that one day his quarterback is going to throw passes just as far as that lawyer tells him to."

Mick Mayflower heard the words, put his own layers to actions and motives, and knew in one dazzling second that he hadn't murdered a boy five years ago at a wild Hollywood party. But now there were other problems.

"Clark's calling in all the markers this weekend, isn't he, Mick?"

"Last year, he told me to start having arm problems," Mayflower said matter-of-factly. "It was easy enough. I knew Makaris was one of Clark's clients. The team was becoming a joke with Phyllis running it. When Phyllis brought in the reverend and started talking about triangles and holy sand, Clark told me I should go along with the 'miracle cure.' I've got to hand it to him the way it's worked out. The team coming back, the fans behind us. We're favored to beat the 49ers by two this Sunday. All I have to do is make sure we lose."

"You don't have to do anything, Mick. Sterling's got nothing on you now."

Mayflower laughed to himself. "When he told me Sunday night there was no way we could win the next game, I told him I couldn't do it anymore. I said I didn't care what he told the police about that boy. I was finished. He told me it was no longer in his control. There were investors, the kind who didn't like being let down. Last night, he called me again to tell me what happened to Dr. Makaris. He said, 'That's what happens when you let down your investors.'"

"You could go to the police."

"Great. And admit I've been underthrowing receivers the last three weeks? Get real, Lujack. If it comes to going to jail or losing a game, I'll lose the game."

"What about me, Mick? I know the truth."

"You're a bookie, Lujack. The police won't believe anything you say."

"But the FBI will."

"The FBI?"

"They've been after Sterling's partner, Frank

Nimmo, a Las Vegas mobster, for the past three years. It started before the murder of Charlie Randolf."

"So why don't they pick the bastards up?"

"They need witnesses, Mick."

"Oh, no. I don't want to end up in front of a Chinese restaurant with a takee outtee sign around my neck."

"You don't have a choice, Mick," Lujack said, showing the quarterback a small tape-recording machine he'd concealed under his shirt.

"I don't believe it. You're a goddamn fed."

"Not likely—but as long as I have this tape, you're going to cooperate."

"What if I call Buddy right now and tell him to take you apart?"

Lujack tapped the bulge under his suit coat. "I'll shoot him."

Mayflower considered his options. Lujack was reminded of his conversation the day before with Kyle Thurgood.

"What do you want me to do?"

"I want you to play the best game of your life this Sunday. I'll take care of the rest."

Chapter 19

THE SIERRA MADRE CLINIC was a large, rambling home in the foothills behind Santa Anita at the foot of the Sierra Madres. In the fifties, a wealthy woman had left the home to the Los Angeles Police Department because her favorite TV show had been "Dragnet" and she wanted to leave a place where Joe Friday and Frank Smith could spend their waning days. The department converted the home into a twenty-bed mental hospital for officers and family members who, for whatever reason, had trouble adjusting to reality after working for the LAPD.

Lujack hadn't been to the clinic in the last three weeks. He usually managed to stop by twice a month. As he pulled in the gate, it occurred to him that the change he had always hoped for might be his, not hers. Today would be a test of that.

It was Friday. Since his visit to Mayflower's beach house on Wednesday, no one had seemed to be following him. Not the FBI. Not Frank Nimmo's soldiers. He could speculate on the reasons, but after what he'd been through the last fifteen days, speculation might be dangerous or useless or both.

The grounds were cool, shaded by the large oak and sycamore trees that had been watching over the estate since before the turn of the century. Lujack had heard that the house had once belonged to a mistress of Lucky Baldwin. Of course, that could be said about many houses belonging to pretty girls who lived near the legendary oil man's Santa Anita ranch. When Baldwin died in 1912 of a heart attack at the age of ninety-two, he was riding in a "hug me tight" carriage with four young women. Lucky didn't come by his moniker without reason.

"Lujack! Lujack!" a roly-poly man with brown hair and a matching beard called to him from the porch as he approached the house.

"How's it going, Clem?" Lujack said, reaching into his coat pocket.

"Did you bring it, Lujack? Did you bring it?" Clem shouted.

Lujack surreptitiously handed Clem a Snickers bar. The plump man looked around as he stuffed it in his pocket. It was a game they had played many times before.

"I owe ya, Lujack. Clem don't forget his friends."

"I know you don't, Clem," Lujack said as he had said many times before, each time struck by the irony that Clem was in the clinic because of bribes accepted from the merchants on his beat. Clem's defense was that he hadn't wanted to hurt their feelings by rejecting their gifts.

"I been readin' about you, Lujack. The way you took care of things at the Pearl. That must have been some shoot-out."

"Don't believe everything you read, Clem."

"It's too late for that, Lujack."

"I know what you mean, Clem."

Lujack walked up to the second floor. Miss Gerard was busy at her desk. She looked up and saw Lujack. Her mouth tightened.

"You didn't call, Mr. Lujack," she said accusingly. "You know I need a little time to prepare her."

"I'm sorry, Miss Gerard. I had some business out this way, and . . ."

"Have you spoken to Dr. Barnes yet?"

"He's out to lunch."

Miss Gerard made a noise that indicated "out to lunch" was hardly a temporary condition with Dr. Barnes.

"How is she?"

"She has her good days and bad days. Just like the rest of us."

Lujack had heard that answer before.

"Let me tell her you're here," Miss Gerard said, getting up from her desk.

Lujack watched her walk down the hall. Third room on the right. The ward was quiet this pleasant fall afternoon. Lujack always appreciated the quiet. Miss Gerard came back a few minutes later.

"All right, Mr. Lujack. You can see her now."

Lujack retraced Miss Gerard's footsteps. The door was open. She was sitting in the chair. Her hair was combed back in a ponytail. Her lips were lightly glossed. Her skin was pale and clear. Her cheeks were hollow but not unhealthy. Her eyes were light blue, the color of a Caribbean lagoon. He had always loved her eyes. She looked very pretty, much like a college girl of twenty, not a woman of thirty-one. The only signs of age were the light streaks of gray in her chestnut hair.

"Hello, Anna."

She didn't move. Her eyes were fixed on the wall next to the window. For four years, he had seen variations of the same look.

"I know it's been over three weeks. Things have been pretty hectic lately. Miss Gerard may have told you. I've been getting my name in the paper a lot."

There had been times over the years when she would look at him, a brief, penetrating glance, then her attention would wander again to the wall or the window. It was at those times he had been most frustrated. Those times he was ready to give up. It was as if she knew.

"What's been happening, Anna, has to do with Marty, with his death."

Both Dr. Barnes and Miss Gerard had said she had been more animated in the last few months, but in the four years that he had been visiting her at the clinic, Lujack had never seen as much as a smile or a nod, and that included the past months. Barnes said all the doctors agreed that she was physically capable of talking, reading, writing. She simply chose not to. Lujack knew it wasn't that simple.

"It also has to do with those Mexican boys. The ones I found murdered in the Temple Arms hotel."

She was wearing a blue nightgown and a robe. Later in the day, she would get dressed and go for a walk around the grounds. Miss Gerard told Lujack that Anna enjoyed her walks, watching the squirrels and the birds.

"I think I know who killed those boys, or who ordered them killed. A lawyer by the name of Clark Sterling. He did it so he could blackmail a football player, Mick Mayflower. My guess is Sterling paid Manny Ramos to kill the boys. Then, when word got

226

back to him that Ramos had talked to me, Sterling had Ramos killed."

He hesitated, wondering if he should have waited and told Dr. Barnes what he was going to say. He had little or no faith in the clinic psychiatrist and often thought that as long as the twenty-five-hundred-dollar check Lujack wrote monthly to the clinic didn't bounce, Barnes would keep her in the clinic until he retired.

"I think you know who Sterling hired to kill Manny Ramos. Don't you, Anna?"

Her eyes moved to meet his. She didn't speak, she didn't nod, but the unblinking blue eyes told him that she knew.

"I talked to Kyle Thurgood a few days ago. He told me about finding the money. I never knew about the money. There were a lot of things I never knew."

Her pale blue eyes kept watching him, pushing him.

"Thurgood said he found three bills under Marty's body. He said Marty was in his underwear, lying face down on the bed, lying on top of the money. I figure you found the money in the closet, and you guessed or else Marty told you where it came from. That's why you shot him."

The eyes he loved began to water, began to cry. He began to try to explain himself in hopes that she would do the same.

"The night I beat up Manny Ramos, I lost it, Anna. I told myself I could make things right. I was a cop. If I couldn't find out who killed those boys, then I didn't deserve to be a cop. I expected too much of myself and of you. I know now that no matter what one person does, he can't make it right. The world isn't built that way. I know how you must feel, being trapped with your own futility. I've been trapped with mine. When I beat up Manny Ramos, I lost my job. When you left me, I lost my life. It's taken a long time to start breathing again."

There were tears streaming down her cheeks. Then she turned away from him. He didn't know what to do. He wanted to be understanding, but maybe she had sensed something else behind his catharsis. Lane.

"Don't turn away, Anna. We can face this together. No matter what it takes. I mean, I can talk to Moe Breen . . . if you want to make a statement. Or if you don't . . . whatever it takes. We can do something."

She was crying now, staring at the wall, tears running down her cheeks. Lujack felt the familiar helplessness, but this time there was no accompanying anger. He wasn't mad at her—for not talking, for leaving him. He put his hands on her shoulders.

"I want to help, Anna. I want you to come back to the world."

"What's going on here, Mr. Lujack?" a very perturbed Dr. Barnes asked, coming into the room.

Barnes was a short, formal-looking man, from his well-trimmed mustache to his highly polished shoes. Lujack had noticed that he never wore the same pair of shoes twice. A psychiatrist with a shoe fetish. He could afford it.

"Nothing's going on, Doctor. I'm visiting my ex-wife."

"I've told you before, Mr. Lujack. Before you talk to Anna, please clear it with me. She seems upset."

"Which is more than you've been able to do in four years."

Lujack immediately regretted saying it. He knew better than to argue in front of Anna. When he looked at her, her eyes were wet, but her gaze was dry. She had left the room for the safeness of the wall.

"I'm coming back next week, Anna. After I've taken

care of the man I told you about. Think about what I said."

She didn't move. He thought her cheeks were flushed; it was good to see the color. His hands were still on her shoulders. He had long stopped thinking about touching her, but strangely, on this day, he took her hand.

"I love you, Anna," he whispered. "I'll always love you." He felt pressure on his hand as he got up. He squeezed back. It was the most communication he'd had with her in four years.

"Please get Anna dressed, Miss Gerard. I think it's time for her walk," Barnes told the nurse, who was standing with him at the door.

"Would you like that, Anna?" the nurse asked.

Anna kept looking at the wall. Lujack followed Barnes into the hall.

"What did you say to her, Mr. Lujack?"

"Don't worry, Doc, I didn't tell her to get a second opinion."

"Always the smart answer. No matter who gets hurt."

"What are you getting at, Doc?"

"I think it might be better if you didn't come back next week. I don't think it's good for Anna or the rest of the patients."

"You've been reading the papers, eh, Doc?"

"Clem keeps me informed."

"You can't forbid me to keep seeing Anna, Doc. Not as long as I keep paying the bills."

"No, Mr. Lujack, I can't forbid you."

"Then I'll see you next week, Doc," Lujack said and walked down the stairs.

Chapter 20

THE NEIGHBORHOOD AROUND THE Chin Up had returned to normal since the last time Lujack had passed through. Tommy had rousted him early that morning, before eight. Thus far, the Good Book had taken over two hundred forty thousand dollars in action on Sunday's Marlins–49ers game, most of it bet on the 49ers. They had dropped the spread to even, and still the money kept coming in on the 49ers. According to Tommy, they were one hundred forty-six thousand dollars heavy on the 49ers and had no place to lay off their action.

Lujack waved to Sid Green, who was out on the sidewalk demonstrating the latest model from Beverly Hills Vacuum to a Korean housewife. She looked interested but skeptical.

Tommy was talking to his brother Winston when Lujack walked in. Winston Chin was only two years younger than Tommy, but he had none of Tommy's capitalistic flair. Winston had lost more money on more bad deals than most Gardena poker players Lujack knew. The problem was that Winston was a businessman, not a gambler.

"Am I interrupting something?" Lujack asked.

"My brother has no confidence in me," Winston complained. "He refuses to give me what is rightfully mine."

"The only thing in this place that is rightfully yours, Winston, is this," Tommy said, holding up a sheaf of unpaid credit card bills. "If you want money, you come back to work here. If you want a handout, go around to the back and ask Wing Fu. He's cooking his famous catfish soup."

"Catfish soup," Winston repeated as if hearing it for the first time. "We could sell Wing's catfish soup recipe to Campbell's! I'll go upstairs and make some calls." Winston headed for the stairs to make the first call of his future catfish soup fortune.

"Just make sure you're on the floor by the first lunch seating," Tommy yelled after him.

"There's no keeping a good man down." Lujack smiled.

Tommy pulled his glasses down from his forehead and pulled out the latest figures. Lujack knew he didn't need to look at them but was doing it for effect. Not unlike Winston's unpaid bills.

"Susie's taken another eighteen thousand on the 49ers since I talked to you. I had her call Irv to see if he knew of anybody we could lay off to. He said the line in Vegas now has the 49ers even or one-point favorite. Some of the smaller casinos have circled the game. He's never seen anything like it. A four-point switch in four days."

"Tommy, I told you not to worry. I've got it handled."

"Jimmy, you're my partner for three years and eleven months. We're close as brothers." Tommy shot a look toward the kitchen. "Closer than brothers. We've made a lot of money together. I don't want to lose it all because you found out the Marlins quarterback is a pansy."

"Tommy, the guy thinks I'm working with the FBI. He thinks I can put him away for thirty years."

"And the other side can put him away forever. You're not messing with Ernie B. or any of the locals here, Jimmy. This is Frank Nimmo, the Chicago family, the New York families."

"They'll never know what hit 'em."

Tommy put a hand through his black mane. "I don't like it, Jimmy. I haven't liked it from the start."

"Look at it this way, partner. We don't have a choice."

"I was afraid you were going to say that," Tommy said with a weak smile.

"Relax, Tommy. Mayflower can do it. He's a natural."

"You just told me he's a queer. What's natural about that?"

"You told me yourself Irv said there was no place to lay off."

"We can still circle the game. Cut our losses. We have enough in the reserve fund to cover our losses."

"And we'd be down four hundred fifty thousand for the year with no money to open next week."

"I might be able to get a loan. From my cousin Fong Liu."

"Oh, no, you don't. I'd rather deal with Frank Nimmo than owe money to the Hong Kong Triad."

"Fong is a very honorable man."

"So was Sitting Bull, but that didn't do much for General Custer," Lujack observed.

The light behind the bar started to flash. Another bet coming in on line 3. Tommy groaned.

"I never thought I'd see the day when you didn't want business, Tommy."

"This game isn't business. It's a benefit for the Mafia."

Lujack had seen Lane only once since their impromptu picnic at Will Rogers Park. The night of the Paul Makaris murder, he'd gone over to reassure her and ended up spending the night. He hadn't told her about his conversations with Kyle Thurgood—only that, after this weekend, everything should be over. She had seemed relieved but apprehensive.

"Not everything, I hope," she'd asked.

Lujack didn't know how to answer. He knew he couldn't live without her, wanted to be with her all the time, but he'd been around the block enough times to know realistically there was no such thing as a woman you couldn't live without. Not unless you married her. He had leaned over and kissed her, hoping that was answer enough, knowing it wasn't.

The last time they talked, after he had been to visit Anna, she had wanted him to come over. He told her he was busy, bookie business. But he hadn't been busy; he had been afraid. Afraid of how strongly he felt about her. He had made a promise to himself that after Anna he would never again put a woman in that position. The position of being his wife.

That night, he was meeting her at the Griffith Park Equidome. He drove there half expecting to propose. She was going to be in a celebrity charity polo match. She said she wasn't crazy about arena polo, the current rage in Los Angeles equine circles, but she had promised to play because she was the highest-rated— four goals—woman player in Southern California.

Lujack agreed to meet her at the Riding and Polo Club adjacent to the Equidome. Then they would watch the professional polo match that followed Lane's match.

He pulled off the Ventura Freeway and turned onto Riverside Drive, following it along the remains of the Los Angeles River. The L.A. Equestrian Center was built in 1982 by a consortium of San Fernando Valley politicos and developers in hopes of being chosen as the venue for certain equestrian events in the 1984 Olympics. The center's backers oddly hadn't figured on Prince Philip, as president of the site-selection committee, being more impressed with Santa Anita's tradition than the Equestrian Center's enthusiasm.

The Equestrian Center soon found it didn't need real royalty, not when there was Hollywood royalty. Since the Olympics, the sport of kings had become the sport of the stars. With polo enthusiasts like Sly Stallone, William Shatner, and Stephanie Powers supporting them, the Los Angeles Colts were soon playing in the American Polo League. Lujack had been hearing about the spring and fall games for the past year. Burt Masters and a few other clients had been after him to put betting lines on the APL matches. Lujack told them the people in Vegas didn't know much about polo and didn't like sports they didn't know about, but he'd look into it. So there were two reasons he showed up at the Equidome that night: to see the woman he loved and to check out potential bookie business. If indeed there was a future with either.

It didn't take long to learn that there was a lot more going on at the Equidome on these warm Saturday nights than polo. Lujack had seen a lot of hot-looking women in his years in Los Angeles and Hollywood, but seldom had he seen the quantity and quality of female talent that he did on this night. The smell of perfume and hair gel and leather and sex was every-where.

The Equidome was set back behind a disco, artfully named Horses. The Riding and Polo Club was be-tween the disco and the dome. There were as many people outside the Equidome waiting for the *après* polo music to start as there were inside watching the match. Lujack gave his name to the maitre d'-bouncer at the door.

The Riding and Polo Club reminded Lujack more of the Pearl than of Palm Beach. He was immediately sorry that Hiram hadn't lived to spend Saturday night at the polo matches, rubbing elbows with producers in lizard-skin pants, girls in riding breeches who he knew didn't ride anything more than the two-legged beast, and more Armani, Montana, Valentino, and de la Renta than you could ever find on the Via Venneto.

"What are you doing here, Lujack?" Burt Masters asked him from down the bar. "The only horse you ride is Johnnie Walker."

Lujack's favorite movie star was standing at the bar talking to a sultry young blonde in a tight cashmere sweater. Lujack assumed she wasn't Masters's wife.

"How ya doing, Burt? Made any blockbusters lately?"

"Fuck if I know. Ask my agent." Masters laughed.

Burt made no motion to introduce the blonde, which meant he either couldn't remember her name or he didn't want Lujack to know it.

"This is quite a scene," Lujack said, studying her braless form.

"I told you it was a hot sport. Come on out to the dome, and I'll give you a tour."

Burt grabbed Lujack's arm, telling the blonde he'd be right back. Lujack saw she was nearer thirty than twenty, which meant she would probably wait, unless a bigger star came along.

"Nice girl. Wish I could remember her name," Masters told him as they walked past the outdoor tables to the arena itself.

"I'm sure it'll come to you."

"When you get to be my age, Jimmy, nothing is for sure," the actor said.

Masters and Lujack stood behind the boxes between the club and the dirt arena floor. There was a five-foot wall around the field. The pro game had already started—the L.A. Colts against the Chicago Panthers.

"Arena polo is played on a smaller field. It's more violent, more explosive, it has more scoring, and it's better for the spectators."

"How about for the horses?" Lujack asked, watching a red-jerseyed Colts player and two Panthers push against the wall, their mallets swinging crazily at the yellow ball. The game reminded Lujack of hockey.

"Yeah, you need stronger horses. There's more contact and less speed than outdoor polo."

As Masters finished talking, the ball squirted out of the corner, and a Colts player literally pushed the ball at the painted goal in the middle of the far wall. The umpire declared a goal. The fans cheered.

Lujack noticed that there was quite a difference between the spectators in the seven-fifty bleacher seats and the holders of private boxes that ringed the stadium. The people in the boxes were more intent on the game and each other, while the folks in the bleachers were more intent on the people in the boxes.

"Each team's players are rated. For this game, the Panthers were given a three-point handicap because the Colts players have higher goal ratings."

"Like the Marlins being favored over the 49ers."

"Yeah, except they actually give you the points in polo. This game started three to zero in favor of the Panthers. But see, the Colts are now ahead seven to six. That means they've outscored them seven to three in the first two chukkers."

"I hope the Marlins do that well tomorrow," Lujack said.

"Forget it, Jimmy," Masters told him. "Everybody in town knows the Marlins are going to fold. There's some very heavy juice going down on that game."

"So I've heard," Lujack said.

"I don't want to run your business, Jimmy, but if I were you, I'd lay off your 49er action."

"I didn't become a bookie to let the mob tell me what games I lay off," Lujack told the actor, though the truth was he couldn't lay off if he wanted to.

"I just thought that after Hiram . . . Hey, it's your business," the actor told him, letting the sentence finish itself. It's your business, but it's my money.

Another Colts player suddenly burst out of the pack at Lujack's end of the arena and in two beautiful swings sent the ball flying down the course, scoring a goal.

"That was pretty impressive," Lujack told Masters.

"That's why I married him," came a woman's voice behind him.

Lujack turned and saw Lane Randolf. If possible, she was more beautiful than usual. She was wearing a white sleeveless dress and white shoes. She looked showered and fresh and elegant amidst the more revealing outfits around her.

"Was he the one who didn't like being pushed?"

"I forget," Lane said, studying him. "Did you get here in time to see me play?"

"No, I was tied up."

"Bookie business?"

"You looked great, Miss Randolf," Masters interjected. "But next time, try to get Sly Stallone a little closer to the wall. It would do wonders for my career." Masters smiled. "Well, Lujack, I'll leave you two. I want you to think about this," he said, nodding toward the polo match in progress.

"The people in Vegas don't like sports they don't know anything about, Burt."

"They set odds on where Skylab would crash, and the last time I looked I didn't see any rocket scientists working at Nevada One," Masters countered.

"Maybe I'll look into it," Lujack said. "Give my best to the blonde."

"I'll try," Masters said and disappeared into the Riding and Polo Club.

"You're not really going to make odds on polo?" Lane said after Masters left. "I can't think of anything worse. It's bad enough with all these professionals," she said with disdain.

"I thought you were starting to like bookies," Lujack said.

"I like you, Lujack. I don't like bookies."

"So where do we go from here?" Lujack asked.

Lane hesitated, catching the long and the short of it. "That depends on you."

"How about your place? Or my place?"

"How about Horses? I've never seen you dance."

"That's because I can't."

"I'll be the judge of that."

The disco was packed. The younger, prettier, female members of the polo crowd plus every loose pickup artist in the Valley. Lujack figured the guys let the girls spend money on tickets to the match and hoped those who escaped the clutches of the polo producers would then fall into their waiting jeans jackets on the Horses dance floor. Lujack hadn't seen so much hair compound since Fabian and Bobby Rydell shared a head shot on "American Bandstand."

Lujack maneuvered Lane near the bar, which seemed to be the least crowded area of the place. Although ID was required, the dance crowd looked to be an average age of twenty. A decidedly younger crowd than inside the Equidome. Saturday night in the Valley. An age-old tradition.

"You know, I used to come to places like this when I was in high school," Lujack shouted to Lane over the strains of "Louie, Louie."

"So did I." She smiled.

She took his hand and pulled him in the direction of the dance floor. Lujack went into his one basic dance step. The same quasi–"Soul Train" move he had learned at the Pearl dancing with the cocktail waitresses. Hiram had always insisted that Lujack had more rhythm than he let on, but being a good cop, he'd rather drink than dance. Lane, for her part, moved easily, seductively, on the floor. For a girl in her late twenties with three marriages under her belt, she looked great. Of course, the twenty million didn't hurt.

Lujack was thinking about boogieing over to the bar when he felt a tap on his shoulder. He turned abruptly, in no mood to be cut in on. Instead, he found himself staring into the round, slightly lecherous face of Kyle Thurgood.

"What are you doing here?"

"We have to talk."

"About what?"

"About tomorrow."

"Can't you see I have a date?"

Thurgood nodded in a surprised Lane's direction.

"Rule is in the parking lot," he said under his

breath. "I'll be waiting at the door. Say good night, Gracie."

"Wait! Thurgood, hold on!"

The lieutenant didn't stop.

"What was that all about?" Lane asked.

"You're not going to believe it but . . ."

"You have to leave."

Lujack nodded. "Louie, Louie" had stopped. The kids were catching their breath. Lujack was trying to control his temper. Helping Thurgood was one thing. Having his love life ruined was quite another.

"Who is that man?"

"An old acquaintance."

"Don't tell me. The bookie business?"

"In a manner of speaking."

"Does it have to do with tomorrow's game?"

"I think so."

"Can't it wait until tomorrow?"

"It should, but I guess it won't."

Thurgood was at the door. He motioned for Lujack to hurry.

"Don't worry. I brought my car," Lane said.

"I hate to leave you like this."

"I'll see you tomorrow at Phyllis's engagement party."

"We'll go out tomorrow night and celebrate," Lujack said.

"Celebrate what?"

"Engagements."

He kissed her on the mouth.

"Let me walk you to your car."

"No, you go with that man."

He kissed her again and took a step.

"Lujack," she called after him. "Take care."

"Always," he told her.

* * *

Quentin Rule was sitting in the driver's seat of his GS-13 mobile. Lujack was wrong. Rule's car stood out in the Equidome parking lot. The car next to his was a Mercedes 450, license plate: "MR. PERFECT."

Thurgood and Lujack got in the backseat. There was another man in front with Rule. Lujack figured it had to be a Feeb.

Rule stepped on the gas as soon as the two men got in.

"Where are we going?" Lujack asked angrily.

"Rehearsal," Rule said in an equally inhospitable tone.

"What are we rehearsing?"

"Busting Nimmo. And you staying alive," said the man in the passenger seat.

Lujack knew who it was before the man turned around.

"It's been a while, Chief."

Police Chief Tom Bane studied Lujack. Lujack studied the chief back. The face was the same: stern, disciplined, but not cold. The hair was grayer, the eyes older. He had seen Bane on TV enough times over the past five years not to be surprised.

"Almost five years."

"You have a good memory," Lujack said.

"From what Lieutenant Thurgood tells me, so do you," the chief said as they drove into the darkness of Griffith Park.

Chapter 21

"I BORROWED THESE FROM my sister's husband. He's a bird watcher," Tommy said, showing Lujack the elegant Zeiss field glasses as he climbed into the Mustang.

"I can't believe you're breaking down and actually going to a professional football game."

"When I have three hundred and eleven thousand dollars riding on one game, I figure I'd better be there in person. Winston can look after the restaurant."

"How's his catfish soup deal coming?"

"Believe it or not, Campbell's didn't think catfish soup would fit their image. Winston's thinking of going with one of the generic brands."

"Safeway's Own Catfish Soup."

"My wife thinks all bottom fish are a hard sell."

"She may have a point."

"Jackie has many points, most of them sharp," Tommy said about his wife of seventeen years.

Lujack had been sent a parking pass along with his invitation to Phyllis's engagement party. Traffic around the Coliseum was heavy because the game had been a sellout for the last week. Marlins fans were coming back in droves to support their rejuvenated team. Everybody loves a winner.

"There will be ninety-two thousand people in the Coliseum today, and ninety thousand of them will be rooting for the Marlins. How can we lose?"

"Yeah. Only the big bettors will be rooting for the 49ers," Tommy groused.

"It'll make for an interesting party."

"Interesting! My stomach hasn't been this tight since I played Nathan Detroit in my high school's great production of *Guys and Dolls*. If the Marlins don't win, it's all over for us, Jimmy."

"Trust me, Tommy. They'll win," Lujack told him, not knowing what else to say.

Tommy grunted noncommittally.

"You were really serious about that singing career, weren't you, partner?" he asked, hoping to change the subject.

"Luck be a lady tonight," Tommy began singing in a passable baritone.

"Hold that thought," Lujack said, handing his parking pass to the attendant.

Lujack parked next to Phyllis Randolf's limousine. He reached into the glove compartment and pulled out a box of .38 shells, emptying them into his sport-coat pocket. Thurgood had told him he should bring his gun. He would have anyway.

Both men looked up at the giant wall which formed the skeleton of the Coliseum. Built for the 1932 Olympics, refurbished for the 1984 games, it was one of L.A.'s most impressive structures. Lujack wasn't sure what that said about Los Angeles priorities.

They walked over to the circular art-deco entrance to the private elevator which would take them up to the press box. That week, the press box had been converted into a giant, hundred-seat private box for Phyllis and her friends. Now only the television media were allowed to work in the enclosed portion of the press box. The print media had been relegated to a makeshift outdoor press box nearer the field. Like most of Phyllis's moves during her three years as the Marlins owner, it didn't do much for her popularity with area newspapers.

A uniformed guard checked Lujack's invitation when the door opened onto box level. The guard nodded, and Lujack and Tommy walked into the world of NFL opulence. Before Lujack could look around, a comely hostess wearing a "Go Marlins" sash served him a glass of champagne.

"If I'd known football games were like this, I'd have started coming years ago," Tommy said, picking up a glass of the bubbly.

"Believe me, Tommy, I've been going to games since I was seven years old, and this is the first time I've ever been served champagne and caviar," Lujack said.

The party took up the entire first level of the renovated press box. Milling between the split levels of the huge private box, dressed to the nines, were at least a hundred of Phyllis's closest friends. Seventy rows below, down on the field, the players were finishing their warmups. In the stands, ninety-two thousand common folk were filing into their seats. Putting on their sun hats, checking their thermoses, putting down their cushions, ordering peanuts and beer. Many of them, Lujack thought, talking about America's favorite sport—gambling on pro football.

"Mr. Lujack, you made it," came the earthy lilt of Phyllis's voice as she walked toward him.

Mrs. Randolf was always an outrageous dresser, but on this day she had outdone herself. Her dress was black satin, full length, with a V cut to show off her ample cleavage. If that weren't quite enough, her dress was also slit to midthigh.

"What do you think of my Elvira costume?"

"It's, uh, rather vampish."

"That's the point." She smiled. "After all, it is Halloween."

Lujack hadn't even thought about the date.

"October 31. All Hallows' Eve," Tommy said glumly. He and Phyllis exchanged polite nods.

"The only day of the year when the devil is called on to intervene in matters of luck and marriage," Phyllis said.

"What does Reverend Moore think of your calling on such a sinister force to bless your marriage?" Lujack asked.

"To be truthful, Mr. Lujack, we haven't discussed the matter," she said.

Lujack noticed she wasn't wearing her gold pyramid. He wondered if this was the day she was going to call on her own personal devil, Frank Nimmo, to intervene in matters of business, inheritance, and murder.

"Is Lane here yet?" Lujack asked.

"She called this morning. One of her horses is having trouble again."

"She's not coming then," Lujack said, not sure whether he was relieved or not.

"I doubt it. Between you and me, I don't think she likes football."

"Between you and me, I think you're right."

"Well, gentlemen, enjoy yourselves." With that, Phyllis kept moving, weaving her way through the guests, heading in the direction of NFL Commissioner Dick Pressley.

"So, what do you think of our owner?"

"She's a very formidable lady," Tommy said.

"You don't believe that Halloween stuff?"

"It doesn't matter what I believe. It's what she believes."

"I think I should check on Lane at the stables."

"I think I should check out the buffet," Tommy said, walking toward a ten-yard-long table of food in front of him. Lujack should have known better than to consult Tommy concerning his relationship with Lane.

Lujack left Tommy picking up a particularly large lobster tail. He found a bank of phones in the corridor that separated Phyllis's box from the television announcers' booths. He dialed Lane's number. There was no answer. He dialed the stable number. No answer there either.

"Calling your bookie, Lujack?" Quentin Rule said, coming up behind him. Rule's blue blazer and Fordham tie showed he was in deep cover.

"Love the tie, Rule." Lujack smiled. "I was calling Lane. I hear she isn't coming to the game."

"Don't worry about Miss Randolf. I put a man on her last night after we left Horses."

"So you're beginning to believe."

"Like all good FBI agents, I'm covering my butt," Rule said with a trace of humor.

"Is Nimmo here yet?"

"He's coming up the stairs right now."

The agent pointed to a group of flashily dressed men hiking up the stairs near the fifty-yard line. In the center of the group was Frank Nimmo. Under the warm, late October sun, the gangster looked resplendent in his casual clothes—the black Nino Cerruti linen coat, pleated slacks, pearl-gray loafers. Next to him was Johnny Stella, followed by two very Vegas showgirls, striking six-foot beauties. Surrounding the entourage were four bodyguards. Lujack guessed two of them were the Guerrero brothers, the men who had deposited Paul Makaris in front of the Chin Up.

"He dresses almost as sharp as you do when you're out of uniform, eh, Rule?" Lujack said as Nimmo took his seat a few rows in front of Phyllis's box.

"Are Bane's men on the roof?"

"And down on the field. If any of Nimmo's gunsels try to get near Mayflower, they'll be intercepted," Rule answered.

"Is Sterling here yet?"

"He's in the TV booth talking with Summerall and Madden. I think he'd like to represent one of them."

"Old Clark represents all the biggies."

"We're hoping that after this afternoon, his client list will be considerably smaller."

"Yeah," Lujack said, "like maybe the softball team at San Quentin."

Lujack made his way past the buffet looking for Tommy. Instead, he found Reverend Moore, who was demonstrating the power of the Christian triangle for the very handsome but not very blond wife of Burt Masters. The actor watched with some skepticism, although his wife was quite serious.

"When did your wrist start hurting, Mrs. Masters?" Reverend Moore asked.

"When she bought that damn bracelet. The heft of that bauble would put a strain on Arnold Schwarzenegger's wrist," Masters said, referring to the spectacular gold bracelet on his wife's arm.

"Don't listen to him, Reverend Moore. It's been

hurting since I had my skiing accident over a year ago."

Reverend Moore produced a little white bag and pressed it on her wrist. Burt Masters gave Lujack a bemused wink.

"Now, Mrs. Masters, just put this on your wrist when you go to bed at night. Believe in the power of Christ and the triangle, and your wrist will heal itself."

"What is it, some drug?" Letitia Masters asked, holding the bag with trepidation.

"It's sand, Mrs. Masters," Moore said, "from the desert east of the Mojave and west of the Colorado."

"Like Giza is east of the Sahara and west of the Nile," Lujack said pleasantly, "except there are no great pyramids where your sand comes from, Reverend."

Moore gave Lujack a surprised look. "There will be one day, Mr. Lujack. The greatest pyramid of our time. A pyramid topped with a cross."

"The only way you're going to build a pyramid in the California desert is when the IRS rules that the Marlins are part of a tax-exempt religious organization and the cross is a TV antenna."

Moore's gaze hardened. "God's will be done," the reverend said.

"So that's the hook." Burt Masters laughed.

"Burt, what is your friend talking about?" Letitia asked.

"He's talking about a scam," Masters said, "and I'll bet your bracelet he's right. Jimmy knows."

"Oh, no, you won't," Letitia said, handing Reverend Moore back his sand bag.

An amused Burt escorted his wife back to their seats.

"You're getting in way over your head, Lujack.

Remember what happened to the armies of the pharaoh," Moore warned him.

"So are you, Reverend. Remember what happened to your fiancée's last husband."

Lujack's hand caught the reverend's fist just before it could reach his jaw. At that moment, Dick Pressley walked up with an empty plate in his hand. The two antagonists stared fixedly at each other.

"You're becoming a regular friend of the family, aren't you, Lujack?" the commissioner calmly observed.

Lujack felt the reverend's fist relax.

"Who do you like today, Commissioner?"

"I like both teams, Mr. Lujack," the commissioner said, deftly serving himself a shrimp aspic.

"That's right," Lujack said. "It's your job to protect the integrity of the game . . . and it's my job to protect the integrity of the point spread."

Pressley frowned. "Good day, Mr. Lujack. Reverend." Pressley made his way toward one of the hostesses.

"Keep the faith, Reverend," Lujack said and excused himself.

By the time he got back to Tommy, the game was about to begin. He and Tommy were sitting on the lower level of the large box which ran from one forty-yard line to the other. Directly in front of them, five rows down in the stands, were Frank Nimmo and friends. One section over, Lujack spotted Ernie Barbagelatta and his friends. The two groups seemed oblivious to each other.

"Look who's sitting a section away from Nimmo," Lujack said, pointing in Ernie's direction.

"Don't seem too friendly," Tommy said, cutting a piece of roast beef with his fork, then piling some salad on top of it. There was nothing in the world

Tommy enjoyed more than eating non-Chinese food that was free.

"You'd think that when the head of one gambling syndicate shows up in another syndicate's city, certain formalities would be observed."

"Unless one's there to put the other one out of business."

"You'd think by now Ernie'd figure out he's been set up."

"Maybe that's why he's here. If the Marlins lose and he starts shooting in Nimmo's direction, then we'll know," Tommy said, attacking a turkey breast and a wedge of brie.

"I thought you were nervous," Lujack said, watching in fascination as Tommy inhaled an oyster.

"I'm feeling better now," Tommy said happily. "This is a very nice party."

"The party's about to get serious, my friend," Lujack said as he watched Rafael Caesaro tee up the ball. The game was about to begin. The game that would decide whether or not the Good Book would stay in business. Whether or not Jimmy Lujack would lay to rest the ghosts that had been following him for the last five years.

The ball left the tee and floated end over end above the players toward the opposing end zone. A cheer went up as the crowd rose to its feet. The 49er return specialist caught the ball on his own two-yard line and began running upfield to the ten, to the fifteen, to the twenty. Then, boom, three powder-blue Marlins uniforms smothered his red jersey. The Marlin fans exploded. The special teams jumped up and ran off the field.

"Way to stick 'em," Tommy yelled.

"Better in person, eh, Tommy?"

Tommy gestured with his champagne glass in the

direction of the waiter who was keeping Phyllis's guests' glasses brimming. "Damn right, Jimmy, only way to go," Tommy said, letting the waiter top his glass.

Tommy's exuberance notwithstanding, Lujack had always loved going to football games. Starting with the USC games he'd gone to with his father, to his college days in Strawberry Canyon in Berkeley, to the Marlins games he had gone to with Marty. There was nothing more typically American than watching football in a full stadium on a beautiful autumn day.

Despite the champagne flowing at Phyllis's party, Lujack didn't see professional football being replaced by polo any time soon. Pro football was America. It was teamwork. It was violent. It was beautiful. It was celebrity and money and winning in a time when the country was consumed with such pursuits. It had the richest owners, the biggest audience, and the most vocal fans. It had the most money bet. As Lujack once told Tommy after too many scotches, "If it hadn't been you and me, it would have been somebody else."

The 49er quarterback, Jack Street, rolled to his left. Street was a great rollout quarterback and had the Super Bowl rings to prove it, but the Marlins left-side linebacker, Cletus Frames, put his helmet hard between Street's numbers and sent him back for a six-yard loss.

"Stick 'em!" Tommy yelled. After two plays, Tommy was on his way to becoming a classic obnoxious fan.

Street remained on the ground as Tommy reached for his glasses. "Maybe he's hurt," Tommy said hopefully.

Lujack looked to the right and the left at the other people seated in the first row of Phyllis's box. Two people to the left, sitting next to Dick Pressley, he saw the angular countenance of L. Clark Sterling. The lawyer was looking down on the field with apprehension. Lujack watched him and waited until Sterling looked over. Their eyes met briefly. On the field, Jack Street got to his feet. The Marlins fans clapped politely. Tommy swore under his breath. Clark Sterling nodded at Lujack.

Street completed four straight passes and moved the 49ers into Marlins' territory before Horace Sims, the giant Marlins defensive end, caught Street as he was trying to slither out of the pocket. Sims squeezed the 49er quarterback like a tube of toothpaste, sending the ball squirting into the air and into the waiting arms of Cletus Frames, who ran it down to the 49er thirty-eight-yard line before being tackled.

"Let's go, Mick," Tommy yelled with ninety thousand other Marlins fans as Mick Mayflower and the Marlins offense came onto the field. Seeing number 12 on the field kneeling before his teammates, cool and confident, the unquestioned leader of the Marlins, Lujack remembered the way Mayflower had looked at him three days before on the beach. He remembered the anguish—he also remembered the edge. Lujack knew Mayflower had what all great athletes needed. The question was whether he would risk his life to prove it.

The first play was a play-action pass. Mayflower put the ball in Tim Woodard's stomach, then pulled it out, dropping back almost casually before setting up and throwing a perfect spiral down the center of the field toward the goalposts. Fleet White had run an up and in, turning the defensive back around, and was open by four steps. The ball nestled snugly in White's arms for a touchdown.

"All right, Mickey, baby!" Tommy yelled, grabbing

Lujack's coat. "Did you see that pass, right on the fuckin' money!"

"I saw it, I saw it," Lujack said, watching Frank Nimmo out of the corner of his eye. As the other players mobbed White, Nimmo turned around and looked up into the box. Lujack wasn't surprised when the gangster's gaze settled on Clark Sterling. Frank didn't look happy. Neither did Sterling.

After the opening touchdown pass, Mayflower and the Marlins never looked back. By halftime, they led thirty-one to three. Mick Mayflower was playing the game of his life. Frank Nimmo was getting a sore neck from looking up at the Randolf box, and L. Clark Sterling was looking more and more like he needed a change of underwear.

By now Tommy had his own champagne bottle and was singing Broadway show tunes when he wasn't making lewd remarks about the anatomies of the Marlins cheerleaders.

"We have to do this more often, eh, Jimmy," he said with a slap on the back, after Rafael Caesaro kicked a forty-seven-yard field goal with no time left in the half.

"Right, Tommy. I'm sure after today, Phyllis will be dying to have us back," Lujack said, standing up.

"Where are you going, Jimmy? Don't you want some more champagne?"

"I think I'll wait until after the game, partner."

"But it's in the bag," Tommy said in a stage whisper. "That limp-wristed quarterback of yours has made us rich."

"To quote an old American proverb, 'It's not over until the fat lady passes out.'"

"I haven't heard that one," Tommy said as Lujack made his way in the direction of the elevator. He had seen Sterling get up as the official raised his arms signaling the field goal good.

He followed Sterling through the crowd. He could see Thurgood's man, Detective Sears, standing in front of the elevator door. Sterling had two options. He could pay a call on his star client and persuade him to throw five interceptions in the second half, or he could make a run for it. The second option was unlikely because not even Clark Sterling could run far enough or fast enough to get away from Frank Nimmo.

"Heck of a first half, huh, Clark?" Lujack said as Sterling impatiently pushed the elevator button.

"Yeah, great," Sterling answered, watching the elevator light which showed the car was on the ground level.

"Your boy Mick is playing the game of his life."

"Where's that damn elevator?" Sterling snapped, seeing the light still showing the ground floor.

"Too bad about Dr. Makaris," Lujack said, continuing the small talk. "He seemed like a credit to his profession."

"What's the matter with this elevator, buddy?" Sterling said to Detective Sears, who was wearing the uniform of a Coliseum security guard.

"It may have broke down again. It gets purdy tired on Sundays," Sears drawled, playing his part to the hilt.

"Jesus Christ, what happens if there's a fire?"

"You can go down through the front door, sir, if you don't mind the walk," Sears said, pointing to the glass doors which opened on the stadium stairs and would take Sterling right past Frank Nimmo. Sterling considered going through the stadium but thought better of it.

"I'm Mick Mayflower's agent. I have to talk to my

client," he snapped at Thurgood. "Can't you hurry this damn thing?"

"I'm sure it'll be back in order soon."

"If I were you, Clark, I'd enjoy the party," Lujack said casually. "Mick's not going to throw any interceptions for you in the second half anyway."

Sterling froze Lujack in his sights. "I didn't hear that, Lujack."

"You heard it all right, Clark. The party's over. Best thing for you to do is take your medicine like a man."

Clark jabbed the elevator button again. "I don't know what you're talking about."

"I'm talking about Frank Nimmo. Frank doesn't like it when people fuck up."

A shadow of doubt crossed over Sterling's face as he realized that somehow Lujack had set him up. "You bastard. What have you done?"

"I made Mick an offer he couldn't refuse." Lujack smiled. "I might do the same for you."

"Get away from me!" Sterling yelled and stalked back to his seat.

"Mean son of a bitch, isn't he?" Rule said, joining him.

"He's not as mean as the guy sitting in row 62 with the pearl cufflinks."

"Right now, all we can do is wait. Your friend Mayflower's making it easier for us. That kid's got a lot of guts."

"Does that mean you're going to cut him a deal?"

"I told you last night, Lujack. If, that's *if,* we get Sterling to roll over on Nimmo, I'll do everything in my power to see that Mayflower is kept out. Besides, to convict, we'd probably need your testimony, and I don't think Chief Bane is any more anxious than I am to tell the press we've been working with an established bookie."

Lujack began to make his way back to Tommy, afraid of what he'd find. When he got to his seat, his worst fears were confirmed. Tommy and Phyllis were doing a Vegas lounge act—a duet of "Memory."

Lujack stayed toward the back of the group that had crowded around them. His only consolation was that when singing with Phyllis, Tommy's voice didn't sound quite as bad as usual. They finished the number to polite applause, including her fiancée, who was standing a few feet away.

"Thank you very much. I'm glad you could come today and help us celebrate. This is a very big day for me, especially if Mick and the boys keep putting those touchdowns on the scoreboard. I want you all to know that Billy and I haven't quite fixed a date yet, but if things keep going the way they have been, I'm hoping that we can be married in New Orleans—maybe during halftime of the Super Bowl." Her friends cheered. "What do you think of that idea, Dick?" Phyllis asked the NFL commissioner. "I know you're always looking for something exciting for Super Bowl halftimes."

"The other owners might feel left out," Pressley said smoothly.

"Not if Phyllis promises to consummate the union on the postgame show," Burt Masters gleefully joined in.

"Only if we win," Phyllis said cheerily, while Reverend Moore listened in horror.

Watching Phyllis in her black, bosomy dress, Lujack guessed the minister might be having second thoughts about his new life-partner-to-be. Wait till he met the Chicago side of Phyllis's family.

The players had come back on the field, and the second half was about to start.

"Tommy Newley strikes again," Lujack said, pulling up a chair next to his partner.

"Did you hear us? Pretty good, eh?"

"I never liked *Cats.*"

"Don't laugh. Some guy sitting behind us works for William Morris. Thinks he might get us a few bookings."

"Anything happen with our friends in the stands?" Lujack asked.

"Nimmo keeps looking up here. He doesn't seem too happy. Ernie B.'s kissing everybody in sight."

"He ought to be. If the Marlins keep it up, he'll win more simoleons than you and I'll ever see."

"What do you mean *if,* Jimmy? This game is over."

"Not till the fat lady passes out," Lujack said as the 49ers kicked off. The ball was fielded by Fleet White on the Marlins six. He started up the sidelines and was all the way back to the thirty when he cut back to the middle of the field. A 49er hit him from behind, knocking the ball out of White's usually sure hands. The 49ers recovered on the Marlins forty-four.

Lujack looked at Tommy.

"Where's this fat lady, Lujack? I want to strangle her."

On the next play, Jack Street hit his tight end over the middle, and the 49ers were on the Marlins six-yard line. Two plays later, Street rolled to his right, pump faked, and ran into the end zone. Just like that it was thirty-one to ten.

"I'm beginning to have a bad feeling about this game," Tommy said, pushing away a dish of strawberries dipped in white chocolate.

Tommy's appetite didn't improve with the Marlins' second possession of the half. Mick Mayflower's second pass was off the fingertips of Tim Woodard and returned for a touchdown by the 49er cornerback. With twelve and a half to go in the third quarter, the score was thirty-one to seventeen. After the Mayflower pass, Frank Nimmo smiled for the first time all day. One section over, Lujack watched Ernie B. fume.

"You think Sterling got to Mayflower at halftime?" Tommy said wanly.

"I know he didn't. But somebody may have."

Quentin Rule tapped Lujack on the shoulder. "Our quarterback seems a little shaky this half," Rule said.

"That pass was Woodard's fault as much as Mick's. Let's wait to see what he does next possession before we get desperate."

"Let's hope you're right," Rule said curtly and walked away.

"Isn't that Quentin Rule?" Tommy asked in shock.

"The very same."

Tommy shook his head. "Have I missed something here?"

"Remember when I told you that Mayflower thinks I work for the FBI?"

"Yeah."

"Well, the FBI thinks I'm working for the LAPD."

Tommy shook his head. "I thought you were working for us," he said.

"I am," Lujack reassured him.

"Where's the champagne?" Tommy said, picking up a nearly empty bottle.

"Better take it easy on that stuff, Tommy. Things might get a little exciting after the game."

"I'm not drinking this stuff because I like it," Tommy said, emptying the bottle.

When Mick Mayflower took to the field on the next Marlins possession, Lujack and Tommy stood up with the sellout crowd to clap and cheer. Everybody in the stadium knew that if the Marlins were to win the game convincingly and show the league they were ready for a Super Bowl year, they couldn't let the 49ers back into the game. They needed to control the ball.

Starting on his own twenty-three, Mayflower proceeded to move the Marlins down the field in one of the best-executed drives Lujack had ever seen a quarterback and a football team put together. The fans cheered progressively louder as each play unfolded, culminating in a perfectly executed play-action pass by Mayflower as he faked a handoff to Woodard, looked left in Fleet White's direction, saw that White was double-covered, and hit Woodard in the right flat for a touchdown. The stadium went bananas. Ernie B. started jumping on one of his bodyguards, Tommy hugged the stranger next to him, and Frank Nimmo threw down his program in disgust.

"That fat lady, she's under the table." Tommy smiled.

"Looks like we'll be around for the year of the Tiger, partner."

"I never doubted it," Tommy said, popping a strawberry into his mouth.

With seven minutes to go in the fourth quarter and the Marlins leading the 49ers forty-four to seventeen, Clark Sterling casually put his binoculars in their case, shook hands with Dick Pressley, and made his way to the elevator. Frank Nimmo and his boys were still in their seats, but when Sterling's head disappeared from sight, Nimmo sent two of them down the Coliseum stairs to the exit.

"If I'm not back by the end of the game, Tommy, you'd better take a cab home," Jimmy said.

Tommy nodded. "Good luck, my friend," he said solemnly.

"Thanks, partner."

One of Tommy's many attributes was that he never asked too many questions.

As he had done at halftime, Lujack followed Sterling toward the elevator. The lawyer stopped briefly to say something to Phyllis. The Marlins owner gave Sterling a perfunctory kiss and went back to her cheerleading pose. She seemed genuinely pleased that the Marlins were winning. Lujack put his Phyllis Randolf wicked-lady theory on hold.

Lujack was waiting at the elevator when Sterling got there. Detective Sears was standing near the door as he had been during halftime.

"Well, we meet again," Lujack said with infuriating cordiality.

Sterling pushed the elevator button, ignoring Lujack. "Isn't the damn thing fixed yet?" Sterling asked Sears.

"It was running a minute or two ago."

Sterling looked at his watch, then at the scoreboard clock. He punched the button again. "Is there another way out of here?"

"Like I told you at halftime, sir, you can take the stairs out front."

"Clark doesn't want to take the stairs. There's a man out there who wants to kill him."

"You're the dead man, Lujack, and we both know it."

The elevator finally opened. Sterling hurriedly entered. Lujack and Sears followed.

"If I were you, I'd step back when the door opens, friend. Bullets are going to be flying," Lujack said to Sears as they began their descent.

"You're crazy, Lujack. You'll know how crazy when Frank gets his hands on you."

"Frank doesn't know I talked to Mayflower, Clark."

"He will when I tell him."

"You won't live that long."

The elevator arrived at the ground level. When the door opened, it was impossible to see who was waiting outside the entrance.

"Be my guest, Clark," Lujack said with a Sir Walter Raleigh flourish.

Sterling hesitated. He looked at Sears. "How'd you like to make a hundred bucks? Just walk with me to my car. It's in the VIP lot just past the main gate."

"From the way this other fellow's talking, a hundred bucks sounds a little low."

A cheer went up from inside the Coliseum. Sterling's voice took on an added urgency. "Make it five hundred, but let's go!"

"I don't know," Sears said, scratching his head, obviously enjoying his new role.

"No wonder you're just a goddamn security guard. As well as no brains, you've got no balls," Sterling shouted and stalked out of the building.

Lujack nodded to Sears, and the two of them followed the lawyer out the curved concrete entryway into the daylight. There was twenty yards of pavement from the elevator entrance to the barbed-wire fence which encircled the Coliseum. The main gate was about forty yards to the left on the Martin Luther King Boulevard side of the park. Very few fans were leaving early to beat the crowd, so the area in front of the refreshment stands was relatively quiet. Lujack spotted the Guerreros before Sterling did. One was at the hot-dog stand almost directly across from them. The other was fifteen yards to his left, lounging near the beer stand. The taller brother began walking toward Sterling, his face behind a hot-dog wrapper, his other hand smoothly bringing up an automatic pistol from his long jacket. He had the Mac 10 in Sterling's stomach before the lawyer knew who he was.

Lujack motioned to Sears to take care of the other brother, who was acting as backup. Lujack kept moving behind Sterling and his kidnapper.

"It wasn't my fault! It wasn't my fault! Let me talk to Frank," Lujack heard Sterling plead.

"Frank says you talk too much already," the Cuban said, pushing Sterling toward his car.

They were almost to the front gate when Lujack put the barrel of his .38 into Guerrero's back.

"Como está, amigo?"

Guerrero's body froze at the touch of the gun. He glanced in his brother's direction and saw that he was being frisked by a security guard.

"What do you want?"

"I want you to keep walking in the direction of that yellow trashcan."

"What the hell's going on?" Sterling asked.

"Shut up and walk," Lujack ordered.

The three-man procession walked to the trashcan.

"All right. Everybody stop," Lujack instructed. "Now, Mr. Guerrero, I want you to slowly, very slowly, drop your machine pistol into the trashcan."

Guerrero hesitated.

"Either the gun goes into the garbage or you do."

Guerrero's right hand slowly lifted the gun above the trashcan. He held it for a second, then dropped it in.

"Now, let's go over and see how your brother is doing. You too, Clark," Lujack said.

"This son of a bitch was going to kill me," Sterling said with a mixture of relief and disbelief.

"He still might," Lujack said.

Sears was handcuffing the second Guerrero brother to the fence.

"Here's another one for you," Lujack said, pushing his man against the fence.

"Chinga tu madre," the Cuban screamed.

"Save it for your parole officer, Paco," Sears said, expertly cuffing the second hit man to the fence.

"What the fuck is going on here, Lujack? Who is this man?" Sterling demanded to know, coming to the conclusion that things weren't exactly what they seemed.

"His name is John Sears, and he works for me," Kyle Thurgood said, strolling up to the five men as if he were mingling at a cocktail party.

"Kyle, I can't tell you how glad I am to see you. These bastards tried to kill me."

"Why would anyone want to kill you, Clark?" Thurgood asked easily.

"I don't have the slightest idea. It could be robbery or mistaken identity," Sterling said, regaining his confidence.

"We can't get a conviction based on 'could have beens.' John, maybe you should let these gentlemen loose," Thurgood said.

"You can't release them. You're a sworn officer of the court. You're supposed to protect me," Sterling protested.

Sears pulled out the key to the handcuffs and began fiddling with the lock.

"These men are killers! They have a contract on me!"

"A contract on you?" Thurgood said. "I thought you didn't know them. Who do they work for, Clark?"

"Oh, no," Sterling said, shaking his head. "I'm not going to incriminate myself to help you people."

"Then I guess we aren't going to inconvenience ourselves by missing the end of the football game. Turn them loose, Sears."

"But they were armed. You have to book them for possession of a concealed weapon."

"Did you see any guns, John? Lujack?"

Neither man said anything. The Guerrero brothers looked at each other, thinking perhaps this wasn't their unlucky day after all. The taller one, who had jabbed the Mac 10 in Sterling's stomach, gave the lawyer one of the most malevolent smiles Lujack had ever seen. That was what did it.

"All right, all right. I don't know why I should protect the bastard—he just ordered me murdered. They work for Frank Nimmo. As if you didn't know. But I want a deal. I want immunity if I have to go to court and testify."

"I'll bet you do, Counselor, but you're not in a position to make any deals."

Sterling considered his options, including the Guerrero brothers. "Nimmo wants to take over the L.A. bookmaking scene," he finally explained. "He planned to put Ernie Barbagelatta out of business by fixing today's game through one of my clients—Mick Mayflower. Nimmo told Mick and me that if the Marlins win, we'd end up like Paul Makaris."

"Nimmo had Makaris killed? Can you prove it?"

"Match the guns these guys were carrying with the bullets in Makaris's body, and you'll have your proof."

Another cheer went up from inside the Coliseum, as if to endorse Sterling's case.

"Why didn't Mayflower go along?"

"Ask your friend Lujack. He seems to have all the answers."

"I'm asking you, Sterling," Thurgood said.

"I don't know why he didn't. The kid's a competitor. He doesn't like to lose."

"But Nimmo said he'd kill both you and Mayflower if the Marlins won."

"That's right, Lieutenant. These guys are proof of that. Between their testimony and mine, you should be able to put Nimmo away for a long time."

"Twenty years would be enough," Thurgood said. Then he pointed up to the press-box roof. "You see those three men on the roof, Sterling?"

Sterling looked up and nodded.

"The two with the rifles work for the LAPD; they're sharpshooters. The guy in the middle, the one who looks like Ollie North without the medals, that's Quentin Rule. He's the special agent in charge of the Los Angeles FBI office. You're going to go up and tell your story to him. If he likes it, we'll all go downtown and make our statements."

"I'm going to need protection, Lieutenant. You don't testify against an animal like Frank Nimmo without protection."

"You can talk to the FBI about protection. Nimmo is their baby."

"Of course," Sterling said politely, looking a little more composed. Lujack knew that Sterling's devious mind was at work, looking for a legal loophole to wriggle through.

Another cheer went up inside the stadium, and more and more people began coming out of the tunnels.

"Nimmo's coming out," a black vendor yelled to Thurgood. Lujack saw the man was holding a walkie-talkie.

"Thank you, Sergeant."

"I guess Frank wants to leave early too."

"You aren't going to let him see me?" Sterling asked incredulously.

"What do you think, Lujack? Do you think we should let Nimmo see our star witness?"

"It's only fair Frank gets to see his accuser. It also might give Mr. Sterling more incentive."

"He'll kill me with his bare hands if he knows I'm talking to you."

"He was going to kill you before, don't forget." Thurgood smiled, enjoying Sterling's panic as much as Lujack.

At that point, Nimmo, Stella, the two blondes, and two bodyguards emerged from the tunnel. Lujack put his hand in his pocket, but Thurgood said quietly, "No. We've got enough guns on Mr. Nimmo."

Nimmo had assumed he'd at least be walking past the dead body of Clark Sterling as he left the Coliseum. A small consolation for the four or five million dollars Sterling had cost him. Instead, he saw the lawyer chatting with the LAPD, his two hit men handcuffed to a fence. Nimmo's handsome olive complexion turned the color of provolone.

"Hell of a game, wasn't it, Frank?" Lujack said as Nimmo approached them.

Nimmo ignored Lujack's remark. He was looking at Clark Sterling. The lawyer began moving backward. The force of Nimmo's black eyes seemed to keep pushing him back until Lujack grabbed the lawyer's arm.

"This is Lieutenant Thurgood of the LAPD, Frank. If I were you, I wouldn't try anything heroic. There are thirty guns pointed at you." Lujack motioned to the various cops and SWAT team sharpshooters who had a bead on Nimmo.

"Frank, I was set up. We both were. Lujack got to Mayflower," Sterling blurted.

Nimmo smiled at Clark Sterling. It was the same kind of smile that one of the Guerrero brothers had given Sterling a few minutes before. A smile that said, no matter how long it takes or no matter who I have to break, I'll kill you before I die.

"Are you going to book me, Lieutenant? Or am I free to leave?" Nimmo asked Thurgood.

"Aren't you going to say hello to the Guerrero brothers?" Thurgood asked, motioning to the two men chained to the fence.

"I've never seen those men in my life," Nimmo said imperturbably.

"Maybe this will refresh your memory. It's a picture I took of them talking to you during the game this afternoon."

"Oh, yeah, they were sitting near me."

"Here's a picture of them talking to Mr. Stella the other night when he picked them up at the airport."

Nimmo looked at the second picture. He handed it to Stella. "I may have met them somewhere."

"I'm sure you'll remember by the time you get to court, Mr. Nimmo. For the time being, you are free. Agent Rule will be in touch," Thurgood said, pointing to the man on the roof.

Nimmo followed Thurgood's finger, then nodded.

"Rule, of course," he said and motioned to his party that it was time to leave.

As he passed Lujack, he stopped.

"You and I, we aren't through, Lujack."

"Don't bet on it, Frank. You've already lost enough money today."

Nimmo and his entourage made their way to a waiting limousine. Thurgood thrust his fist in the air signaling victory to Rule. Nimmo wouldn't be causing any trouble in Los Angeles.

"Lujack, you and Sears had better take Mr. Sterling up to see Agent Rule before this crowd makes a run for it. I'll get my detectives to get the guns out of the trashcan before they're covered with beer and mustard."

The three men walked back toward the elevator entrance. Lujack was beginning to feel like a yo-yo, but he knew there was going to be one more jerk on Sterling's chain before it was over.

"You've been a cop all along, haven't you, Lujack?" the lawyer said as they reached the alcove.

"I was suspended almost five years ago. I never went back."

"So what are you helping these assholes now for?"

"You haven't figured it out, have you?" Lujack asked the lawyer.

"Give me a clue, Lujack."

"The Temple Arms Hotel, January 12, 1982. Three dead boys were found piled in Room 206. Chief Bane told me if I helped him get Frank Nimmo, he'd help me get the man who ordered a pimp named Manny Ramos to shoot those boys in the head. The same man who, a week later, paid my partner one hundred thousand dollars to kill Manny Ramos."

Lujack watched Sterling's mouth fall open as the other shoe dropped on his last hope.

"That's how you got to Mayflower," Sterling said flatly.

"That's why you owe me a thousand dollars, you chicken-shit little creep," Lujack said with more satisfaction than he'd felt in a long, long time.

The elevator door opened, and the three men stood back as a crowd of Phyllis's friends piled out. Lujack nodded to Burt Masters and his wife.

"Remind me to stay away from inside information," Masters said to Lujack, referring to his losses.

"I'll remind you, Burt, but it won't make any difference."

Masters laughed. As the actor went by them, Clark Sterling made a surprisingly quick move, pulling Detective Sears's revolver from his holster. By the time Lujack had his .38 drawn, Sterling had a gun pointed at John Sears's head.

"Drop the gun, Lujack, or this cop dies."

The elevator crowd made collective sounds of fear and disbelief while they huddled against the wall. From where Lujack stood, there was no clean shot at Sterling. Not without endangering Sears or the others.

"Don't make it worse than it already is, Sterling."

"It can't get any worse, Lujack. Now drop the gun."

"Shoot him, Lujack!" Sears yelled as Sterling pushed the detective to the edge of the sheltered entrance while Phyllis's friends looked on in horror.

"I've heard of sore losers, Clark," Burt Masters said, "but this is ridiculous."

"Shut up, Burt," his wife yelled.

"She's right, Burt. Shut up," Lujack said, watching Sterling's unsteady hand holding the gun under Sears's right ear.

"I'll tell you once more, Lujack, drop the gun. Then tell Thurgood I want all his sharpshooters away from the roof, or the detective dies," Sterling ordered.

"You're crazy, Sterling. You'll never get out of here alive."

As soon as Lujack said it, he realized that Sterling had a better chance than he thought. The game would be over in less than two minutes. Ninety-thousand happy, excited fans would be streaming out. Even with the sharpshooters in place, they would be ineffective with the hordes of people hurrying to the exits. There wasn't much time.

"Let everybody else go, then we'll deal," Lujack said firmly.

"Tell Thurgood to clear away his men! Go on, get out of here!" Sterling yelled at the startled guests.

"See to it, will you, Burt?" Lujack snapped.

"Come on, folks," the actor said, ushering his wife and the others out of the entry. Once in the clear, they frantically started looking for Lieutenant Thurgood. Lujack measured his shot. It was a tough chance. He still needed an edge.

"You're slipping, Clark. You should have taken Masters. A movie star is worth a lot more than a junior-grade detective."

"Next time I take a hostage, I'll remember that," the lawyer said. "Now drop the gun."

Lujack bent down slowly, holding the gun palm down, making eye contact with Sears. His gun was less than a foot from the concrete floor when the final gun sounded and a huge cheer went up from inside the Coliseum. At precisely the same second, the elevator doors opened. Sterling's brain was momentarily overloaded, and Lujack used that moment to flip his hand and fire a .38 slug a half-inch above Sterling's right eye. The force of the bullet sent him back as Sears lunged forward. Sterling's reaction was too late. The bullet from Sears's gun flew harmless into the alcove.

Lujack looked over the barrel of his gun to see Tommy, Phyllis, and Reverend Billy Moore staring at him in shock.

"We were going to the locker room to congratulate the players," Phyllis said, thinking Lujack deserved an explanation or he might shoot her too.

Lujack stepped back. "Don't let me stop you."

Phyllis looked at her lawyer's body, for one of the few times in her life not sure what to do.

Thurgood and the other officers arrived at the entrance.

"What the . . ." Thurgood began, then, seeing Sterling's forehead, "Rule's not going to like this. This was his star witness."

"You still have the Guerreros," Lujack said.

"It was either Sterling or me, Lieutenant," Sears said hoarsely.

"That's what I was afraid of," Thurgood said.

"All right, folks," Thurgood continued. "Move around Mr. Sterling and get on out of here. Let my detectives secure the area."

The dazed people moved mechanically around the body.

Tommy came up to Lujack.

"Jimmy, does this mean I have to take a cab home?"

Lujack laughed.

"We can afford it."

Chapter 22

LUJACK DIDN'T GET HOME until after six. He was something of a hero with the LAPD but had no intention of changing professions. Chief Bane had made an oblique reference to the way things had turned out, leaving an opening for Lujack if Lujack wanted to take advantage of it. Lujack wasn't about to volunteer, and the chief didn't press it. After officially adding up the take on the Marlins win—three hundred seventeen thousand five hundred dollars—Tommy reported they were actually ahead for the year. Lujack's frustration and boredom with the sixteen- and seventeen-hour days of a bookmaker were nothing that couldn't be cured by a good dose of winnings. And, as Tommy pointed out, their big months were just coming up with the holiday season and bowl games.

He was meeting Lane at the Bel Air Hotel for a drink and their victory dinner. Lujack had suggested the Beverly Hills Polo Lounge, but Lane said she'd had enough of polo and polo ponies for one weekend. He hadn't told her on the phone about Clark Sterling. He was getting tired of telling her about people he killed, even bastards like Clark Sterling.

There had been one more call to make. Irv Katz wasn't hard to find. Less than two hours after the last game, he was hard at work putting together the lines for next Sunday. Irv was happy to hear of Nimmo's misfortune but said he had been in Las Vegas too many years to believe in the invincibility of the FBI. With or without Frank Nimmo, Nevada One would continue to put out the best betting line in the country. No matter who was sitting in the plush office in the penthouse, forty million Americans were going to bet on football games next week, and it was Irv's job to make sure the house got its points worth. Katz said he had heard Ernie B. chartered a jet to Vegas after the game and was last seen entering the Nero suite at Caesar's with six bodyguards and every showgirl he could rent. To the victor go the spoils.

Lane was sitting at the bar. She was wearing a rich burgundy-colored dress, her brown hair piled on top of her head, a gorgeous necklace around her tan neck, sipping a glass of champagne. As usual, she looked right out of the pages of *Elle*. Not a horsehair in sight.

"You don't look like a big winner," she said, kissing him.

"I don't think it's quite sunk in," Jimmy said, sitting down.

"Marvin, would you get Mr. Lujack a scotch with a splash?"

"Certainly, Miss Randolf."

"They know you here too?"

"This was always Daddy's favorite bar. He used to walk Kurt and me around the pool and give us crackers to feed the swans. It seemed like the right place for us tonight."

"To finish or to start?" he asked.

Her dark eyes asked him the same question. "I don't know, Jimmy. I was hoping you might have the answer."

"You heard about Sterling?"

She nodded. The bartender brought him his drink. He hadn't had a cigarette in eight years and suddenly found himself dying for one. The scotch would have to do. Lujack took the check out of his pocket. He slid it over to her.

"You know how I felt about Sterling, even if you don't know why. Let's call us even after the first installment."

"But you earned it. Clark was part of your earning it."

"Sterling was a separate deal," he told her. "There are better places for thirty-five thousand dollars. The Brotman Burn Center could certainly use it."

"What's the matter, Jimmy? You seem different," she said, putting her hand in his.

"I'm always like this after I win three hundred thousand dollars," he said, forcing a smile.

"Three hundred thousand! That's a nice piece of change."

"Of course, Tommy and I were almost down that much for the year."

"What would you have done if you lost?"

"I'm not sure," Lujack said, telling the truth. "Tommy has a cousin in Hong Kong who could have kept us in business, but that would be like selling our souls to the devil."

She looked away.

"Can we have dinner now? I'm so hungry I could eat a hor . . . a cow," he corrected.

She laughed. He enjoyed making her laugh. He enjoyed almost everything about her.

The maitre d', Michael, showed them to a table looking out on the beautiful patio. The wood-paneled dining room was warm and comfortable. The walls were covered with elegant oil paintings of the English countryside. If there was a more serene and genteel dinner setting in Los Angeles, Lujack didn't know about it.

Lane suggested the menu and ordered the wine. Lujack felt comfortable with her taking charge; it gave him more time to think. When they had finished the soup course, she looked up.

"When you said Clark was a separate deal, what were you talking about?"

"Remember when I told you about those three boys I found in the hotel room? The Temple Arms?"

"Yes, but . . ."

"Clark Sterling was the man who ordered them murdered."

"No, that can't be true."

"It's true. Later he paid my ex-partner one hundred thousand dollars to kill the boys' pimp. All of that so he could blackmail a football player—Mick Mayflower."

"I can't believe it. Clark was a mean, crafty lawyer, but he wasn't a murderer."

"When you work for people like Frank Nimmo, it's not easy to draw distinctions."

Lane shook her head. "Why would someone with Clark's connections get mixed up with a man like Nimmo?"

"My guess is greed and power. They seem to be popular motives these days."

"So is revenge," she said softly.

"I plead guilty. I've been after Clark Sterling a long

time. Even though I didn't know he was the man I was after," Lujack said. "Sometimes it happens that way. You're too close to see what's right in front of you."

"What do you see now?"

"I see a beautiful woman."

"Is that all?"

Lujack didn't answer. The waiter brought the main course, some kind of veal with an Italian name surrounded by hard vegetables. Lujack was getting tired of vegetables he couldn't cut with his fork.

The veal was very good, almost making up for the undercooked, undersized vegetables. He stayed away from the wine, preferring to punctuate his meal with scotch. There seemed to be more commas than usual, as he and Lane didn't have much to say. Or at least they weren't saying it. He didn't know if she was expecting him to propose or disappear. He almost wished he could . . . disappear.

After dinner, he ordered a brandy, knowing that he couldn't leave the table without saying something.

"What is it, Jimmy? You've been looking at me all night as if I just ripped off the church poor box."

"It's about Phyllis."

"With Nimmo out of the way, she can't do too much harm, can she?"

"The truth is, she's harmless."

"But I thought you said she was working with Nimmo. That's why they had Makaris kill my father."

"I was wrong."

Lane laughed. "You mean, after all we've gone through, Phyllis is innocent?"

"I don't know about innocent. But she didn't have anything to do with Nimmo or your father's death or your brother's."

"I'm sure she'll be happy to hear that," she said. "Although I guess that means I'll have to start going to her parties again. It was easier to make up excuses when I thought she was going to have me murdered for my share of Daddy's estate."

"She would never have been able to get your money. It was the remarriage clause that threw me, but when you told me that your father had taken it out, I had a feeling you were safe."

"So you've been scaring me just so you could protect me, eh, Jimmy?"

"Pretty dumb."

"I don't know. I kind of liked it."

"As long as I thought you were in danger, I never thought of you as being dangerous."

"What's that supposed to mean?"

"It means that Frank Nimmo did have a partner. But it wasn't Phyllis."

"It was Clark obviously, with help from Paul."

"No. They were supporting players. Put into place once the plan had been worked out. Makaris owed Nimmo because of his Rancho Verde deal. My hunch is Sterling's ties to the mob went back even before Nimmo set his foot in Vegas."

She was watching him now with a cold understanding. He could see the toughness that made her so unique. The intelligence that gave her entree to a world dominated by men.

"So who was Nimmo's partner, Jimmy?" she asked in a final dare.

"You, Lane. You were his partner."

"You're insane," she said without fury.

"Stupid, blind, in love, but not insane," he said. "Maybe I should have known sooner. Maybe by making me fall in love with you, you made sure I didn't. But you're the one, Lane."

"You're telling me that you love me and you think I'm a murderer? Is that what you're saying, Jimmy?"

"There was always something wrong about Phyllis, but I never could put my finger on it. She came from Chicago, and she had a motive to kill her husband, but everything else about her was wrong. Phyllis is the kind of woman who dances with crippled children and dresses up like TV stars. She's selfish, but she's also generous. She's outrageous, but she's real. She's not a murderer. She wouldn't knowingly do anything to hurt the Marlins; she's too vain to hurt something she's identified with."

"And what kind of woman am I?" Lane demanded.

"The kind of woman who would conspire to plan her father's murder to get his money and then, when your brother started to suspect you, you had him and his family killed. You were the only person who had a motive for killing Kurt's wife and kids, Lane. That meant you got all the money."

Tears were forming in her eyes. Lane looked across at him as if he had betrayed her and had betrayed himself. He kept talking because if he stopped he might also stop believing he was right.

"It was the little things. They kept adding up. You told me you'd never met Frank Nimmo. Yet there is a picture of you and your father with Nimmo in his office in Las Vegas. The night I saw you playing cards, the way you acted at the table—it was like you were in another world. I'd seen that look on compulsive gamblers before, but, of course, with you I never thought to make the connection. Until the other night, during the polo match, when Brit Falstaff made the breakaway and you said that was why you had married him. Then I remembered the name, Elaine Falstaff. A friend of mine in Las Vegas told me years ago he fell in love with a gambler one night watching her lose fifty thousand dollars. He said she lost it without so much as a frown. I called him back this afternoon;

he described you down to the diamond posts in your ears."

"There's no law against gambling."

"So I called another friend in Vegas. It seems Elaine Falstaff is a regular at the best tables in town. Sometimes she wins, sometimes she loses. But the lady has unlimited credit because she's guaranteed by Frank Nimmo. Word was that she slept with him. But I know not even Frank Nimmo pays fifty thousand a night for a woman. That's when I made another call to a friend in the real estate business. He said you'd been selling off your share of your father's estate bit by bit for the past two years. It must be expensive keeping thirty or forty horses and two homes, not to mention having to pay huge gambling debts. What my friend thought was funny was that you didn't sell through your brother but used a firm in Santa Barbara. It probably was the real estate sales that tipped Kurt off about you. Maybe that was why he came to me, hoping I could find another suspect."

"No one will believe you, Jimmy."

"They'll believe it, Lane, because it's the truth."

"The truth." She laughed. "What do you know about the truth? What do you know about my drunken father bringing girls home and chasing them naked around the house when I was growing up? My father was a miserable son of a bitch. He didn't deserve to live as long as he did."

"What about your brother, Lane? What did he do to deserve to die?"

"My brother was afraid of my father. He enjoyed the humiliation," she said. The tears had dried. Lane had been suddenly transformed into the composed, controlled woman he had seen at the poker table. She was going to play this losing hand for all it was worth.

"And his wife and the two little girls? What did they

do to deserve to die, Lane, except to stand between you and another twenty million dollars?"

"You'll never prove it, Jimmy. Everything you've said is hearsay. You'll never prove it, and you'll hurt us both if you even try."

"I'll prove it, Lane. I'll prove it because, whatever the sickness is that makes you gamble, that makes you kill, that sickness won't let you go free."

"You want to destroy me like you destroyed your wife. Is that it, Jimmy?"

"I can't destroy you, Lane. It's too late for that," Lujack said.

She threw her glass of red wine at his face. He moved to his left, and it went over his shoulder. When she ran out of the dining room, he didn't follow. She wasn't going far. After he paid the check, he stood up and saw that most of the wine she had thrown at him had ended up on the oil painting behind his head. The painting was of a polo match.

He thought Anna would get a kick out of that.